Praise for *Submarine*

"Brilliant . . . laugh-out-loud enjoyable. The sharpest, funniest, rudest account of a periodically troubled male teenager's coming-of-age since *The Catcher in the Rye*. . . . [Recaptures] a time when the ordinary so often looked and felt extraordinary."
—*The Independent* (UK)

"Funny, smart . . . Dunthorne's writing rings bitingly true."
—*Harper's Bazaar* (UK)

"Dunthorne's creation is a true original."   —*Publishers Weekly*

"Supremely funny."   —*Esquire* (UK)

sub•ma•rine (sub'mə rēn')

a novel

joe dunthorne

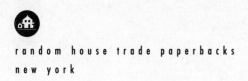

random house trade paperbacks
new york

2011 Random House Trade Paperback Edition

Published in the United States by Random House Trade Paperbacks, an imprint of The Random House Publishing Group, a division of Random House, Inc., New York.

RANDOM HOUSE TRADE PAPERBACKS and colophon are registered trademarks of Random House, Inc.

Originally published in hardcover in the United Kingdom by Hamish Hamilton, an imprint of Penguin Group UK, London, and in the United States by Random House, an imprint of The Random House Publishing Group, a division of Random House, Inc., in 2008.

Grateful acknowledgment is made to Casarotto Ramsey & Associates Ltd. for permission to reprint an excerpt from *Ghetto* by Joshua Sobol, translated and adapted by David Lan, copyright © 1989 by Joshua Sobol and David Lan. All rights whatsoever in this play are strictly reserved and application for performance, etc., must be made before rehearsal to Casarotto Ramsey & Associates Ltd., 7–12 Noel Street, London W1F 8GQ, England. No performance may be given unless a license has been obtained. Reprinted by permission of Casarotto Ramsey & Associates Ltd.

Library of Congress Cataloging-in-Publication Data
Dunthorne, Joe.
Submarine: a novel/Joe Dunthorne.
p. cm.
ISBN 978-0-8129-7839-1
eISBN 978-1-5883-6670-2
1. Teenage boys—Fiction.   2. Imagination—Fiction.   3. Family secrets—Fiction.   4. Parent and child—Fiction.   5. Marital conflict—Fiction.   6. Swansea (Wales)—Fiction.   I. Title.
PR6104.U58S83 2008   823'.92—dc22   2007014069

www.atrandom.com

9 8 7 6 5 4 3

Book design by Carol Malcolm Russo

For my mum and dad

sub·ma·rine

1.

triskaidekaphobia

It is Sunday morning. I hear our modem playing bad jazz as my mother connects to the Internet. I am in the bathroom.

I recently discovered that my mother has been typing the names of as-yet-uninvented mental conditions into Yahoo's search engine: "delusion syndrome teenage"; "overactive imagination problem"; "holistic behavioral stabilizers."

When you type "delusion syndrome teenage" into Yahoo, the first page it offers you is to do with Cotard's Syndrome. Cotard's Syndrome is a branch of autism where people believe they are dead. The Web site features some choice quotes from victims of the disease. For a while I was slipping these phrases into lulls in conversation at dinnertime or when my mother asked about my day at school.

"My body has been replaced by a shell."

"My internal organs are made of stone."

"I have been dead for years."

I have stopped saying these things. The more I pretended to be a corpse, the less open she became about issues of mental health.

I used to write questionnaires for my parents. I wanted to get to know them better. I asked things like:

What hereditary illnesses am I likely to inherit?

What money and land am I likely to inherit?

Multiple choice: If your child was adopted, at what age would you choose to tell him about his real mother?
A) 4–8
B) 9–14
C) 15–18

I am nearly fifteen.

They looked over the questionnaires but they never answered them.

Since then, I have been using covert analysis to discover my parents' secrets.

One of the things I have discovered is that although my father's beard looks ginger from distance, when you get up close it is in fact a subtle blend of black, blond, and strawberry.

I have also learned that my parents have not had sex in two months. I monitor their intimacy via the dimmer switch in their bedroom. I know when they have been at it because the next morning the dial will still be set to halfway.

I also discovered that my father suffers from bouts of depression; I found an empty bottle of tricyclic antidepressants that were in the wicker bin under his bedside table. I still have the bottle among my old Transformers. Depression comes in bouts. Like boxing. Dad is in the blue corner.

It takes all of my intuition to find out when a bout of my father's depression has started. Here are two signals: One, I can hear him emptying the dishwasher from my attic room. Two, he presses so hard when he handwrites that it is possible, in a certain light, to see two or three days' worth of notes indented in the surface of our plastic easy-clean tablecloth.

Gone to yoga,
Lamb in fridge,
Ll

Gone to Sainsbury's
Ll

Please record Channel 4, 9pm
Lloyd

My father does not watch TV, he just records things.

There are ways of detecting that a bout of depression has finished: if Dad makes an elaborate play on words or does an impression of a gay or Oriental person. These are good signs.

In order to plan ahead, it's in my interests to know about my parents' mental problems from the earliest age.

I have not established the correct word for my mother's condition. She is lucky because her mental health problems can be mistaken for character traits: neighborliness, charm, and placidity.

I've learned more about human nature from watching ITV's weekday morning chat shows than she has in her whole life. I tell her, "You are unwilling to address the vacuum in your interpersonal experiences," but she does not listen.

There is some evidence that my mother's job is to blame for her state of mental health. She works for the council's legal and democratic services department. She has many colleagues. One of the rules in her office is that, if it is your birthday, you are held responsible for bringing *your own* cake to work.

All of which brings me back to the medicine cabinet.

I slide the mirrored door aside; my face cross-fades, replaced by black and white boxes for prescription creams, pills in blister packs, and brown bottles plugged with cotton wool. There's Imodium, Canesten, Piriton, Benylin, Robitussin, plus a few suspicious-looking holistic treatments: arnica, echinacea, Saint-John's-wort, and some dried-out leaves of aloe vera.

They believe that I have some emotional problems. I think that is why they do not want to burden me with their own. What they don't seem to understand is that their problems are already my problems. I may inherit my mother's weak tear ducts. If she walks into a breeze, the tears come out of the far corners of her eyes and run down toward her earlobes.

I have decided that the best way to get my parents to open up is to give them the impression that I am emotionally stable. I will tell them I am going to see a therapist and that he or she says that I am mostly fine except that I feel cut off from my parents, and that they ought to be more generous with their anecdotes.

There's a clinic not far from my house that contains numerous types of therapist: physio, psycho, occupational. I weigh up which of the therapists will provide the least trouble. My body is pretty much perfect so I plump for Dr. Andrew Goddard, BSc MSc, a physiotherapist.

When I phone, a male secretary answers. I tell him that I need an early appointment with Andrew because I have to go to school. He says I can get an appointment for Thursday morning. He asks me if I've been to the clinic before. I say no. He asks me if I know where it is and I say yes, it is close to the swings.

I am amazed to discover that there are detective agencies in the Yellow Pages. Real detective agencies. One of them has this slogan: *You can run but you can't hide.* I fold the corner of the page for easy reference.

Thursday morning. I usually let my Mum wake me up but today I have set my alarm for seven. Even from under my duvet, I can hear it bleating on the other side of my room. I hid it inside my plastic crate for faulty joysticks so that I would have to get out of bed, walk across the room, yank it out of the box by its lead, and only then jab the snooze button. This was a tactical maneuver by my previous self. He can be very cruel.

As I listen to it, the alarm reminds me of the car alarm that goes off whenever heavy-goods vehicles drive past. It wails like a robotic baby.

The car is owned by the man at number sixteen on the street below us, Grovelands Terrace. He is a pansexual. Pansexuals are sexually attracted to everything. Animate or inanimate, it makes no odds: gloves, garlic, the Bible. He has two cars: a Volkswagen Polo for every day and a yellow Lotus Elise for best. He parks the VW in front of his house and the Lotus out the back, on my road. The Lotus is the only yellow car on my street. It is very sensitive.

I have watched him many times as he jogs up through his back garden, swings open the gate, and points his keys at the road. The wailing stops. If it happens late at night, he looks up to see how many lights have come on in the windows of the houses on my street. He checks the car for scratches, tenderly sliding a large hand over the bonnet and roof.

One night, it cried intermittently between the hours of midnight and four in the morning. I had one of Mrs. Arlington's maths tests the next day and I wanted to let him know that, in our community, this behavior is not acceptable. So I came home at lunchtime—having performed poorly on the test—went into the street, and made myself sick on the bonnet of his Lotus. It was mostly blueberry Pop-Tart. The rain that afternoon was fierce and by teatime the lesson had been washed away.

When I make it down to breakfast, my dad asks me why I am up so early. "I'm going to see a therapist at eight-thirty—Dr. Goddard, BSc Hons." I say this as if it is no big deal, this newfound responsibility taking.

He stops dead in the middle of slicing a banana onto his muesli. The open banana skin sits in his palm to protect him from the downward slash of his spoon. This is a man who knows about maturity.

"Oh right. Good for you, Oliver," he says, nodding.

Dad admires preparation; he leaves his muesli overnight in the fridge so that it can fully absorb the semi-skimmed milk.

"Yeah, it's no biggie, I just thought I'd like to have a chat about a few things," I say, all casual.

"That's good, Oliver. Do you want some money?"

"Yes."

He pulls out his wallet and hands me a twenty and a ten. I know when I am spending Dad's money because he folds the top of his twenties back on themselves, like a bedsheet, so that they fit inconspicuously into his wallet. Blind people also fold their banknotes.

"Eight-thirty," he says, looking at his watch, "I'll drive you there."

"It's only on Walter's Road. I'll walk."

"It's okay," he says. "I want to."

In the car, my dad treats me gently.

"I'm very impressed," he checks his wing mirror, signals right, and turns onto Walter's Road, "that you're doing this, Oliver."

"It's nothing."

"But you know, if you want to talk about anything then, me and your mum have been through quite a lot; we might be able to help."

"What sort of thing?" I ask.

"You know—we're not as innocent as you think," he says, with a little sideways glance that can only mean sex parties.

"I would like to have a chat sometime, Dad."

"Oh, that'd be great."

I smile because I want him to believe we have a chummy rapport. He smiles because he thinks he is a good father.

Dad stops outside the clinic and watches me walk across the forecourt. I wave at him. His face is tensed in a mixture of pride and sorrow.

The practice looks nothing like a hospital. It reminds me of Gran's house: all banisters and carpet. On the wall is a poster of a spine rearing up like an adder, about to shoot venom. I follow the signs to the waiting room.

No one is at reception. I thumb a doorbell that has been nailed to the desk. It has "Press for Assistance" written next to it.

I keep ringing the bell until I hear footsteps from upstairs.

I pick up *The Independent* from the newspaper rack and sit down on the seat next to an Edensprings watercooler. Although I'm not thirsty, I pour myself a drink just to watch the translucent jellyfish gurgle to the surface.

The seats are shaped to improve posture. I straighten my back. I pretend to read the paper. I am commuting.

A voice tells me I must be Mr. Tate. I look up and he is standing in front of me holding a clipboard. He has large hands. I recognize him.

"If you wouldn't mind filling out this form then we can get started," he says, handing me the clipboard. "You live at number fifteen, don't you? You're Jill's boy?" he asks.

I realize that he's the pansexual who lives on Grovelands Terrace. I'm surprised that pansexuals are allowed to work as receptionists.

I reject the impulse to write a false address.

"Okay, that's great. If you'd like to follow me."

We enter a room with a stretcher-type bed in it and a skeleton standing in the corner. There is no one in the room but us. The pansexual sits down in the doctor's chair.

"Sorry, I don't know if I've introduced myself. I'm Dr. Goddard," he holds out his hand, "but please call me Andrew."

His hands are even bigger up close. Not true—merely a matter of scale.

"So then," he glances at my form, "Oliver. What's the news?"

I tell him it's my back. That it hurts.

"Right, if you wouldn't mind taking off your gear—everything but your pants—then we can have a look at you." By *we* he means *I*.

I tell myself not to feel sexually threatened. I am of no special interest; he could just as easily be angling for the printer.

I take off my shoes, then my jeans, but I leave my socks on. Then I take off my jumper and T-shirt in one, saving time.

"A bad back is often partly to do with lifestyle." He taps some keys on his keyboard. "Do you spend a lot of time sitting down?"

"I sit down in school," I say. "And I sit at my desk in my bedroom in the attic."

He nods and turns to his computer screen.

"I can see into all the back gardens on your street," I tell him.

He's reading something, squinting.

"Uh huh," he says.

He keeps tapping the down arrow key.

I let the information catch up with him. He stops and turns to me. He nods, blinks, then he points at my legs. "Oliver, you are tall for your age and you have long femurs. This means that most chairs won't fit you."

I rest my hands on my thighs.

"You'll find yourself slouching or leaning back too much."

I straighten up in my chair.

"If you could just hop on the bed for me then we'll see what we can do."

By hop he means sit. I sit on the bed with my legs dangling over the side.

"Do you know about pansexuals?" I ask, on my guard.

He stops. "No, I don't think I do." He moves round the bed so that he is behind me. "Someone who has a thing for pots and pans?"

This is a joke.

He spiders his fingers up and down my back while talking. "Why do you ask that?"

"You know your next-door neighbor, the man at number fifteen?" I ask.

"You mean Mr. Sheridan?"

"He is a knacker. A knacker is someone who slaughters horses."

He doesn't say anything. He rubs my back at approximately the sixth vertebra.

"Would you mind lying on your front for me, Oliver? You can put your face here." He could have said "lying prone," saving two syllables.

He points to a small hole, a bit like a toilet seat, at one end of the bed. I shift onto my belly and poke my nose through the hole.

"Here, Andrew?" I ask.

He nods. I swing on to my front.

"I'm going to lower the bed now, Oliver." The bed lowers, becoming briefly animate. I wonder if he lied about not understanding the word *pansexual*.

He massages the area surrounding my eighth vertebra. "I know Mr. Sheridan quite well, Oliver," he has moved up to my neck now, "he's a painter decorator."

He rubs my back at approximately the ninth vertebra.

"Andrew, he has the eyes and overalls of a killer," I say.

My mum says that if you want to remember someone's name you should be sure to address them by their name at least twice during your introductory conversation.

I can only see this tiny patch of light blue carpet. I think about spitting on it. Or trying to vomit.

He applies a little more pressure on my neck.

"The family at number thirteen are Zoro." I lose my breath as he kneads my back. "Zoroastrians. Zoroastrianism is a pre-Islamic religion of ancient Persia."

I can't stop myself from grunting. I hope he doesn't think I'm enjoying myself.

"Hmm, I'm fairly sure that they are Muslim, Oliver." He presses harder on my neck. If I wanted to throw up, I could.

"Okay," he says. A machine bleeps like a television being turned off. "I'm going to do some ultrasound on your back." I don't know what the word *ultrasound* means. Normally, I would note the word on my hand but in this instance, I am forced to bite a chunk from the inside of my cheek as a reminder.

"This is cold," he says and it feels like he is breaking eggs on my back. It is not unpleasant.

I think about what he has told me about the family at number thirteen and the man at number fifteen. I think about the way he touches my back and the model skeleton and that he said I have long femurs.

I could easily throw up.

He rubs the gel into my spine and shoulders with what feels like an underarm deodorant roll-on. I don't need to use deodorant yet. Chips says that roll-on is for gays.

"I was sick on your car," I tell him. He stops rubbing.

"What?"

It is quite difficult to speak; my cheeks are squished together.

"On the bonnet. But it didn't stick because of the rain."

"You were sick on my car?" he says. This is like speaking to a baby.

"Yes, I was sick on your car. The yellow one. Your car alarm had been going off all night and I wanted to teach you a lesson."

I really feel like I might be sick. My face is starting to feel numb. There is another bleeping sound. I think he has turned something off. I hear him pacing. I am very vulnerable. I occasionally glimpse one of his loafers. Then he stops. I wait for him to say or do something.

"You can sit up now, Oliver. We're done."

Afterward, the doctor was very nice to me. He told me that I am really very healthy and my back isn't bad at all. He gave me a free lumbar support, a salami-shaped cushion, because, he said, he wants us to be friends from now on.

I hide the lumbar support under my shirt as I open my front door.

Mum is waiting inside, sitting on the bottom-but-one stair.

"How did it go?"

"Great—I feel really relaxed."

She has half dried her hair. The tips look darker brown than the roots.

"Good. Will you go again?"

"Nah, it turns out I only had a small bit of childhood trauma; it didn't take very long to sort out. He says that one of my main problems was that I don't feel close enough to my parents. They don't share enough with me."

She watches me. She's wearing a terrible purple fleece.

"What's under your jumper?" she asks.

I look down at my barrelled chest.

"That's a new pillow."

"What?"

"So I can sleep at night. I've been having trouble sleeping. It's mostly your fault."

"Can I see it?"

"No. I lied. It's rolled-up porn magazines."

She squints at me.

"Tell me what's under your jumper, Oli?"

It's times like this I am thankful to be a teenager.

I take advantage of my parents' current stance on swearing—that it is *up to me.*

"Fuck sake!" I yell, barging past her and taking three steps at a time. Thank our Lord for long femurs.

I run up to my bedroom, sit down at my desk, and start writing a short story:

There are nine planets in our solar system, Saturn being the largest. The life forms of Saturn are silent. They don't need mouths because they communicate using thoughts, not speech.

"I want to stay in my room," a young Saturnian thinks to his mother.
His mother understands completely. She comprehends his meaning in
a way that spoken Earth monosyllables could never replicate. She knows
that he feels like having some time to himself—no need to ask if he's okay
or worry about him or leave booklets around the house.

I tongue the small notch in the wall of my mouth. Then I look up the word *ultrasound* in the encyclopedia.

Ultrasound uses high-frequency sound waves to study hard-to-reach body areas. Ultrasound was first developed in World War II to locate submerged objects: depth charges, submarines, Atlantis, and such.

The first thing I ever stole was three pounds and forty-five pence from the mantelpiece at Ian Grist's birthday party. I spent it on Copydex.

The second thing I ever stole was my father's *Oxford Encyclopedia*. I caused a small argument between Mum and Dad where he said, "I always put it back in exactly the same spot after I use it and—look!—it's not there."

The next day, he went out and bought two hard-back copies of the encyclopedia, one black and one navy.

"Okay," he said, "now I've bought you your own copy."

I heard the thunk of the book landing on her desk.

Some months later, when Mum was away at a conference, I left his old encyclopedia on the landing outside my bedroom. I wanted him to find it. It was open to pages 112–13, which contain the entry for *cognitive dissonance:*

"Cognitive dissonance is a condition first proposed by the psychologist Leon Festinger in 1956, relating to his hypothesis of cognitive consistency. Cognitive dissonance is a state of opposition between cognitions."

A cognition is basically a thought, belief, or an attitude.

"The theory of cognitive dissonance holds that contradicting cognitions serve as a driving force that compels the human mind to acquire or invent new thoughts or beliefs, or to modify existing beliefs, so as to *minimize* the amount of dissonance (conflict) between cognitions."

Dad read this entry then, without comment, he quietly placed the book back on my bookcase.

For my last birthday, Dad bought me a pocket-sized *Collins Dictionary*. It would only fit in a pocket that had been specially designed.

Last Christmas, in the way that my father tends to when he feels he has hit upon a seam of easy, pleasing gifts, he gave me a blood-red *Roget's Thesaurus*, a square bulge in my stocking.

I have my reference books to hand while gazing in through the windows of our downhill neighbors.

I have the attic room in a building that is partly owned by my parents and partly owned by the bank.

We live halfway up a steep hill in a three-story terraced house. The area is known as Mount Pleasant. The Victorians built the streets in a grid shape so that all the houses face the same way, looking out over the bay. My parents tell me that I have a fantastic view but I don't believe in scenery.

Swansea is shaped like an amphitheater. The guildhall is somebody in the front row wearing an ungainly, clock-tower hat.

From their first-floor bedroom, my dad likes to watch the Cork ferry as it appears from behind Mumbles lighthouse and shuffles out into the bay.

"Here's Corky," he says, as though introducing a game show host.

I like to look into the windows and the back gardens of the houses on Grovelands Terrace, the street below us. I consider myself an excellent judge of character.

The family at number thirteen are still Zoroastrians.

The ugly old woman at number fourteen is a triskaidekaphobic. She fears the number thirteen.

The man at number fifteen is still a knacker.

And there's Andrew Goddard at number sixteen—both an excellent pansexual doctor and a compulsive liar.

Sunday. Me and Dad are at the tip, which is nothing more than a car park full of skips, crushers, and enormous freight containers. The sky is concrete gray. I can smell beer slops, vinegar, and soil.

I'm high-fiving wine bottles through stiff brush. It is a bit like a mass grave and all the green bottles are Jews. There are brown bottles and clear bottles too but not nearly as many. With Gestapic efficiency, I pick out another green bottle from the crate.

All the bodies will be crushed, recycled, and used in building motorways.

"Oliver, we've got something to tell you," Dad says, dumping a cardboard box full of garden waste into a toad green mangler.

Unlike the doctor, when Dad says *we*, he means we because Mum is omnipotent.

"Who's dead?" I ask, shot-putting a bottle of Richebourg.

"No one's dead."

"You're getting a divorce?"

"Oliver."

"Mum's preggers?"

"No, we—"

"I'm adopted."

"Oliver! Please, shit up!"

I can't believe he just said that. I yelp with laughter. He looks flustered and red, cradling a slush of Sunday newspaper supplements. I keep laughing long after it has ceased to be funny.

But what Dad says next cuts my chortling short. Nothing could have prepared me.

"Your mother and I decided: we need a holiday. We've booked for us all to go at Easter. To Italy," he says.

flagitious

In assembly, Mr. Checker announced that these are the best years of our lives. He said that most of our defining memories will be formed during school.

At the end of the assembly, Mr. Checker held up an article from the *Evening Post*. He explained.

"Zoe Preece's mother's beagle has beaten off eight thousand other dogs to win Best in Show at Crufts."

Mr. Checker made Zoe stand while we applauded, cheered, laughed.

Zoe is not the fattest girl in our school; Martina Freeman is much fatter. If you call Martina fat she will push you against a wall and grab your balls. For this reason, Zoe has been appointed fattest girl. When she gets called Fat she scurries away and writes about it in her diary. She has a short dark bob and excellent skin, the color of full-fat milk. Her lips are always wet.

The best kind of bullying is topical. My friend Chips is a topical bully.

It is a well-known fact that on the last day of school before a holiday, or even a half term, there are absolutely no rules.

The path to the school pond runs through a scrubland of ill trees, nettles, and punctured footballs.

Chips adopts the pompous trot of the Crufts dog trainer as he leads Zoe down the path, dropping the contents of her pencil case at intervals like dog chews.

"Good girl," Chips says, tossing Zoe's highlighter pen over his head.

Chips has a grade two all over; you can see the contours of his skull, bulging and ridged.

Jordana, Abby, and I bring up the rear, watching Zoe's bum when she leans down to retrieve her stationery. She is wearing trousers.

"Come on, girl," Chips encourages, dropping a Niceday eraser that bounces out of Zoe's grasp.

Zoe calls out, "Stop it!" as she stoops. Victims lack creativity.

A protractor clatters onto the paving stones. I see Zoe's dairy skin where her shirt has turned transparent with sweat.

"That's it, Fat, almost there." Chips lets a palette of colored pencils fall from the pencil case.

We reach the small, stagnant school pond. It is covered in green algae. A sunken tennis ball, mossy but luminous, glows beneath the surface like a globule of phlegm. The pond is bordered with paving stones; tall brambles encroach on all sides, leaving hardly enough room to walk around the edge. Chips stands on the far side, his mouth slightly open, his tongue bright red. I can see the small dark scar, like an almost healed scratch, on his upper lip. With her left hand, Zoe clutches the retrieved stationery to her chest. Her right hand reaches out as Chips dangles her pencil case over the water.

"Give it back!" she shouts.

"Good girl. Now, roll over."

Bullying is about solidarity.

I don't know which of us puts a hand to Zoe's back first—we are all capable—but once one person commits then the rest must follow: a basic rule of bullying.

I feel the ridge of Zoe's bra strap and the warmth coming off her skin as my hand—our hands—push. She falls, not in the traditional style, belly-flopping, but with a foot outstretched as if the algae might hold her up. The Reebok on her right foot finds the bottom of the pond, which is only eight inches deep. For a moment I imagine that she might just balance there, fat ballerina on one leg, but her foot slips from under her, and she falls on her bum into the shallow gloop. Her ruler, eraser, pens and pencils float on the thick algae.

We all feel proud; as Zoe begins to sob, her shirt splattered green, her stationery slowly sinking, we know that this will be one of those vivid memories from youth that Mr. Checker told us about in this morning's assembly.

autarky

My mother stands by the front gate, talking to a driver's-side window that is wound down halfway. She is explaining, in Italian, that she cannot speak much Italian. Smiling, she tells the window that she is from "Galles." My mother loves being asked for directions.

"They must have thought I was local," she says, sitting back down at the stone table. Her light tan complements the simple wrinkles at her eyes and mouth. My parents and I are near Barga, in Tuscany, staying in a rented villa. Sitting outside on the clay-colored patio, we look down upon a small river and a dried-up vineyard in the valley below. It is warm here but not excessively so. My parents like to come to holiday destinations "out of season." It gives them a sense of individuality.

In the car on the way to Heathrow airport, my parents had a discussion about money. My parents don't argue—they only discuss. I find this infuriating.

They were discussing how much money to transform into traveler's checks. Traveler's checks are a way of letting the world know that you expect to get mugged. It is the equivalent of swapping to the other side of the street when you see some older boys smoking outside the newsagent.

They disagreed about how expensive Tuscany would be: Dad thought quite, Mum thought not very. The debate was reignited today, in the butcher, when I demanded that we buy lamb. Dad said that the lamb was a bit steep; Mum said that it was perfectly reasonable. Regardless, it is my fifteenth birthday tomorrow so we're eating things that I like: beetroot and yogurt, cheesy mash and lamb cutlets of indeterminate value. The lamb is bleeding.

I listen to them talk about their friends and colleagues. I try to let them know that they are boring by turning my head very deliberately from one to the other as they talk, as though I were on Centre Court. They have nicknames for most of their colleagues: Pixie, Queen Ann, and Porko. Porko is my mother's boss.

"Porko's getting married."

"I thought there already was a Mrs. Porko."

"No, he's had various ladies . . ."

"Porkettes."

"Porkettes. Exactly. But this one is the real deal."

"How can you be sure?"

"Well, he announced it at the end of a board meeting."

"No flash in the pan then?"

"Apparently not."

"Not a rasher decision."

"Please, Lloyd."

Anger does not come easy to me. It is something I have to encourage, like a greyhound in second place. My father is pulling a lump of lamb fat from between his front two teeth. He struggles with it, trying to pincer it between thumb and forefinger, pushing it with his tongue. His yellow teeth are enough; I'm out of the traps with a howl:

"Why don't we talk about me?"

My father dabs the edges of his mouth with his handkerchief. Handkerchiefs exist somewhere between the tissue and the flannel. My dad owns eight.

"All you ever talk about is work. What about me? Aren't I interesting?" I say.

"Okay then, Oliver, tell us something."

I slide the slices of beetroot around my plate, turning the splodge of yogurt pink. I like the way beetroot turns your wee pinkish red; I like to pretend that I have internal bleeding.

"It's not as easy as that—you can't just ask me to tell you something and pretend that you're taking an interest. This is not some board meeting where I'm just another bullet point."

I sound impassioned. My father pretends to write down something on his handkerchief.

"My son is not a bullet point," he says, making an exaggerated full stop, looking to me for my reaction. He hopes to defuse the situation with humor. My greyhound is laughing, lagging.

"To be honest, Oliver, I think of you more as a permaculture farm," he says, using a word I don't understand. He sees my discomfort. "Permaculture is a form of very delicate, small-scale self-sufficiency farming. Certain crops are planted next to each other so any nutrients that one plant takes from the soil the other puts back. Like the birds that peck food from a hippo's teeth, you need a careful balance of stimulus—"

I look at my mother. She's watching my father with a familiar expression—a mixture of disgust and affection—that she adopts when she sees me use my own earwax as lip gloss. I believe in recycling.

I turn back to Dad.

"I am not delicate," I say. "And you two are no stimuli at all!" My correct use of a difficult plural spurs me on.

"So we have failed to fulfill a certain need," my father says, in between chews. He looks at me. He has a spot of yogurt in his beard.

"No. You just don't care."

I slam my fist onto the table to no effect. It's made of stone.

I leave the rest of my dinner uneaten and walk down the valley's steep side. The tangled vines are stiff as spider's legs squished in a notebook. I pick my way through nettles to the river's edge. Yesterday, I began to build a dam across to the other side.

I am annoyed that I cannot rouse my holiday parents.

Drinking espressos on the balcony, they cannot see me because of three large pine trees overshadowing the river. I crab-carry the largest rocks out into the center of the current. With each splash, my weir reaches further toward the other bank.

I think about an exhibition my parents took me to at the National Botanic Garden of Wales, where the artwork had been installed in and around the various ponds, streams, and water features. The exhibition was called "Show," which, I discovered, is also a word for a plug of cervical mucus expelled at the onset of labor.

I imagine myself as modern art: I am in the womb. The waters break, plashing on the awkward boulders. The sun on my eyelids glows an amniotic pink. I am a footling breech, coming out feetfirst as if my mum were a waterslide. Forceps nip at my toes. The water turns misty, my feet cloak beneath plumes of silt. I need to be crying; I think of sad things: imagine if your parents were dead.

In history we were shown a photo of Belsen. There were corpses lying beneath the trees, speckling the forest like fallen fruit. Their faces and upper bodies were covered with blankets so that they could have been anyone. I flutter-blink but my eyes stay dry.

The oldest photo my parents have of themselves as a couple is black and white. It is not black and white because there were no color photographs—it was a specific choice they made. The corners are rounded like a playing card. The photo shows them having a picnic beneath some trees during the late seventies. I imagine them setting the camera timer then lying back, pulling the picnic blanket over their heads. Not napping but dead.

My favorite photo, however, is in color. It is my seventh birthday and we are in the back garden. It shows my dad the prankster pretending that he might pour a bowl of strawberry jelly with fruit pieces on top of my mother's head. Mum sits on a camping stool; Dad stands behind her, holding the bowl above her, tipping it slightly. Our au pair, Hilde, myself, and four of my friends sit on the grass around them. We are all grinning, looking up at Dad and hoping his hand will slip.

Dad looks mock worried—pursed lips saying *uh oh!*—while Mum's face displays genuine terror: it's her war face. She looks so ugly. Her hands and arms are slightly blurred, as she moves to protect her lovely hair. It as though she has just realized that, after years and years, her husband dislikes her and—worst of all—he has waited for their son's birthday to let everyone know.

Farther down the river, the bank changes into stretches of glistening, untouched mud, smooth as whale skin. I walk downstream, getting deeper with each step. My feet squelch and fart; the mud takes on the consistency of jelly with fruit pieces. I allow myself to sink. I think of things that bite or sting.

Earlier this morning, a scorpion made a home in one of my father's loafers. Dad put on his shoes in a rush, giving the creature no chance at all. He tipped it out onto the tiled floor; it landed the right way up with its tail and stinger intact, claws slack and open. We watched it, waited for it to start up again. I nudged it with a thin twig but nothing. My holiday dad lifted the scorpion to his earlobe like an earring. He Betty Booped, coyly blowing me a kiss.

My knees slip into the gloop. Where the mud's skin has torn I can see tiny worms, almost maggots, flailing around. As I go to move my right foot, my left foot sinks deeper—up to my paper white thigh. I still myself, like a sculpture, and take a breath. I am in the center of a large hippo's back of mud. I search through my pockets: an English pound and, to my surprise, a tennis ball. I place them on the mud next to me. Neither object sinks.

———

. . . American soap operas do this.

In dramatic situations, I close my eyes very slowly and then re-open them. I stay in the same place, the same predicament, but things change. Where there is no way out, a plan materializes. When I am lost for words, I find them . . .

It is important for my parents that I occasionally put myself in danger. It gives them a sense of being alive, of being lucky. Holiday Dad is always a good person to scream for.

The villa sits halfway up the valley side. I try to sound as if I've got something exciting that I want to show him: "Dad!

"Father!

"Lloyd!" I imitate my mother's voice.

"Pa! Pops!" I bleat—this makes me sink a little further. The mud sneaks under my shorts.

"Help me!"

I hear someone—my father—coming down the hill. When he runs, he makes noises like someone clearing their throat. I listen to the sounds get louder. My father has a bad back. One day, I too will grunt at physical exertion.

My father's bare torso appears above the brambles and nettles. Instead of going the long way round he stomps through them, pretending they do not hurt. He is naked except for his corduroy shorts and brown leather sandals. He has at least ten dark hairs around each nipple.

My father looks frightened. He loves me. He cannot help it.

He says nothing, ignores the tennis ball and pound coin, does not even make eye contact with me. His one concern: prolonging my life. After searching for but not finding a branch—heroes always use initiative—he comes to the edge of the bank, standing where spears of grass pierce through the mud. He leans forward; the mud gives like dog shit beneath his feet.

"Nnngh," he grunts while getting his balance. This is no time for vowels.

I imagine the instrumental guitar music that they play during the cliff-hanger ending of Friday's episode of *Neighbours.* Will I make it to my fifteenth birthday?

Bending his knees, Dad stretches one hand out to me. His arms are tanned like crème brûlée. This is not the moment to mention that the mud in my shorts is warm and sexual. I reach out with both arms, only to slip a little deeper, a little farther away.

My father glances left, right, and up.

I am the only person I know whose belly button is undecided, *um*ming and *ah*ing between in and out—it disappears beneath a pregnancy of mud.

There are seams of orange clay, like spatterings of paint, appearing where the mud has been churned.

My father retreats back toward one of the pine trees. He wedges one foot into a gap where the trunk parts into two main limbs. He climbs up one of the tree's arms, using a rough, protruding knag as a foothold. I am impressed by his style of ascent. As he climbs I can see that he has little underarm hair, almost none.

I imagine he will force a branch down so that I can reach it and then, with a sound like the first volley of arrows being loosed, I will be flung high into the air above the valley. A safety net on the patio, constructed by my mum using the washing line and clean sheets, will catch me and drop me into my seat at the table.

The mud underlines my rib cage.

The next thing that happens is very disappointing. My dad climbs farther up the tree until he is entirely hidden. I can hear the flap of his sandals being heeled down onto wood. I wonder if my mother has phoned the emergency services; it's not every day that she gets the opportunity to use the Italian for "helicopter rescue." Eventually, with a limp-sounding crack and my father's loud exhalation of breath, a long, thick branch falls from the foliage.

The saving of my life takes less time than I had hoped. I grab on to one end of the slightly rotten branch, my father holds the other. We struggle for a bit then there is the sound of a sausage pulled from mash as he yanks me free. I belly-slither onto the bank. My legs are covered in a darker mud—the color of cinnamon toast. I smell like a fridge.

"I'm hungry," I say.

"Your food's still warm."

From his pocket, he pulls out one of his eight handkerchiefs and dabs the corner of my eye.

We walk back to the villa through the dried branches of the vineyard. The sun is still high; I can feel my legs start to stiffen. My father does not tell me to be more careful in future. He must be grateful.

My parents drink their coffee and watch me eat. Tomorrow is my fifteenth birthday. The mud cracks and falls off me in pieces. It looks as though someone has dropped a precious vase.

voodoo

Chips is a traditional bully; he leads us behind the bike sheds. Except they're more like bus stops than sheds. There is one bike locked up, its front wheel stolen, its back wheel kicked in.

Chips, Jordana, Abby, and I stand in a circle or perhaps a square. Chips drops Zoe's diary on the floor and stamps on it with his heel. The lock holds out.

Chips stole the diary during double music. Mr. Oundle, our teacher, used to be a successful opera singer, a bass. He has perfect pitch. Dad even has a CD with his full name on the inlay: Ian Oundle. Dad is sad about Ian's career.

Mr. Oundle was in the storage cupboard and Zoe had her headphones on while Chips, with his sleeve rolled up, rummaged through her satchel.

The diary is covered in purple felt and has a gold-colored lock as if to signpost to bullies: *Reading this book is what will hurt me most.*

Chips stamps on the lock again. This time it breaks.

Picking it up, he scans through, looking for his own name. He tears out each page as he goes through. A small pile starts to form at our feet.

I pluck a page from the air as it falls:

Sunday: B+

Showed Mam the lumps in my armpit. She says there are glands in your armpit, though I am too young to get glandular fever. Which is what cousin Lewis had when he stayed in bed for a month and didn't have to go to school. Must check my armpits every day.

Got an e-mail from D. He says he can't wait to see me at West Glam this summer. He thinks that I should try out for the part of Esmeralda. I told him that they won't give me the part because I'm not skinny.

I think Dad got bored of letting me win badminton this week. We went to Joe's Ice Cream afterwards and I had a Chocolate North Pole.

We visited Nanna. She looks weird with no hair, but she won't wear the beret Mam bought her.

We are all reading separate pages, shouting out the most relevant bits, like a comprehension exercise.

" 'I wish I was dead,' " Abby quotes. You can see the join on Abby's neck between her foundation and her real skin.

"I hate my life," Jordana says.

I grab another page as it falls:

Tuesday: C−

School today was shit except I found a fiver on the way home. Did trust exercises in Drama where four people stand in a circle around you and then you have to close your eyes and let yourself fall. Gareth made heaving sounds and Gemma shouted timber as I let myself go. They didn't drop me though I thought they would.

Came second highest in Mrs. Arlington's maths test. She handed the tests back so that the people with the best marks got given their papers first. Tatiana Rapatzikou came first. Eliot came last. Apparently Eliot's dad ran off with one of his elder sister's friends. The girl is only eighteen. Mam thinks it's terrible.

Got a letter from D today. He had included a Lego figure with four changeable heads that he said I could use as a voodoo doll for anyone.

"Ah ha," Chips says, finding a page upon which he cameos. He adopts a whiny voice that is a bad impression of Zoe: "Jean who works breakfasts understands. She says that I am very mature for my age. She says that she has had a fluctuating waistline all her life and it's never done her any harm. She says that kids can be cruel. I told her I felt like crying in Geography when Chips said: 'I bet you eat your dinner off a tectonic plate.' "

Chips looks up.

"I forgot I said that."

He holds the diary by its front cover and lets the pages hang open.

"This looks like a case for Inspector Zippo," he says but Jordana has already had the same thought—the smell of oil, then flame. Chips waits for the fire to catch hold before dropping the book to the floor. Jordana itches her forearm, scramming it red.

I imagine Zoe thought that recording the cruel things we say to her would be cathartic. A reminder of past embarrassments: like when you don't bother wiping the pus off the mirror.

We watch the diary burn.

"Don't feel bad," says Chips. "It's best that Zoe doesn't remember."

Except for Jordana and me, everyone vacates the crime scene.

We watch the cremation, the flames glow green as the felt burns. Jordana gets smoke in her eyes; she looks upward and blinks. Everything about Jordana reminds me of fire. The skin on her neck is inflamed and, as a symbol of independence, she has singed the end of her royal blue tie.

I see that the diary's lock is burning. It must be made of plastic, not gold.

nepenthe

I have decided to type Zoe a pamphlet explaining to her how to fit in. I am feeling compunctious.

Clearly, she is not getting the guidance she needs from her parents. Last Christmas my parents bought me a book called *Seven Things Every Successful Teenager Should Know*.

I have learned from it that the most important thing about self-help guides is to use nearly every feature that your word processor has to offer: pictures, text boxes, diagrams, abundant subheadings.

Also, the key to being a successful teenager is choosing the correct font. I use Centaur. Centaurs come from Greek myth; they are creatures with a human head, torso, and arms but a horse's body and legs.

How to Fit In with People You Don't Like Even When You Are an Endomorph
or
The Art of Being Two Species at Once

I. Breaking the victim cycle
Victims stay victims because they behave like victims

- Zoe, if something bad happens to you, ignore it. Do not try and talk it out.
- Chips is very astute. He knows you are weak because you chat to dinner ladies at lunchtime. He has also seen you write in your diary and, in the same way that he would want to see the X-rays if he broke your nose, he wants to see his name immortalized.

II. Harnessing your Inner Bully

Bullying is an art form; it can be learned.

Here are some hints on tapping into your latent bully:

- It's all in your attitude.
- Learn to show no shock, nor pain, nor embarrassment.

Here are two examples:

I. Do you remember when Rhydian Bird pulled down his trousers in the playground to fart? When he followed through, curling an unhealthy looking turd onto the tarmac, he didn't look embarrassed—quite the opposite—he screamed with laughter and pointed. Nobody can tease him about it because he is so proud.

II. During maths I famously stabbed Paul Gottlied in the back repeatedly with my compass. He said nothing, showed no discomfort as his shirt blossomed with blood poppies. His stoicism reminded me of the brave men who died in the First World War. Every year, on that day, I hold a minute's silence in his honor.

Exercise I: *How to give a Chinese burn*

Practice on a kitchen roll; how many sheets of KittenSoft extra-absorbent can you twist and tear through? One sheet is poor, five is excruciating.

> Maria, the school counselor, is the chicken. Emotional problems are the egg. Which came first?

III. Finding your special skill

- With some training you will notice that everyone who is not bullied has a special skill. You must find a skill of your own if you wish to fit in.
- Fo Chu should be your idol: he is fatter than you, can hardly speak English, and yet he flourishes on account of combining two special skills:
  I. Firstly, he always wears brand-new trainers.
  II. Secondly, he propagates the belief that he is a respected member of The Triads.

> A nepenthe: something that helps you forget sorrow and suffering, like a bottle of poppers.

IV. Tricking your older self

Bullies don't write diaries

• Bullies never remember all the bad things they have done, they just remember the good times. Part of the reason for this is that they keep no record of their cruelty. Here is an example of a diary that will never exist:

Diary,
I feel so shitty about Zoe—she'd probably be alright if I got to know her. I can be such a meanie sometimes. I just see her as this emotionless blob. How the fuck would I feel, being teased all day? I'm no stunner myself. At least Zoe does something with her life. She helps out with the school plays—painting the sets and stuff. What do I do?
    Exactly.
    Chips

• If you feel that you **must** write a diary, be aware that you are writing not to document your misery, but to make your future self happy. Your diary should be a nepenthe.

Exercise II.

Write a diary, imagining that you are trying to make an old person jealous. I have written an example to get you started:

Dear Diary,
I spent the morning admiring my skin elasticity.
    God alive, I feel supple.

In the late morning, I met a girl in the bandstand. We did cartwheels, headstands, the crab. Then we shared our perfect bodies.

I read small print without squinting. I hear all sorts of minute noises. I never ask the question: am I happy?

Even my imaginary experiences are more real and vivid than the day-to-day lives of the over-forties. Whilst walking home from the park, I annihilated the Death Star, discovered a pan-dimensional portal, and shrank myself to the size of a dust mite. I am not remotely tired.

God alive, I feel supple. I think I will spend the rest of the evening standing on one leg.

Good day,

Oliver

V. "Kids can be cruel"

A mitigation

- In your diary, you mentioned Jean the dinner lady using the phrase: "kids can be cruel."
- Adults use this phrase to trick themselves into not feeling guilty about the bad things they did as children.
- You are expected to be cruel. Put on your pointy shoes.

> If handled carefully, being unhinged can also pay off. I once threaded my fingers into spiderwebs, needling black cotton through the skin on the tips of my fingers, then at each joint until I was webbed. I got sent to the nurse and, from then on, Graham Nash stopped calling me "Oliver Twat."

VI. Only being yourself inside your head

- You must be willing to transform any facet of your personality to fit in.
- After they called me "posh" in primary school I changed my accent to sound more poor; I cut out the vowels like Marks and Spencer's labels from my shirts.
- It is okay to study as long as you do so in private and, whilst in class, you maintain a facade of indifference.

Exercise III.

Look in the mirror. Make your facial expression suggest boredom while you are secretly running through your tenses: *je mange, tu manges, il mange, elle mange, nous mangeons, vous mangez, ils mangent, elles mangent.*

Zoe, I've seen you steal sachets of mayonnaise, I've seen you covertly eat iced buns in class: channel your mischievous streak. Like food, I know you've got it in you. And if you ever feel that you are all alone then remember this: there are more fat people in the world today than there are hungry people. And if I had to use a word to describe you it would be *zaftig*—which means to be desirably plump and curvaceous.

Good luck, endomorph!
Note: in keeping with the above rules, I will not stop bullying you until someone else stops first. That's the way things work.

compunction

Fat's not been in school since we cremated her diary. It's been more than two weeks. She is probably at home, imagining all her classmates reading out loud about the no sexual experiences and the no drug abuse.

I have been keeping my pamphlet in a sealed brown A4 envelope in my bag in case she turns up; it's starting to get a bit tatty. If only she could know how close she is to changing her life forever.

There's only one person who will know what has happened to Fat: Jean the dinner lady, recognizable by her loose forearms and the way you can see her scalp through her hair if you catch her in the right light.

I get up at seven and out of the house by ten past; I tell my parents that a boy can't exist on Raisin Splitz alone, slamming the front door. I get to school by half past seven. Breakfasts start at eight.

I find Jean at the back of the dining hall, dwarfed between two giant steel bins, staring out toward the rugby pitches. She has a cigarette in one hand, the other is deep in the pockets of her faded turquoise smock. In the half-light, she appears to have a full head of hair.

"Morning," I say.

"Up early," she says.

"I came to see you."

She pulls on her cigarette for a long time. I don't think she knows who I am.

"I want to talk to you about Zoe," I say.

The smoke comes out of her nose first.

"Who's Zoe?" she asks.

"Fat," I say. "Some people call her Fat."

"You one of 'er friends?" she asks, exhaling, her jaw angled to the sky.

This might be a trick question. I think on my shuffling feet.

"I'm more of an admirer," I say.

She does not react.

"I've just been wondering, she hasn't been in school for a few days now: Is she okay?"

"She's moved schools to Carreg Fawr," she says, speaking calmly. "She hated it here."

Carreg Fawr School has a bad reputation and an excellent drama department.

"Oh."

The giant wheelie bins cool the air around us. The smell is Cheese Doritos and banana skins.

"There's something I wanted to give to her."

"Well, best go down to Carreg Fawr and find her then."

I wonder how old Jean is. She sounds kind of juvenile.

"But I'd get beaten up," I say.

She shrugs. The skin on her face is powdery, as though dusted with icing sugar.

"Don't you care about Zoe's love life?" I plead.

"It's a love letter?" she asks, leaning against one of the bins.

"Is that so hard to believe?"

The tiniest hint of a smile at the corners of her dry lips.

"All right, give it to me," she says, extending her hand.

"What?"

"Give me the letter; I'll find a way of getting it to her."

A boundary of sunlight pushes its way across the cricket pitch and tennis courts.

I pull the dog-eared A4 envelope from my rucksack.

"That's a big love letter," she says, squinting.

I know what I'm going to say and for a moment I wish there was a film crew documenting my day-to-day life.

"I've got a big heart," I say.

She takes it from my hand, then blows smoke above my head.

The sun repaints the rugby posts from bottom to top.

It is seven forty-one and I am in school.

After lunch, in chemistry, I stare at Jordana as she blackens the rubber on the end of her pencil in our Bunsen burner. We are wearing lab coats.

"You'll catch cancer from the fumes," Mary Pugh says as she walks past. Mary wears her goggles over her glasses: six eyes.

"I like the smell," Jordana says to me, twirling the pencil like a wand through the billowing yellow flame. Jordana and I, knowing that being respected by our peers is more important than our eyesight, wear our goggles on top of our heads.

I inhale. The fumes are caustic and sharp.

Jordana looks at me for a long time. The yellow flame reflects in her eyes.

"Which super power: flight or invisibility?" she asks.

"Invisibility," I say.

"Would you rather be fat or ugly?"

"Depends how ugly," I say.

"Would you rather be fat or unpopular?"

There is the sound of a test tube cracking under heat.

"I'd rather be fat," I say.

Jordana arches her back.

"God alive, I feel supple," she says, looking at me.

I look down at the graffiti on the table. It says: I EAT MEAT.

Jordana wafts the smoldering pencil rubber under my nose. I inhale. The little flap between my nose and my throat starts to sting.

She grabs my exercise book from in front of me.

"I've made some new findings," she says.

"Write them in your own book," I say.

"I think you'll find them interesting."

Opening the book to a new page—it is square lined—she leans down and writes something in pencil. She hands it back to me.

I read her message:

Hey Oprah,
Meet me after school by the tennis courts.
I want to show you my special skills.
J x

The three tennis courts are at the far end of the playing fields, lined up against the mesh fence that surrounds the school grounds. The tennis nets droop in the middle.

On the other side of the perimeter fence is a single-story old person's home. Sometimes, during P.E., one of the old people will come to a window, pull aside the vertical blinds and watch us playing doubles. We are told not to wave at them. When I see them watching I make a point of being young and alive.

Jordana is in the umpire's high chair.

I walk under the rugby posts and onto the tennis courts, stopping a few meters in front of her, in the service box.

Her legs are crossed.

I wait for her to speak.

"I have two special skills," she says.

She pulls a sheaf of papers from under her bum. I recognize the font and the text boxes. It's my pamphlet.

"Blackmail," she says.

She holds up her Zippo in the other hand. I can tell that she has been practicing this.

"And pyromania."

I am impressed that Jordana knows this word.

"Right," I say.

"I'm going to blackmail you, Ol."

I feel powerless. She is in a throne.

"Okay," I say.

"If you don't do what I tell you then I'm going to show everyone in school your little pamphlet."

Her thighs are very white. I am at her service.

"Right, what do I need to do?" I ask.

"So you'd better do what I tell you."

"Fine. I'll do anything."

"Meet me in Singleton Park on Saturday with an instant camera and your diary."

"Okay. I'll have to buy a diary," I say.

"Well, buy one," she says decisively.

"I will."

"Or else I'll distribute this and everyone will know how much you love Zoe," she says, wafting the pamphlet in the air. "Imagine what Chips would say if he saw this."

Chips would probably just do his impression of having sex with Zoe: as an underwater diver, holding his breath, swimming through rolls of flesh.

"Did Jean give it to you?"

"Ah ha, that's for me to know and you to find out," she says.

If I miss the first two buses home then I have to wait half an hour for the next one. I've already missed the first bus.

"Oh. Well, I'll see you tomorrow then. I'm going to catch my bus now," I say.

"And if you do what I tell you then I promise to burn this document," she says.

"That's fair."

I see the second bus through the fence at the top entrance.

"I've got to run to catch this," I say.

It disappears behind the old people's home.

"Guess what?" Jordana says.

"I need to leg it."

"You were right. Jean mistook me for one of Zoe's friends. She handed it to me in the canteen."

"Pardon me but I've gotta run," I say and I turn to move off.

"Wait. We could burn the evidence now?" she says, holding her Zippo in the air.

I am one of those servants—butlers usually—who respectfully points out when their master is about to do something stupid. "You should probably only burn the document once the blackmail has been completed, m'lady."

I see the bus pull in at the bottom bus stop.

"Don't bother, you've missed it," she says.

She might be right. My only chance of catching it is if there's already a few people at the bus stop and one of them does not have the correct change and he has to run to the Sketty Park newsagent and buy a toffee crisp to break a fiver.

"You've missed it," she says.

I'm going to have to catch the third bus.

"We could burn it now?" she says, from behind me.

I turn around.

She is staring at me.

"Come on, let's burn it," she says.

I could tell her that she is completely undermining the idea that blackmail is one of her special skills.

She holds my gaze as she slowly lowers one leg after the other, descending the laddered steps. She is quite graceful. A breeze ripples her pleated skirt. I imagine this accompanied by big band jazz music.

The bottom but one step wobbles as she stands on it; she panics and jumps to the ground. Her skirt parachutes up to her waist. I see some things I should not have seen.

I don't feel so powerless anymore.

"All right, let's burn it," I say.

osculation

My tongue is in Jordana's mouth. I can taste semi-skimmed milk.

I experience a sudden flash; it is a mixture of true love and a disposable camera.

She retracts her tongue and takes a step back. She's wearing a black top with red arms and a denim skirt with pockets.

"You better not 'ave had your eyes open," she says, winding the camera on. The sound of the flash recharging is like a tiny plane taking off.

We are in the center of the stone circle in Singleton Park. Basically, just a few uneven rocks sprinkled about the place. Fred, Jordana's parents' ancient sheepdog, is off his lead; he is sniffing and pissing on the boulders.

The green light starts to glow.

"Right, now try to look a little less gay."

We engage. Her tongue is warm and strong. I skim along her incisors. They feel enormous. I check out her premolars and have a scout around for wisdom teeth. There is a *cluck* sound as light pulses on the backs of my eyelids. We disengage.

"I thought you said you weren't square," Jordana says, wiping her mouth with her sleeve. "You snog like a dentist."

"That's my style."

"What—the drill?"

She expects me to have a witty reply.

"Let's try no tongues," she says, setting the camera on a nearby monolith.

She looks through the viewfinder, then points at a spot on the ground.

"Kneel on the grass there."

I go to ground. The grass is damp; it cools my knees.

"Beautiful," she says, pressing a button on top of the camera.

She kneels down in front of me.

"Right," she says. "No tongues."

We go at it like fish. She puts her hand on the back of my head. I put my hand on her neck. Various birds are communicating. One of them sounds like a modem. My lips feel swollen. The flash goes off. We keep going. After a while, Jordana pulls back. Her lips are bright red and the skin around her mouth is starting to look inflamed.

"Okay, that should do it," she says. "Now we need your diary."

I bought a Niceday hardcover ring-bound diary in Uplands newsagent. It has a comprehensive map of the British Train Network in the back.

I sit cross-legged on the grass with the book in my lap; she sits above me and opposite, on a boulder.

Again, I have the feeling of powerlessness. It is just a matter of seating.

"Turn to today's date, please," she says in the voice of Mrs. Arlington, our maths teacher. "I'll dictate."

I turn to the sixth of April and let my pen hover at the top of the page.

"Dear diary," she says, "I can't stop thinking about Jordana Bevan."
I nod and start writing.

Dear diary,
I can't stop thinking about Jordana Bevan

I look up. She finishes rubbing Vaseline into her lips.
"I know I'm not the only boy who fancies her," she says, which seems reasonable enough. I write:

I know I'm not the only boy who fancies her.

"Jordana dumped Mark Pritchard and now he has had to settle for Janet 'cum-tub' Smuts."
I stop transcribing.
I feel like she is going off-point a little. Plus, I'm not entirely comfortable with calling Janet "cum-tub."
"I sit by Janet in geography," I say.
Jordana is biting her thumbnail.
Janet Smuts used to be Jordana's best friend. And Mark Pritchard used to be Jordana's boyfriend. The word in the playground is that Mark cheated on Jordana with Janet at the Blue Light Disco, which is run by police officers who pretend to be your friend. Apparently, Mark fingered Janet during the slow dance and they've been together since.
"Jordana?" I say.
She's really working at that nail, trying to get it clean off in one.
"It doesn't sound like something I would write," I say.
She has the scrag of nail between her front teeth. She spits it at me. It clings to my blue jumper. I leave it there.
"All right, all right, what have we got so far?" she says.
" 'DeardiaryIcan'tstopthinkingaboutJordanaBevanIknowI'mnottheonlyboywhofanciesher.' "
"Okay," she says. "Take this down: I was so lucky to get the snogs in."

"I would never say snog. I would say osculate."

She looks at me as if to say: *Why do you exist?*

"It's a good word," I tell her.

"It sounds like a word a dentist would use."

"That's my style."

She frowns.

"Okay, Shakespeare, I'll dictate, you translate."

"Right," I say.

"Ready?"

"Yup."

"Seducing Jordana was solid—she's got such high standards—but when I finally got the snogs in it was all worth it."

I transform Jordana's blather into high-level discourse:

Lounging in a post-osculatory glow, I knew that all those months of hard-chivalry had been worthwhile.

I look up.

"Jordana is so . . ." Jordana says, shaking her head, looking to me for adjectives.

"Tender?" I suggest. "Intrepid? Accomplished?"

She nods.

Jordana is so tender, intrepid, and accomplished.

"Snogging her was such a score that I had to get a photo of it," she says. "One for the grandchildren."

I took a photo of us, mid-embrace. When I am old and alone I will remember that I once held something truly beautiful.

I turn the diary around and hold it up so she can read it.

"Yeah," she says. "Then: And to think that mong, Mark Pritchard, would rather go out with cum-tub Janet than Jordana just seems ridiculous."

You can tell Jordana really means something because she starts to roll her *r*'s.

I put the diary down.

"You really want me to call Janet a cum-tub, don't you?" I say.

"Yes."

"And you really think Mark's a mong?" I say.

"Yes."

I have respect for Mark Pritchard: he has been using deodorant for two years already; he brings an electric razor to school; he has hair like Elvis.

"You sound like you're a bitter and wizened fifty-year-old," I say.

Jordana tenses her jaw. There is a repetitive scraping sound. *Scritch. Scritch. Scritch.* Her hand is in the small front pocket of her skirt. I can see a muscle in her wrist pulsing. *Scritch. Scritch.*

"Jordana?"

The sound stops. She looks at me.

"Make your hands into a ball," she says.

I do not question her.

I cup one hand around the other like I've trapped a moth.

"Okay," I say.

She slips off the boulder and sits cross-legged in front of me.

Pulling a purple Bic lighter out of her skirt pocket, she forces the top of it into a gap between my thumbs. She holds down the button on the lighter; there is the hiss of gas escaping.

"Keep it airtight," she says.

"Are we making a bomb?"

"This is a trust exercise, like in drama," she says.

"Are we making a bomb as a trust exercise?"

"Ready?" she says.

"No."

"Ready?"

"No."

"And go."

She scrapes back the flint wheel. I feel the spark against my skin and instinctively open my palms. For a moment, I am master of the elements. I am Ryu from *Streetfighter II*. A small blue-yellow fireball in my hands.

It disappears in the air between us.

My hands are not charred.

She has a special skill. And it is not blackmail.

"I've got an idea," I say.

"Okay," she says.

I pick up the diary and write:

I asked Jordana about her ex-boyfriend.

She said: "He is a really sweet guy but there was just no physical spark. Mark Pritchard—bless him—he may have the jaw line but he snogs like he's searching for cavities."

I asked her the big question: "So you didn't shag him then?"

Jordana shuffles around and sits next to me on the grass: legs tucked beneath her, thighs angling toward me. I wish I were studying GCSE body language.

I hand her the diary. Her eyes jolt as she reads. I wait for her to catch up and answer the question.

"Technically . . . no," she says, handing me back the diary.

I nod and carry on writing:

"God no!" she said. "Minging!"

"And what about Janet?" I asked. "Aren't you angry with her—she was your best friend?"

Jordana's reply was so magnanimous:

"I know I should be angry but, honestly, I wish Janet all the luck in the world. She's a nice girl. She's not had a lot—if any—luck with boys in the past. I remember when I had to teach her how to give a love bite. You never know—they might end up getting married and staying together forever."

Jordana has such a great attitude.

Jordana shuffles closer and rests her chin on my shoulder. The wind whips her hair up under my nose. It smells of burned sugar. I keep writing.

Jordana is sex talent. She can do things with a lighter that you wouldn't believe.

She slides her hand along my back and around my waist. I keep on writing.

Her body is exceptional: fully-developed breasts, a definite neck, legs like a Top Shop mannequin.

She squeezes her boobs against my arm: shape and weight and warmth.

Thank you God, thank you Janet and thank you Mark Pritchard!

She bites my neck and sucks a little.

Yours smittenly,
  Oli T.

She detaches with a slurp.

"That's perfect," she says, reaching over and tearing out the page. "You make it sound as if I couldn't give a toss."

"What are you going to do with it?" I ask.

"Distribute it."

"How?"

"Chips."

There is the sound of her sheepdog barking at another dog.

"Are you going to tell him that it was all a setup?"

"No."

"Oh."

"What are you complaining about?" she says, taking hold of

my fingers and kissing the back of my hand as if I were a princess. "This is conclusive proof that you've actually snogged a girl."

28.4.97

Word of the day: Propaganda. I am Hitler. She is Goebbels.

Dear Diary,
They are calling for you.
The results of Jordana's "leak" have been two-fold:

- Firstly, my heterosexuality has been established whereas, up to this point, it has been a point of discussion.
- Secondly, and contradictory to my being a lady killer, I am now known as the sort of boy who writes about his emotions and uses words like osculate.

All this has led to three distinct types of playground goad:

1) Hey Adrian, where's your diary?
2) (To the tune of the musical) Oliver, Oliver, never before have I thought you weren't gay.
3) Tatey, Tatey, Tatey: have you shagged her yet?

It is a form of respect to have the letter *y* added to the end of your surname.

So this leaves me a distinct dilemma—just the sort of problem for which a diary was intended. Do I keep "leaking" sections of my diary and try and create a more beefy persona? Or do I cut my losses, burn this diary right now and just be pleased that I am known as an attentive lover?

Hmm,
Oliver

zugzwang

I've decided that I'm not going to write a diary. It puts my reputation in danger. I'm going to keep a "log." It's going to be seriously buff: there will be no emotions; there will be no emoticons; it will be sprayed with bullet points like the wings of the Luftwaffe after the Vickers K machine gun was introduced.

I scribble out the word *Diary* on the front cover, so it just says: *Niceday.* Then I Tipp-Ex out the word *day* and the left-hand arm of the capital letter *N.* Now it just says *Vice.* I write my name on the inside front cover. And a sinister anagram of my name: *O evil treat.*

When I am very old I will be able to look back through my logbook and clearly recall the taste of a fifteen-year-old girl's mouth.

12.5.97

Word of the day: Flagitious—characterized
by extremely brutal or cruel crimes.

Dear Logbook,

All the people I've ever kissed, latest:

- Arwen Slade—She wears a brace and is deeply unattractive. I kissed her on the bus on the way to Dan-Yr-Ogof Show Caves. She'd just eaten half a bag of flying saucers. Her saliva tasted like coins. Arwen is proud of her fillings; she has one for every year of her life.

  Arwen's best friend, Suzie, told me that Arwen thought, on a kissing scale of one to ten, ten being the best, I rated a ten. She asked me how I would rate Arwen's kissing. I told her ten to save her feelings but I was thinking three or four.

- Rhian Weld—Rhian Weld was square. I wanted to help her out. It was after a school disco. I told her that, if we were going to do it, we had to hide behind the tall kitchen bins. It was snowing and I have bad circulation. I remember that she closed her eyes, stuck her tongue out and waited for me to reciprocate. Her tongue was blue from black currant squash. It was smoldering in the cold. I put my lips around it—the world's worst lollipop.

- Tom Jones—not the singer. He was a friend of mine who moved to Brighton last year. I kissed him at a wedding with my mouth full of vol-au-vents. He could do a very convincing impression of a girl.

- Jordana Bevan—It was a pleasant kind of blackmail. Her mouth did taste of milk. The boys at school call her Banana Heaven.

  Jordana's pros: She never speaks about herself. She could, therefore, be anything. Perhaps she is a Fabian. This makes her a socialist who advocates gradual change. She owns very nice, small breasts that I have not touched. Her moderate unpopularity makes things easier. She is a girl; to be seen with her makes me more acceptable in the eyes of my peers. She has not met my parents. My parents have not met her.

Jordana's cons: When she imitates the voice of Janet, her exfriend, she sounds like my mother—not necessarily a bad thing—but when I kissed her and looked at her breasts this made me feel uncomfortable. She is not a Fabian. A shame. She is fifteen and has probably never heard of socialism. I'm too young to be tied down. I want to play the field. The playing fields.

Other things that are true:

- Jordana's mum works as an invigilator: a security official in a public gallery.

- People sometimes say that I am posh because I say "Mum" not "Mam" and "Grampa" not "Bamps." I do not tell them that my mother is of English descent.

- If a graphologist were to examine my handwriting, they would note that I am creative, sensitive, and destined for a modicum of success.

- Cod liver oil is good for the joints. Taking it every day may help to keep you supple in old age. I take two capsules before breakfast and one before tea. The capsules are the color of piss. Which reminds me: if you eat/drink Berocca vitamin supplement tablets then your piss will turn the fluorescent color of a high-visibility jacket.

- I write cryptic crossword clues on the backs of my hands to solve during maths or religious education. If a supply teacher gives us a word search, I try and find words which we are not supposed to be looking for. The word *zzxjoanw:* a Maori drum.

- I was born in a hospital with both parents present. My first word was *is,* a conjugation of the verb "to be."

- Some lunchtimes I help the student teacher build a Tudor house out of matchsticks for the year eleven display table. We have even created a matchstick maid who throws excrement down into the street from the house-top window. Her name is Ethel.

- Copydex sticks to your hands but then peels off like the skin of a snake. You can see your fingerprints in it.

- This is not a diary.

Goodbye,
O

Jordana and I are on the swings. It is Wednesday lunchtime. She says, "I bet I can swing higher than you." This is her way of flirting. She wants to boff me.

We swing until we get dizzy then we lie out beneath the climbing frame on the wood chip. It smells like rain.

"Remember when Arwen said you were a ten-out-of-ten kisser?" she says coquettishly.

"Hmm," I say.

"You're not ten out of ten."

Again she tries to bed me.

"I'd give you a six and a half," she says.

I lean over and put my palm on her belly.

"Get off!" she says, grabbing my wrist. Jordana sometimes lacks intelligence.

"Oliver?" she says.

"Yes."

She looks a bit like a beautiful woman. She has hipbones that stick out and make me want to do handstands on them. She smells of milk and estrogen.

"Sunsets or sunrises?"

Jordana always asks things like this: Knife, fork, or spoon? Full fat or skimmed? Money or good looks?

Fork, full fat, money.

"They're both pretty shit, but if I had to choose, I'd go for sunsets—they are less supercilious." Sometimes I think that I might give Jordana a dictionary as a Christmas present.

We share a chocolate Pop-Tart at my house. Jordana asks if she can have a look around my room while I go to the toilet. I sometimes take up to and beyond five minutes on the loo. I will change.

14.5.97

Word of the day: Echolalia—meaningless
repetition of another's words.

Dear Log,

• The problem, I think, with diaries is that they make you remember things you'd rather forget. I prefer to use the space for recording the times when I've got the Countdown conundrum before the contestants:

  reference—14.01.96
  speedboat—4.04.96

  Facts:

• Jordana carries cartons of milk in her backpack. She likes the taste of milk and says she wants to have strong bones when she's older. She has never broken a bone.

• When I was four years old I used to climb onto the windowsill—during my parents' dinner parties—pull my pants down and perform a genital display. In my subsequent research I have learned that this sort of behavior is perfectly normal for a five-year-old boy. And so, when my parents recall this story I remind them that, if anything, I was ahead of my peers.

- In sex education they show us photos of all the STDs. I think they want us to feel disgusted by sex.

- My favorite was the man with the anal warts which looked like a bad outbreak of bubble wrap. There was a man with thrush; it gave his bell-end a kind of polka dot pattern like a hat that no one would wear.

- When I have sex with someone I will be thinking about the unnecessary number of words there are for intercourse: shagging, fucking, screwing, bonking, porking, nobbing, consummating, boneing, boffing, copulating, dicking, bedding . . . I could go on.

- Chips says that sex is like a wet wank.

Thursday afternoon.

Sometimes it is important to skip school for an afternoon. We are missing Welsh and maths. Our classmates will notice that we have disappeared and they will respect us. Our Welsh teacher thinks he is young. He tells us that the Welsh for skiving in town is *mitchio yn y dre.*

We lie on our backs in the wood chip beneath the kids' climbing frame. She shows me the photos of the time we snogged in the stone circle. She says she is going to e-mail them anonymously to Janet.

"Are you using me?" I ask.

Jordana thumbs through the pictures and laughs. In the photo it looks as though I am eating her face.

"You have a massive head," she says. Normally I would say that this is just her trying to get into my pants.

"I said are you using me?" Sometimes Jordana doesn't hear very well.

She puts the photos down, turns onto her front, and leans up on her elbows.

"You wish I was using you," she says, smiling.

"Just because we have a tryst doesn't mean you can take me for granted," I say.

Jordana stands and clambers up the red ladder that arcs over the climbing frame. Once at the top she carefully lowers herself between the two uppermost rungs so that she hangs upside down by her legs. She looks like a spider at the center of a web. Her long brown hair falls down toward where I am lying, almost touching my nose. It smells of bubble gum.

"Banana Heaven. Is that really what they call me?"

Jordana's mammary glands look bigger from this angle.

"You kissed Rhian Weld," she says, starting to sway back and forth. I think that Rhian must have told Jordana although they are not friends. I was afraid this might happen.

"And Tom Jones. You snogged Tom Jones."

I pick up a handful of wood chip and throw it at her.

"Not likely," I say. I sound like someone who is lying. I roll onto my front and start to examine the soil beneath the wood chip. There is a worm, half squashed, writhing about. Worms find it difficult to tell the difference between the vibrations made by rainfall and those made by a human foot stomping rhythmically on the soil above them. A worm makes its way to the surface only to discover that it is a beautiful, sunny day.

I pick up the worm and, returning to my supine position, throw it at Jordana's hair. All of which, with a worm's tiny intellect, is entirely unfathomable. I feel young.

"I read your diary, Oliver. While you were on the loo."

"What diary?"

"You are such a shit liar. Adrian."

"Don't call me Adrian."

"Adrian."

"It's a logbook, anyway."

"Adrian."

In school, we looked at an extract from Adrian Mole's diary. Chips said, "When do we get to the bit where he realizes he's gay?"

Jordana's face is turning red as the blood starts to collect in her skull. She may also be blushing—sexual nervousness can do that. She turns her head to look at me. This creates a kind of tunnel of her hair between my face and hers. A spot lives in the hairs of her right eyebrow.

"Open your mouth," she says.

I open my mouth as though I am screaming. Jordana concentrates. She pouts. One minute she's hot to trot, the next she's not. I don't know what she is planning. Then, slowly, delicately, Jordana allows a thread, a thermometer of spit to stretch from her lips. It dangles for a second, a few inches from my face. The cord snaps and I feel the cargo hit the back of my throat. I try not to cough. Or be sick.

Jordana pulls herself back up onto the top of the climbing frame. Her hair looks as though she has just had rough sex. I swallow. She climbs down and lies next to me. Her face glows strawberry red.

"Oliver?" she says, staring up at the sky, or the climbing frame.

"Yup."

I feel postcoital.

"You should write more about me in your diary."

15.5.97

Word of the day: Pederast—the American version of a pedophile. It took me the entirety of a double lesson of religious education to solve this cryptic crossword clue: "Deep transformation turns a lost rasta into child lover."

Dear Log (and Jordana),

- Jordana's new cons: her spit is thicker than mine. I do not want to be in an unequal relationship.

- New pros: she has very good aim.

- In double chemistry we were doing potassium. Everyone fears Eliot Shakespeare—he laughs at explosions.

- During geography I solved this clue: "move rhythmically when boy goes to church." Five letters. I thought of DANCE straight away but then thought that was too easy. Whilst Miss Brow was explaining about oxbow lakes I made sense of the rest of the clue. The boy is Dan. His religious denomination is the Church of England.

- Sam Portal is Church of England. I tell him that the Bible is a work of fiction. I ask him why he chooses Christianity over the other religions. I write him Post-it notes from God and stick them on the inside of his physics textbook. It is important to keep duplicates of good deeds. See below:

  Dear Sam, don't listen
  to your friend Oliver
  Tate, I put him on earth to
  confuse you. Keep it on
  the hush-hush. Much love,
  the one who signs
  off with a cross. X

- I got home from school to find my mum had cooked a lemon sponge where the middle had risen too much and popped like a volcano or a spot.

- Each Saturday, and now on Wednesdays as well, I imagine what lottery numbers I would pick if I were of legal gambling age. I write them down on a sheet of paper. My numbers for last night's midweek rollover were 43, 26, 17, 8, 9, and 33. My numbers didn't come up. I saved a pound.

Behave,
Love, Oliver

pederast

I have changed my mind. I'm going to go back to writing a full-blown diary, rather than a log. I have brokered a deal with Jordana whereby she is allowed to read my diary as long as she promises that, in future, she will not distribute it to my classmates.

I am feeling a little emotional.

I had a conversation with my mother. She wanted to have a "chat." Mum knows I have a girlfriend but, as yet, I have refused to disclose the name Jordana Bevan. When I go to meet Jordana, I usually tell my parents that I'm going out for pudding. They think this might be a nickname for heroin. Mum made the international face for: Is there anything you want to tell me?

17.5.97

> Word of the day: Compunction—a strong
> uneasiness caused by a sense of guilt.

Hi Diary!
Hi Jordana!
News:

• I've discovered that masturbating in the darkness of my empty wardrobe is excellent, particularly because of that newborn feeling as you stumble back into the well-lit room. A kind of Narnia.

• For some time now, my parents have been slowly coming round to the idea that they can speak to me about anything. I've been very careful to remain in the mode of a well-adjusted young man. I wrote a log, not a diary. I acquired a girlfriend, of all things.

  But my good work was undone this afternoon. Mum sat at the dining room table with a glass of Rose's Lime Cordial glowing like kryptonite. She said that she'd spoken to my therapist. That she'd bumped into him on our street when his car alarm had been going off.

  I was next door, in the kitchen, fixing myself a dessert island.

Oli T's Famous Dessert Island Recipe

Ingredients:

    One wooden hut (chocolate muffin)
    One sandy beach (custard)
    Utensils: Microwave, bowl, spoon

Mum said: "I am worried about you."
I said: "That's good to know."
She said: "I spoke to Doctor Goddard, across the road, about your consultation."
I said: "Yes."
She said: "It was very kind of him to give you that lumbar support."

This was clever—she let me know that I'd been uncovered but, by not making a big thing out of it, she made me believe, for a few hundred milliseconds, that we have an open and honest relationship.

I said: "Look, Mum, I've got to tell you something big."

I thought that probably, the best thing I could do was tell her some sort of enormous secret. I knew that—deep down—she was hoping there would be some sort of highly classified information, a disturbing formative event, which would explain all my weirdness. And then, if she felt that I was being fully honest, she would unveil all the family skeletons.

Like all of history's great orators, I stood up and walked in slow circles around the dining room table as I spoke. Here is a transcript of my speech:

Remember, Mum, when Keiron last came over. I was eleven and he was seven. He had one upper tooth that poked outward, giving him a permanent Elvis lip. You were having coffee with his mum in the front room and we were in the music room.

We were playing the perennial classic: hot or cold. Except I didn't really know what it was I wanted him to find. I got him to open up Dad's viola case. I got him to lift up the lid on the piano. I got him to search through the cupboard full of board games and shove his hand into the cloth sack for the Scrabble letters. I made him open the jar full of dice, tiddlywinks, and golf tees. Then I laid out in the middle of the rug, in a star shape. Whenever he came close to me I said Warmer until, eventually, he knelt by my side and put his hands on my chest. Temperate, I said. Then he searched my hair. Hyperborean, I said. Then he touched my chest. Thawing. Then he touched my stomach. Clement. Then he went down my right leg. Algid. And my left leg. Gelid. Until there was nowhere left for him to go. He cupped both his hands over the lump in my jeans. Magma, I said.

And then when he put his hand on my zip, I said Thermal. And when he unzipped me I said Igneous. And then he looked at me for a moment and he seemed a little unsure. Then he put his clammy hand inside my trousers and flopped out my wazzock. It's hot, he said.

Please don't be angry, Mum; I came onto the Turkish rug.

Keiron asked me: What is it? And I said: It's glue. Like Copydex. And he said: I like Copydex. He rubbed it on his hands. It peels off like skin, he said.

Afterwards, I didn't want to do anything but stare at the ceiling rose. He sat on my chest and fed me back my own cum off his fingertips, laughing and saying: This'll glue your throat closed!

Jordana, if you're reading this, the truth is that I don't even know what cum tastes like. And I did not tell my mother any of this. I made up that whole soliloquy. Diaries are gullible.

In actual fact, the conversation between me and my mother was much longer, we talked for what seemed like hours and I drank sugary tea. She wanted to know if I was okay. She wanted to know about my emotions. She wanted to know if anything had been worrying me. I said that I was worried about a number of things: global warming, GCSEs, and girls. She seemed to buy it. She hugged me and did some crying and said she loved me and called me her little pot of clay.

Out,

O

quidnunc

It is Sunday. My parents have gone to Gower for a walk. They didn't ask me to join them. They did not say that I would enjoy myself once I was there.

Jordana is lying on her front on the large Turkish rug, reading my most recent diary entry. She's about a third of the way through.

I'm sitting on the piano stool, watching her read and thinking about the relative merits of being a convincing liar. It may seem like a useful life skill but it has its downside. Part of the process of sounding like you are telling the truth is that, in some way, you have to believe in what you are saying. This leads to all sorts of problems.

Yesterday, Jordana and I caught the train to Cardiff. It was slightly romantic. We couldn't meet at each other's house because I didn't want her to meet my parents, she didn't want me to meet hers, and there would have been too many school friends in town or the park—so we went to Cardiff.

We planned to dodge the ticket collector by hiding in the toilets. But we were too busy kissing and groping—we didn't hear the hiss of the carriage doors—and he asked us for our tickets. I made up a story about how, earlier that day, we had got mugged on the High Street. I said they'd taken my wallet, which contained both our tickets. I said that it was Jordana's birthday and that I was taking her to Cardiff as a gift. Jordana was tapping my leg as if to say, *Don't bother, he'll never believe you.* But I carried on and I talked about our visit to the police station to report the crime. I mentioned a female police officer who said that there had been a spate of muggings. I used the word *spate.* Jordana slyly pinched my side as if to say, *Give it up.* She was about ready to fork out for tickets when I burst into tears—man tears—and started sobbing about how one of the boys punched me in the neck. The neck, of all places. And the other boy had said that he was going to knife my girlfriend. On her birthday. And how they had Irish accents. It all just came to me, off the cuff. I felt genuinely traumatized.

And even though I saved her a tenner, Jordana hardly spoke to me for the rest of the day.

"The word *custard* always makes me think of cancer," she says. "I don't know why."

She is reading my recipe.

"Maybe that's what tumors are made of," she says.

I don't feel well.

In my diary, I pretend that the episode with Keiron's clammy hand is just another of my ridiculously imaginative lies. This was a kind of double bluff. It was something that actually happened except I didn't say all those long words. Seven-year-olds do not understand words like *gelid.*

One of the icebreakers that teachers use with a new class is: tell us one thing about yourself that is true and one thing that is not true. And I am always jealous of people who have done something in their life that is so remarkable you assume it must be a lie. Abby King came second in Junior Masterchef. Fact. Tatiana Rapatzikou was in the Russian circus. Fact. I cannot say I have had sexual relations with a seven-year-old boy. They would make me go and see Maria, the school counselor.

Jordana traces across the page with her index finger. She's about to get to the confession. My face is heating up. Tricking Keiron into unzipping my trousers is the single worst thing I have done in my life, thus far.

Recently, I've been thinking more about Leon Festinger's theory of cognitive dissonance. I think of myself as a thoroughly good egg. And yet the incident with Keiron is the behavior of a bad egg—a splodge of blood in the yolk. I have the sort of brain that can just forget things or pretend that something was a dream, if it suits me. It would probably be easier for me to believe that this event did not happen.

I think about the time Chips was suspended from school for flooding the toilets and writing the word SHIT in feces across four mirrors. His mum sent him back to school the next day with a note saying that she knows her son and he would never do such a thing.

Jordana turns a page. She is near the end of my confession.

"Oliver, I didn't know you were a pedo," Jordana says casually. She thinks she is making a joke.

When I was round at Chips's dad's house—Chips lives with his dad in the week and his mum every other weekend—we watched a program about an American murderer slash rapist whose name was Curly Eberle. The program focused on his most famous crime, whereby he raped and murdered a nineteen-year-old girl at a bus stop then phoned the victim's mother to tell her about it.

In court, they had evidence to spare. His fingerprints on the girl's mobile phone. His sperm in the usual places. Her blood on his clothes. The testimony of the driver of the car that cruised past but was too wimpy to stop. They even had a recording—somehow—of the phone call he made.

And they showed footage of the court case. It may have been a reconstruction. The camera focused on Curly Eberle's face as they played him the recording. He listened to it. Listened to himself describing the girl's facial expression, telling the girl's mother how her daughter had sounded, doing a squeaky-voiced impersonation. All the while the girl's mother is freaking out at the other end of the line: squealing, wailing, animal noises.

They asked him: Mr. Eberle, do you recognize this phone conversation? No, he says. Everyone in the courtroom made their give-me-strength-in-the-presence-of-evil face. Mr. Eberle, is that your voice? No, it's not. Curly already knows he's going to be in jail forever. The evidence is overwhelming. It's not going to change the verdict either way. Is that your voice? No, it is not my voice.

The program tried to make out that this made him an even worse person but I was thinking fair play to him, he's just being pragmatic. The series is called *America's Most Evil Killers* and maybe Curly thinks of himself as a decent chap, on the whole, apart from one or two fairly major slipups. And here he's being asked to admit to being the devil, and if you agree to that sort of thing, then it tends to swallow up your whole self-image.

"Ha," Jordana says, shaking her head at the page in front of her. "You're mental."

Maybe a lady fainted on the train—it was the hottest day of the year—and Curly caught her under her arms as she fell. She was dead weight. And with the help of another passenger he lifted her out onto the platform. She came to and Curly gave her some of his bottled water. She thanked him, said she was okay, then Curly got on the next train and went about his business.

But if he admits to being one of America's most evil killers then all his memories—even the really sunny ones—will start to be tainted. He'll start to remember being aware of his fingers near the sides of her breasts as he carried her out of the carriage. And that he liked the way her shirt and skirt had ridden up a bit in transit. He'll remember hoping that she would need mouth-to-mouth resuscitation. More than that, he'll remember that the only thing keeping him from tearing her tights off and doing something demonic right there on the platform was the crowd of commuters that had gathered to watch. He'll have to go through this process for every single memory. Rewrite his entire life story. Draw little devil horns on every childhood photo.

"Well, well, well," Jordana says. She's close to the end of the entry.

I don't want to lie to myself like Curly Eberle. I want to have a realistic picture of myself. The truth is that Keiron did come round and we did play hot or cold and I don't even remember why— maybe I thought it would be funny—but I made him unzip my trousers. Maybe I just thought it would be interesting. It is the worst thing I have done in my life, thus far, and I will never forget about it or pretend it didn't happen.

Keiron's eleven and next year he's going to be in the same school as me and I've got this image of him standing up in assembly and telling everyone. Then the police will come round and shine an ultraviolet light onto the Turkish rug, which never gets washed because it is too delicate and valuable.

"Weird," she says, slapping the book closed and pushing it away. "I don't buy it. Gelid, algid. How would a seven-year-old even understand all these words?"

"Exactly," I say. "It's totally ridiculous."

Sometimes, if my mind tries to tell me that the whole incident was a dream or a fantasy, I feel around on the rug for the small patch of stiff, tough bristles.

Jordana turns onto her back and spreads her arms and legs into a star. She starts writhing.

"Warmer, warmer," she says, in the posh voice that is supposed to be an impression of me. She makes me sound like a homosexual. "Magma! Magma!" she says, laughing.

She is kicking her arms and feet in the air like an overturned lady bird. She is wearing a red polka-dot skirt, too. The backs of her knees are scratched raw.

"Come on! What's wrong?" she says, holding out her hands and legs to me. "Don't leave me stranded."

I can see her knickers, clear as day. White cotton knickers, crinkled in the crotch. I feel nothing. Sex-purse. I am cold.

"Pederasty is a very serious offense," I tell her.

"You're no fun," she says, sitting up into a cross-legged position.

I drop to my hands and knees and start feeling around on the carpet for the patch of dried cum.

"Lost a contact lens?" she says.

I turn my back to her and keep on searching.

"Cor blimey, sir," she says, in the voice of a Victorian orphan, "feel the 'eat off 'em."

I look over my shoulder. She has the palm of her hand cupped near the crotch of my jeans. Fred, her sheepdog, has notoriously warm balls.

She beams. Like this is the happiest day of her life.

"Come on. The fuck's up with you?"

Jordana is good at swearing.

My face feels hot. I am alight with guilt.

"Jordana, I have something to tell you."

I turn and sit opposite her on the carpet. I make the serious eyes.

"You love me?" she says.

"No, not that."

"You have bought me a moped."

"I have not done that."

"You love me."

"About Keiron."

"What?"

"The story is true. I was lying that I was lying."

"Your face is puffy," she says.

"I needed to tell someone."

"Are you going to cry again?"

"You can't understand Oliver Tate without knowing his dark secret."

"Ha."

"You're not taking me seriously. His name's Keiron. He's a family friend."

"I think that you just think it's cool to have a dark secret."

I move my tongue along my bottom teeth.

"I am morally damaged," I say.

"You're a good liar."

"I'm not lying."

"Prove it."

"The proof is beneath you."

"What are you trying to say?"

"I mean it's on the carpet."

Jordana frowns and rolls out of the way.

I run my hands over the patch where she had been sitting. Something scrapes against my palm. I open my eyes.

"Rub here," I tell her.

She rubs her right hand back and forth over the same spot of carpet, flicking at it with her index finger. It makes a *scritch-scritch* sound.

"What does that prove?" With a great deal of effort, she raises one eyebrow.

"That's dried cum. You must recognize it. Abby King's sleeves are covered in this stuff."

"So he actually wanked you off?"

I bow my head.

"Yes."

"How would a seven-year-old boy know all those words?"

"I was lying about the words—I only said hotter and colder."

"And he actually wanked you off?"

"Keiron started things off but his technique was very poor so I ended up doing most of the work."

"So he didn't wank you off."

"Morally, he did."

She puts a finger under my chin and lifts my head up.

She's smiling.

"Have you told anyone else?" she says.

"No, just you."

"You do love me."

She takes my hand.

"I do," I tell her.

"Ha. So what did you say to your mother?"

"She thinks I am worried about the ice caps."

"Ol, it's okay. Don't look so bad."

I stare up at the ceiling rose. I think about my parents.

"It's nothing," she says. "He didn't even finish the job he started."

She puts her hand behind my neck and kisses me lightly on the chin.

I echo her. "It's nothing," I say. "Now you know my only secret."

"That's a rubbish secret," she says.

She grabs both my hands and falls back onto the Turkish rug, pulling me on top of her. I lie in between her legs. She snogs me aggressively. Her hair is laid out on the carpet in rays from her head. She spreads her legs so that I can rub my fly zip against her knickers.

My hard-on is back, it strains against my jeans. The guilt is lifting.

She pushes me up into a kneeling position and puts my hand against the crotch of her knickers.

I want to say: *Hotter.*

"Hotter," she says.

She pulls aside the crotch of her knickers like a curtain. It is the first time I have seen one in the flesh. It is not so pretty. I remind myself that I like the taste of shellfish.

With her other hand, she grabs my right index finger and traces it around the lips like someone applying Vaseline. She makes some noises. I close my eyes.

She guides my finger inside of her, where it is wet and warm. As I break the surface tension, she breathes jerkily. She helps me at first, her hand on mine until I get the hang of it—as though teaching me the knack for unlocking a difficult front door.

She lets go of her knickers and lets her arms lie, wrists up, on the rug; the knicker elastic rubs against the side of my hand. I put up with the discomfort.

She is squirming a little, arching her back, rubbing the crown of her head against the carpet. Her mouth is agape; I can see the back of her top teeth.

The games cupboard is open. I see Risk, Cluedo, Rummikub, Monopoly.

I close my eyes. My wrist is getting tired. I slow down.

"Fuck," she says.

I speed up.

"Fuck," she says.

I am reminded, again, of Chips's advice. One is an insult, two is a courtesy, three's a pleasure, and four is a challenge. I upgrade to two fingers.

"Futch," she says.

I have moved her beyond language.

"Ung," she says.

Evolution means nothing.

"Uh, stop, stopstopstop," she says, grabbing me by the wrist.

I open my eyes. She looks scared, standing on the edge, peering into the dark. We will take this step together. Not right now. But soon: next week is half term.

I want her first sexual experience to be perfect. I want her first sexual experience to be before I turn sixteen.

shadoof

I have heard my parents having sex. I've even heard my mother laugh during sex; I hope I've not inherited my father's problem.

Dad cooks grilled prawns in yogurt and lime as an aphrodisiac, on nights when my parents have been apart for a few days. My parents traveled to Goa before I was born, where they ate this dish.

"Do you remember them pulling the limes straight from the tree?" my father asks, knowing that my mother remembers. "And the smell of the sea and the decomposing limes?"

I imagine it smelling like The Body Shop.

"All the prawns were fresh, caught that morning," my father tells me.

"We couldn't understand why the prawns were gray." She turns to me. "Uncooked prawns are gray," she says.

A philter is a drink that stimulates sexual desire. My father pours my mother red wine and, instead of saying *when*, she just smiles. On these occasions they give me a small glass of wine. Alcohol can also act as a sedative.

I hear them through the thin floorboards.

My parents begin by laughing and chatting. Seven minutes pass, mostly in silence but occasionally broken by my father's low voice like a radiator grumbling. This is foreplay.

Jordana's father owns an extensive video collection. She has never heard her parents having sex. He stores the videos in a bin bag on the top shelf of the wardrobe in their bedroom. My parents' copy of the *The Kama Sutra of Vatsyayana* is not even illustrated; it lives on the bookcase in the sitting room. You may also find a book called *The Rough Guide to Prague* and *Am I Too Loud? Memoirs of an Accompanist* on the same shelf.

There is a short transition period between foreplay and penetration. At this point, I can hear weight being transferred as the bed frame groans, mattress sighs.

The Kama Sutra of Vatsyayana was translated by a man called Richard Burton. Under a subsection titled "Men Who Obtain Success with Women," the book claims that "men who know their weak points" will get all the ladies. My two main weaknesses: rounders and encouraging Jordana to set things on fire. She has burned my leg hair, the *Evening Post,* and an old, dried-out Christmas tree that went up like a jet engine.

Some other groups of men who will be successful with women: "men who like picnics and pleasure parties." I despise picnics. Also, "men well-versed in the science of love." And love *is* a science.

Coitus. It lasts for ten minutes. During sex my mother sounds as if she's being given a deep tissue massage. Is she having an orgasm? I'm certain my father cannot tell.

When it's over, my father, understandably, sounds relieved. He has outperformed the national average by two minutes. He will sleep well.

I have done some research on Tantra.com. It turns out that Tantra transports your sexuality from the plane of *doing* to the plane of *being.* It can last for up to fifteen hours.

Tonight, Jordana is coming round. I shall cook her a meal. I even told my parents about my plans. At this early stage in proceedings, I am doing my best to minimize any contact between my parents and Jordana. Mum said it was "terribly sweet" and promised to take Dad out for the evening.

So far, they have only glimpsed Jordana at the door a few times and, on one other occasion, when Jordana accepted the offer of a cup of tea. I am always careful not to let them start a conversation. It would not take more than three of my father's jokes for an icy wind to blow through our relationship.

My parents are going to see a performance of *Richard III* at the Grand Theatre. My dad told me the play contains a scene where Richard, an evil, unattractive man, seduces the recently bereaved wife of his brother, whom Richard also murdered, while the corpse is still in the room.

"Now there's seduction," he said.

I want the evening upon which we lose our collective virginities to be special. I'm no parthenologist but I suspect that Jordana's virginity is still intact. Her biological knowledge is minimal. She thinks that a perineum is to do with glacial moraine.

One of the factors here is that, in school, there have been rumors that Janet Smuts and Mark Pritchard have consummated or, at the least, are very close to it. There are also three other couples who are moving quickly from base to base, looking to make a name for themselves. I figure we might as well get involved before it seems like we're just jumping on the bandwagon.

The meal will set the tone. Jordana will be put at ease, confident in my sexual prowess, because cooking and lovemaking (as it will be known for this evening) are, after all, interchangeable skills.

For weeks now, with this evening in mind, I have been making a list of foods that she does not like. I sometimes go to school early to meet her for the breakfasts that they serve between eight and quarter to nine. Her parents don't eat breakfast.

I open my diary and write myself a reminder about Jordana's culinary habits:

J's culinary dos and don'ts

- Egg white. (I have told her that chocolate cake and pancakes contain egg white but she doesn't care.) She only likes the yolk.

- Sausages must be well cooked. She ruthlessly checks the skin for any telltale transparency.

- She does not like posh food. She has confirmed that the following foods are posh: paté, frankfurters, porridge, mushrooms, mussels, scallops, cockles, octopus, black pudding, hake, haddock, ratatouille.

- She only likes very soft cheese: overripe brie/camembert is acceptable if the rind has been removed. I asked her if a melted hard cheese is okay. It's not. I asked her if she could say which cheese lies on the cusp between hard and soft, just so I can get an idea of the boundaries. She said nothing.

I tear out the page and use the power of magnets to stick the list to the fridge door.

Jordana doesn't like the most traditional aphrodisiac, seafood, so I have decided to go for a safe, contraceptive option: homemade burgers. A burger with no bun and a perfectly round nose of egg yolk, no white—just to show I listen.

But there has to be a sense of ambition to the meal too. We have bundles of fresh asparagus in the fridge, which I will grill. I will also make creamy mash, partly because Jordana makes Smash for herself at home and partly because it is easier to overcook potatoes than boil them well.

"Anything you need from the shop before we go?" my mum asks.

"I've got it under control thanks," I say.

"Anything you need from the chemist?" my dad says.

"Lloyd, please." My mum opens the front door and pulls him outside by his elbow.

I bought a packet of Trojan Ultra Pleasure Extra Sensitive condoms: *No. 1 in AMERICA.* They smell nothing like a positive first sexual experience. I tried one on to check the fit. There are eleven left.

As with many things, good food relies on preparation. First, I wash eight small potatoes that are speckled with warts of dirt. My mother says that these potatoes taste better; she buys them from a farm where a woman wears Wellington boots at all times. I quarter them.

Finely chopping half an onion, I hope to cry but it does not happen—similar to Uncle Mark's funeral. I add the onion in with the worms of mince in a bowl. I practice kneading breast-sized patties, which, I'm almost certain, will benefit Jordana in the long run.

I crack an egg and use the shell halves to disrobe the yolk. The transparent white slops down into the sink. It does not run easily through the plug hole so I stir at it with my finger until it disperses. Jordana will benefit from this also.

I roll the elastic band down the bundle of asparagus—again, good practice—and lay the stalks out on the chopping board. Finally, I turn the electric grill to full, knowing that it takes a long time to heat up. If Chips were here, he would tell me why a woman and an oven are similar.

Now I wait for Jordana. When she comes, I will simply need to pop the potatoes on the heat, wait eight minutes, slide the burgers under the grill, wait four minutes, lay out the asparagus beneath the grill and turn the burgers, wait two minutes, maneuver the yolk onto the red spot in the center of the frying pan, break in my egg as well, drain and mash the potatoes, take out the burgers and asparagus: serve it all, *et voilà.*

My parents' room, situated on the first floor at the front of the house, contains the only double bed. Their bedroom has two large wooden framed windows looking out to sea. You can see the curve of Swansea bay, marked out by the seafront lights, tapering off to the glowing pier and the lighthouse. Out in the bay the Cork ferry may look like civilization but it probably contains at least one person vomiting. In between the two windows stands a dressing table made of smoky wood. It looks older than both Jordana and I put together. *Jordana and I put together.*

The queen-sized bed has a wooden frame and a dark orange duvet cover and pillows. The bedside tables on both sides are identically stocked: three books, a lamp, and a glasses case. I wonder if this allows my parents to swap sides during the night. I turn on one of the lamps, lighting the room like a sexy library.

A fireplace in one wall holds pinecones, not logs, in the hearth. A picture of me, six years old, wearing a beret and a stripy top like a sailor, stands on the mantelpiece. I turn the photo facedown. The scene is set.

I have one other, major concern: sex words. Mrs. Profit, our sex education teacher, has not tackled the difficult issue of knowing which words to use when describing the sexual act. Some words have the mark of an amateur: *nob, todger, willy.*

Penis and *vagina* are fine nouns but when overused they tend to make me think of the coffee tide-marks on Mrs. Profit's teeth.

We asked our Welsh teacher, Mr. Llewellyn—who is almost young—to tell us the Welsh sex words. The Welsh word for sex is *Rhyw.* It sounds like coughing. He said that, in general, Welsh speakers use English words. When pressed, he gave us a couple of examples to show us why this might be. *Llawes goch* means "red sleeve." *Coes fach* means "small leg." The phrase would be "put your small leg in my red sleeve."

Some euphemisms make you sound like Martin Clove, a boy

who for psychological reasons doesn't have to use the communal showers after rugby. When we ask Martin what is wrong with his wang he gets defensive and refers to it as his little man. This implies a kind of distant, seemingly friendly relationship between him and his penis.

In the *Kama Sutra* the penis becomes the *lingam* and the vagina becomes the *yoni*. These words will add a certain mystical resonance, like very poor lighting, to the congress. *Congress* is an ancient word for sex.

Chips says that "anal sex is for the connoisseur." He heard me use the word *connoisseur* once and said that he liked it. Now he uses it most days.

There are some much-underrated words used in Chips's porn magazines. *Razzle* contains a very candid letters section where readers describe their sexual enterprises. Often, as the sex becomes more passionate, the words become more evocative. "Lick my shaft" gives a sense of strength and an implication of coal mining. My rock-hard cock. My throbbing rod. You couldn't fail to be good in bed if you were the proud owner of a raging love-pole. One more word that may be useful in the heat of passion: *dong. Dong* sounds like someone very important has just arrived.

Describing the vagina throws up just as many, if not more, problems. I have been trying to think of my own words. I came up with *undermouth*. I came up with *undermouth*. I came up with *undermouth*. I'm not sure what this sentence means.

The doorbell rings. She is early, eager.

I open the door.

"Hey," she says.

She's not wearing makeup. We must have a modern relationship. She wears a black skirt, slightly crumpled and, like all her clothes, starred with dead skin. Her red zip-up top has got the hammer and sickle in yellow on the left breast.

In the seventies there was a female Russian weight lifter named

Yvana Sfetlova who was fed so many male hormones and steroids that she grew internal testicles. Jordana uses hydrocortisone—a steroid cream—for her eczema.

"You're crying again," she says.

"Onions," I say, blinking.

Sometimes the process of mourning a loved one can take years.

"You're still crying," she says and points at my nose. She wears a square green bracelet.

The dining room looks like the sort of room in which healthy, stable relationships form. On the mantelpiece sits a vase of fresh chrysanthemums that I bought from a house on Tavistock Terrace. In their porch they also had roses and rhododendrons in buckets with an honesty box hung from the door knocker. I bought chrysanthemums because they smelled least like an apology.

A blue tablecloth drapes over the large dining table. I have laid out our heaviest cutlery and two cork place mats next to each other, not at opposites like my parents. For Jordana's enjoyment, and because her skin looks smoother in the half-dark, I have lit five small candles.

"Posh," she says.

"I've made you dinner."

"It better not be scaloops."

She pronounces *scallops* wrong. I do not correct her.

Jordana circles the table, examining it. She's humming a song badly.

This reminds me that I forgot the romantic music.

"You can put some music on," I tell her. "The stereo's in the music room."

"Nah, I'm going to read your diary," she says and stomps upstairs to my bedroom.

I fill a pan with the recently boiled water from the kettle and carefully drop in the potatoes. The recipe says "toss them in" but I think that irresponsible. I place the pan on a hob.

The food is ready and on the plates, still she has not come downstairs. The asparagi look perfect: crispy, brown at the edges. The burgers, although a little dry, have held together. The mash is hairgel thick.

I put the plates out in the dining room and sit down. Jordana is a slow reader so I decide to start eating.

I hear her coming down the stairs; her clammy hands squeak as she slides them down the banister.

She stops and stands cowboy-style, framed in the doorway.

"Why didn't you write about fingering me on the carpet?" she says.

"Um. Because I have so much respect for you."

I would be good at faking an orgasm.

"No. You're *supposed* to write about the important moments in your life."

"Once our relationship's over, I'll be sure to write the whole thing up."

She cocks her hip, squints at me as if I don't make sense and looks huffy. She wants romance.

I cut off my fried egg's coattails, spear them with my fork, cut off a hunk of burger, stab that with my fork, cut the head off an asparagus, balance it on the bits of egg and burger, and finally dip the lot into the mash. I look into Jordana's eyes as I direct the fork into my mouth.

"Christ," she says, sitting down. She stares at her plate of food.

"Toyourtaste?" I ask, between chews.

She picks up her fork with her left hand and passes it to her right. She doesn't touch the knife.

"Oliver," she says, piercing the egg yolk—it bleeds over the edges of the burger and drips onto the plate—"why have you done all this?"

I hold my knife in the air as I take a few more chews. Swallowing is a bit of a struggle.

"Because we are going to make love tonight," I say.

Jordana puts down her fork and places her hand on my wrist like a nurse to an old person.

"No, Oli, we're not."

"Where shall we go?" I ask.

"Oliver," she looks into my eyes as if she means it, "no."

She moves her left hand toward the candle and passes her forefinger slowly through the flame. It blinks and ducks. I think she's lying.

"We could use the coffee table," I suggest.

The underside of her forefinger starts to darken; she pulls her finger back from the flame.

"The airing cupboard?" I suggest. "We can snuggle in amongst the beach towels."

Jordana picks up a limp asparagus spear with her fingers.

"Beneath the apple tree in the garden like Adam and Eve?"

"Oliver—fuck off." It suits Jordana to swear.

She dips the asparagus tip in a little egg yolk and simulates oral sex with it. She bites off the end and smiles.

"Stay here," she says, and as she speaks I can see a film of egg yolk on her teeth. She scrapes her chair back from the table, stands up, and leaves the room.

She returns, holding my diary and my pen.

"You need to get the beginning right," she says.

I cannot speak; I have just put a large glob of gelatinous mash in my mouth; I look slapped.

She pushes my plate out of the way and places my diary open on a blank page.

"Tomorrow's date," she says, handing me the pen.

I write the date in the top right-hand corner, while swallowing.

"Go on," she says, standing over me.

"What?" I say, looking up at her.

"Pretend that it's the day after you lost your virginity," she says.

I write:

Word of the day: Parthenologist—a specialist in the study of virgins or virginity.

Dear diary,
Chips lost his in the toilets of Riley's Snooker Club.

"Cross that out," she says. "This is supposed to be about me."
I put a line through.
"Let me start things off for you," she says. "Jordana is." She stops.

Jordana is . . .

"Go for it," she says.

. . . fully symmetrical. I can confirm that now.

"Never," she says. "You got one more chance."
I tear out the page and throw it at the wicker bin next to the dresser. It slips straight in. I take that as a good sign.
I have read that sometimes it is sexy if a man expresses his emotions:

19.5.97

Word of the day: Jordana

Oh diary,
I love her. I love her. I love her so much. Jordana is the most amazing person I have ever met. I could eat her. I could drink her blood. She's the only person I would allow to be shrunk to microscopic size and explore my body in a tiny submersible machine. She is wonderful and beautiful and sensitive and funny and sexy. She's too good for me, she's too good for anyone!

I stop for a moment, expecting her to interrupt me, tell me that she doesn't buy it. But she stays silently watching. I carry on:

All I could do was let her know. I said: "I love you more than words. And I am a big fan of words." This was a cheesy thing to say but being in love with Jordana, I have discovered, tends to make me cheesy. I told her: "I will happily wait forever for you."

(I confess that I did think, if only for a moment, that waiting forever would be a bit of a waste of our lithe and supple bodies but, nevertheless, I was willing to hold out.)

By some mad, intergalactic fortune, she said that she was ready. We made perfect, flawless love. We were no longer virgins. But it wasn't like losing anything.

"Okay, stop. Stop there."

I look up at Jordana. She blinks. A moment passes where I'm wondering what she is thinking about and she's wondering what I'm thinking about.

"All right," she says, slowly raises her index finger, and points at the ceiling. "Your parents' room."

Jordana looks through a small drawer on top of my parents' dressing table.

I am trying not to think about the food I prepared going cold and, in particular, the congealing egg yolk. I tell myself that if sex lives up to its reputation, food—not to mention breathing, talking, sleeping, and so on—will seem like nothing more than a tedious interlude between ruts.

Jordana finds a pair of Mum's earrings kept on black felt in a box. They are turquoise. She lifts one up to her ear and bats her eyelids. I am so ready.

The alarm clock on the bedside table claims that the time is four minutes past eight. The room is lit by my mother's bedside lamp. The curtains are open but, unless we end up making love directly against the window, nobody will be able to see us.

I stand next to Jordana in front of the dressing table. We are framed by the oval mirror. I'm about to kiss her when she kisses me first. She tastes of egg yolk, not milk. After a while I stop noticing the taste or I get used to it: synthesis. Our teeth knock together.

My hands move to her sides, she puts her hands on my neck. It is very passionate. Her eyes are closed, mine are open. In the mirror it looks as though she loves me more than I love her.

We sit on the bed and kiss for a long time; my lips feel swollen, as though I've eaten tomatoes. She lifts up my T-shirt and puts her hand on my stomach, which has bunched into four small rolls of flesh like a fat lady's neck.

She rubs her hand over my chest, brushing against my nipples. I have hardly any underarm hair and no chest hair but I have an erection. That is something that has happened.

I kiss her neck, this reciprocates an earlier action. One of her hands rests on my inner thigh. Next to her hand, under the blue denim of my jeans and my black boxers, lives my penis.

An unopened jar of Bonne Maman Strawberry Jam.

She lifts up the hem of my T-shirt with both hands. I put my arms up in the air and feel like a six-year-old as she pulls the shirt over my head.

Holding the collar of her red zip-up top with one hand, I unzip with the other. She shrugs her shoulders and the top falls down her back and off her arms as if she has done this many, many times before. Her shoulders are freckled; I want to grab her collarbones as if they were handlebars.

Roasted, stuffed, red and yellow peppers.

She hugs me with her skin and we fall backward onto the bed. She sits up momentarily on her knees, straddling my waist, and pulls off her vest. Her black, frilly bra reminds me of the net curtains at number thirteen. She reaches behind her back as if she's going to ask me which hand the surprise is in. There are two surprises: her bra falls off toward me.

I still have an erection. She has three striations on her stomach. I have seen these before. She says these lines appear when you overuse hydrocortisone cream. They look like the marks left on the skin of a leg of pork when it's been tied up with string in the oven.

I touch her left jubbly and then the right.

She rests herself on top of me; her breasts feel water-bottle warm.

Yvana Sfetlova.

She unbuttons and unzips my trousers. It surprises me that she has not noticed that I am hard. She looks at me with what I take to be admiration.

"Lift up," she says, nodding to my trousers, which she holds by two belt loops. I raise my crotch into the air and she yanks my trousers down to the knee.

"Off," she says, and I shuffle my jeans down my calves and kick them off my feet. Nice to still be wearing socks.

She takes a moment to unbutton her skirt at the side, then she whisks it off, matador-style.

St. Ives Exfoliating Apricot Scrub.

Her knickers are green. A couple of spider-leg black hairs poke through the cotton. It is common knowledge that every human eats six spiders a year while asleep. I still have a stiffy; her hands squeeze it through the material of my boxer shorts.

I put both my hands on her breasts, her tits. I caress them as you would the presents in a lucky dip box at the school Christmas fete. She makes a sound that can only mean arousal.

She places my right hand between her legs. I hope she knows what she's doing. I try to relax, it being vital that I remain spiritually involved. Her hands dip inside my boxer shorts, she strokes my lingam. She skips chapters of sexual etiquette but I forgive her.

Lamb shank.

My arm starts to ache as I hold my hand between her legs. I can feel the heat of her yoni but she is not sopping yet. Words from *Razzle:* sopping, juicing, dripping. Jordana is none of these.

On the bedside table I notice a book titled *A Guide to Daily Practice of Ohm Yoga.* Jordana thinks that I am lost in the moment. She laughs.

"What are you doing?" She looks down at my hand in between her thighs. She makes judgments with no frame of reference.

Falling down on the bed next to me, still laughing a little, she pulls off her knickers. Her pubes are longer than I imagined, and smoother.

"Come on," she says and tugs at my boxer shorts. I pull them down, wriggling like a worm, and kick them off. Just my Wilson sports socks remain. My own pubic hair, sparse and dry, looks more like a beard.

She smiles as if to say, *Wow.*

"Socks?" she says.

I lift my knees up and pull both socks off. We lie naked together.

I repeat Chips's rule of thumb: One finger's an insult, two's a courtesy, three's a pleasure, and four's a challenge.

I slide my hand down her chest and into the space between her legs, which she has opened slightly. I touch her yoni; it has the tacky texture of a Powerball. I find her clitoris with ease. I know I've found the clitoris because she tenses up and looks away.

She takes hold of my hand and moves it in a vaguely circular motion. Then she leans back again. Dad owns more pairs of shoes than I realize. Eight pairs sit on a shoe rack in the corner. The Cork ferry is going outward, not docking, I can see that now. This also means time has passed. Seven minutes in.

Jordana itches her wrist. My fingers feel slightly damp. I can smell her. She must be ready.

She pulls me on top of her but doesn't spread her legs. My cock wags a little.

Collins Pocket English Dictionary.

"You haven't got any condoms, have you?" she says. I notice remnants of egg yolk yellowing her lips.

"I've got eleven," I say. "They are in my room, beneath my Super Nintendo."

She pushes me up by my chest.

"Bye then."

She'll be fine while I'm gone. I swagger down the landing and into my bedroom. It is difficult to maneuver myself under the bed. Having an erection is sometimes like being in a wheelchair.

I still have a rock on when I get back to the room. Jordana lies on her side, facing away from me, her hands in her lap. Her chest is rising and falling. She is in the throes of something. I can see patches, like slap marks, of eczema on the backs of her knees. She doesn't notice me at first. She nuzzles her mouth into the duvet and makes an *nngh* sound.

I rip open a condom packet. The smell of no child support. I pull back my foreskin, which I have a lot of—Vienetta wrinkles—and place the condom on the end. I roll it down the shaft of my manhood. My penis wears its condom like a bank robber wears tights.

Jordana turns over to face me. She looks as though someone has told her a wonderful secret. She covers up her yoni, no, her pussy, with her hands. Perhaps she is embarrassed in my presence.

"Ready?" she says.

She pulls me on top of her. I touch her exactly on the clit—she is suddenly sodden. She pulls me in toward her, my hotrod touches her vag. It is thirteen minutes past. The national average is eight minutes. My father took ten. I watch as she slowly guides me inside as though feeding a crumpled note into a change machine.

Marie Claire had an article on how to make your man better in bed. It said that one of the best ways to prolong ejaculation was to think of strange, unsexual things.

Senile maculation—dark skin patches found upon old people.

Jordana makes the same sound that she made when I saw her brushing her knotted hair after swimming.

I could get used to this. Jordana holds me at the waist, occasionally digging her nails into my side. There is no pop sound like the seal being broken on a jam jar. Chips lied.

Salmagundi—a dish of chopped meat, anchovies, eggs, and seasoning.

The clock flashes twenty-two minutes past eight. That's nine minutes. I am a man. I have a dong. She is woman. Her pussy is wet. I must remember this moment—I will write a letter to *Razzle*. I start to really fuck her and my diction changes, hardens. I have a dong, a wang, a cock of rock. I stuff her, I pump her. I laugh at the faces she makes. She hardly even knows what she is doing. I'm going to come right up inside her. Spray my gunk all over her. She writhes now and we both know it doesn't matter that we have stayed in the missionary position. Next time we screw, I will spin her around like a wheel; the *Kama Sutra* calls this position "the top."

She sounds less and less like Chips's impression of a girl getting fucked.

I feel like a water balloon being filled up under the tap. I try and think of smoker's lungs or insect pupae or an endoscope but the balloon is still filling, pregnant, so I try and visualize a shadoof, an Egyptian irrigation device of a bucket on a pole, or a Hydra, the many-headed snake, but suddenly the water rushes upward so I stop thinking.

The condom is specked with blood the consistency of mucus. I pull the condom off my dong, which is still a dong, and throw it on the floor of my parents' room.

I lie back.

Jordana is here. She looks terrible.

"How many orgasms?" I ask.

She looks at the ceiling and scratches her arm, a plume of dead skin like a puff on a cigarette—postcoital.

"How many?" I say, but I think she lost count.

epistolary

20.5.97

Word of the day: Eugenics

Yes, diary. Yes.

All that training had paid off: fingertip pull-ups on the dado rail, strengthening my pelvic floor by clenching and unclenching on all bus journeys (thank you *Marie Claire*) plus hours of research with the *Kama Sutra* and the Internet.

I'm glad that Chips, my personal trainer, prepared me visually by recommending a strict sex-shaped diet: clams, kebab, wet lettuce.

We didn't even get under the covers.

As *Marie* predicted, we were discovering each other's bodies. I feel like I uncovered a new species.

We made Siamese semaphore. We were a cappuccino milk frother.

Just as I was about to let rip, I remember thinking—shiiit—

and—God!—and then suddenly, nothing, no words, except something vaguely *Cymraeg* at the back of my throat. I feel certain that, one day, the sound I made as I came inside a condom which, in turn, was inside Jordana, will come to mean "winner" in some distant future language.

Jordana did make some of the sounds I'd been expecting. There was something that approximated an oooh. Except with less vowels. More of an uh. But mostly she made sounds like *nh*.

Since we had sex—and with such results—I am drawn to ask the question: When will we do it again? Is there any point? Could we possibly hope to improve?

And now that I smell the way I do, I will not be washing again. My fingertips have the kick of permanent markers.

On that note I leave you.

O

P.S. Afterwards, I was ravenous. I finished off my plate of food then started in on Jordana's.

When I hear the Mazda pull up outside, I am reading the *New Larousse Encyclopedia of Mythology.* It is a book the size of a telephone directory. I rest it in my lap. I am focusing on the following sentence: *One morning Thor woke up to find that his hammer was missing.*

"Hello?" My mother calls from the porch. She sounds like someone entering a haunted house.

I am in the wicker chair by the bookcase in the front room. As my parents enter I look up and then clap the book closed.

"How was your evening?" I ask, nonchalant.

They are wearing their coats: Dad in a navy trench coat, Mum in an orange cagoule.

"Excellent," Dad says. "It was a good production, wasn't it?"

"Your gran would have liked it," she lowers her voice to a whisper, "lots of naked people." My gran gets the Edinburgh festival brochure and circles the performances that have warnings about nudity. She says she likes the human form.

Mum is looking around the room for something to tidy.

"And where's m'lady?" Dad says.

"Jordana went home."

Mum flicks the TV off standby.

"Always rushing off. She can't have been here very long," he says.

If only my father knew.

"I hope you walked her home," Dad says.

I shrug and say, "I put her in a taxi."

My mother straightens out the arm covers on the sofa. My dad smiles. He has his hand up on top of the open door, leaning on it.

"I hope you gave her enough money," Dad says, looking at the back of Mum's head. She picks up the remote control and puts it on top of the TV.

"I gave her three quid."

"Good. And how was the romantic meal?" My dad is grinning, waiting for my mother to look at him. She doesn't.

"It was fine. She liked her asparagi."

They do not even suspect that their bed was an accomplice. Jordana is two months older than me and, as such, she is the criminal mastermind.

I go upstairs. The first piss of my sex life twirls like the corkscrew roller coaster at Alton Towers. And it stinks. Like acid and bins and homeless people. I begin to think I have done something truly terrible for which I am being punished and my insides are turning to mulch but then I remember that we had asparagus for dinner.

Afterward I retire to my bedroom and write a letter to *Razzle*. It contains the metaphor: *I spread her legs as you might the center pages of a porn magazine.*

II.

diuretic

Last week, I found Dad's tricyclic antidepressants in the bathroom
bin. I defeated the childproof lid with an insouciant push-twist
motion. The bottle was half full of chalky white pills.

On alternativemedicine.com, a bookmarked Web site on my
dad's computer, it says that "the emotional lull from coming off
Prozac is often far worse in the patient's eyes than the original depression."

I think that the Web site means "in the view of the patient" and
that eyes are not especially affected.

The first sign was a downturn in Dad's otherwise impeccable
attendance record for Monday breakfasts.

When I got home after school on Monday, I found him at his
bedroom window in his blood-colored dressing gown, watching the
Cork ferry coming in to dock. Their bedroom light was on full
beam.

"Here's Corky," I said, in the game-show voice, as I entered the
room.

"Here is Corky," he confirmed.

He was holding a mug of water with a knobbly stub of lemon floating in it. He was wearing slippers and socks.

"Are you bad?" I asked.

He usually likes to hear me use Welsh colloquialisms.

He turned to me. The pouches under his eyes looked soft and smooth. He wasn't wearing his glasses.

"I don't feel very well," he confirmed. "I'm going to stay in bed."

His pupils were small.

I looked around the room. The bed was made. He had even laid the cushions out in a diamond pattern against the headboard.

I didn't see him then for a couple of days, except when he came downstairs to refill his mug with hot water and, sometimes, change his wedge of lemon. He was using the mug that has the word *Persona* written on it, next to an unimaginative logo: a Ferris wheel of colored dots, fading from red, through yellow, to green and back to red.

On the Monday night, Dad was upstairs in bed; it was just me and my mother having dinner. Although I am often frustrated by my parents' seemingly pointless teatime yakking, I should be thankful that, at the very least, they manage to entertain each other. I spent most of dinner listening to the sound of my own jaw moving. Even the infinite possibilities of my plateful of Alphabites did not throw up any topics for conversation.

In the silence we bore, I decided that I would write and memorize a list of topics of conversation to help us through the rest of the week. I tried to keep a balance of both our interests:

Appropriate	Inappropriate
Fungi	Chips's views on women
Homeopathic treatments for Jordana's eczema	Suicide—a cure for depression
What happened to that nice friend Rick	That time when Keiron came round

Her weight
Sharks
The meaning of the word *Persona*
  on Dad's mug
My metabolism
Jordana's parents
Oxbow lakes
The Mount Pleasant Quarry Group
What happened to that nice friend Zoe

Dad's sexual performance
Chips's views on immigration
Is it okay to have such an elastic
  foreskin?
Sunrises or sunsets?
The rhythm method of contraception
Chips's views on my mother's legs
Dad—hot or not?
Treat 'em mean, keep 'em keen—
  discuss

I can now confirm that the best of these topics was the *Persona* mug.

Mum spoke in the chirrupy voice she uses to answer the phone: "Persona is a brand-new form of birth control that works in harmony with your body." Her head waggled from side to side as she spoke.

"Right," I said.

She turned to look at me.

"Basically, you wee on a stick and it tells you whether you are fertile."

"Is that what you and Dad use?" I asked.

"Sometimes."

I looked at her encouragingly, hoping for a little more information.

"It's very popular in Italy," she said.

And that was the highlight of our repartee.

It is Friday afternoon.

This morning—without warning—Dad turned up to breakfast. He toasted a slice of wheat germ loaf, fried laver bread rolled in oatmeal, and poached an egg to go on top.

I ate half Raisin Splitz, half Golden Grahams. I listened to him chew. I watched his cheeks and filtrum swell and sink as his tongue tried to get bits out of his teeth.

He didn't speak. No mention of his sudden disappearance from dinnertimes. No explanation for the sudden penchant for seaweed. No apology for the fact that, overnight, he turned from being Papa Fun-Love, the Chirpy Chief, the Popsicle, into some sort of citrus-junkie-hermit. He could have at least written us a note, carved into the tablecloth:

J + O,
As of now,
my heart is a cold,
hard stone.
Ll

Dad is back in his bedroom. I am doing some research in an attempt to explain his behavior.

On Encarta, it says: "Depressive disorders are, thankfully, amongst the most treatable in psychiatry. Two major classes of drugs are used to treat depressive disorders: the tricyclic antidepressants and the monoamine oxidase (MAO) inhibitors. The latter require following a special diet because they interact with tyramine, which is found in beer, wine, cheeses and chicken liver and other foods, and causes elevation of blood pressure."

Which may explain the seaweed.

"A major development in drug therapy is the drug Prozac, which blocks the reuptake of serotonin in the brain.

"Electroconvulsive therapy is considered the most effective treatment for depression that is not susceptible to drugs."

I also read that "In 42% of cases, a placebo is as effective as genuine antidepressants."

I remember that last year, in the fairground, there was an arcade game called shocker where you sat holding these conductors and it pretended to give you an electric shock.

I think that it might work as a kind of electroconvulsive placebo.

Also, from my own experience, I have always felt that it is very difficult to be unhappy in a fairground. Even last year, when Chips and I were mugged behind the hot roast pork van, it didn't spoil our mood.

The boy had said, "Givuhsue money then boys," and he showed us a blunt-looking blade with a deer-hoof handle.

He had caught us at a good time, having just come from a bumper afternoon on the two-pence machines in the marina.

We paid out in fistfuls. The front pockets of his army-style coat became saggy copper tits. He walked slowly away, making the sound of sharpening knives.

The fair is on gravel at the recreation ground on the seafront. You can see the top of the Skyliner from my bedroom window. I bound downstairs, five at a time, parallel barring between banister and border rail.

It's dusky outside. I find my mum in the kitchen, lit up by the light from the open fridge, unpacking a Sainsbury's bag that slouches on the surface top.

I start simple: "Mum, can we go to the fair as a family unit?"

She stacks Apricot Muller Fruit Corners on the top shelf.

"It'll be fun!" I add.

"I don't fancy it, Ol," she says, transferring free-range eggs to slots in the fridge door. "Why don't you go with one of your friends? I don't mind giving you a few quid."

I stand behind her as she slides the natural Greek yogurt— Dad's favorite—in beside the Tupperware cheese box. I put on my orphan face and lean around her shoulder, into the angelic fridge light, and say, "When was the last time we had a family outing?"

She ignores me. Her mouth opens and closes. She huffs out through her nose, "Well . . ." She stands a carton of apple juice in the door.

"We never spend quality time together anymore," I add.

Her eyes flinch at this; I employ emotional shock therapy.

"I don't think your father will be in the mood for the fair right now," she says.

I stand back as she swings the fridge door shut.

She turns round and addresses me straight on.

"Me and you could go if you like?" she says.

There is the smell of cheese in plastic.

I say, "Ah, no, I don't think so."

I didn't mean it to come out like it did.

She holds my gaze. Her lips thin.

The phone rings.

"I'll go," she says, not going.

We listen to it bleat.

I notice a faint dew on her upper lip.

"I'll go," she says, going.

I listen as she answers. It's her friend, Martha, who wears green crystal earrings.

There are two phones in my house: one downstairs, in the music room, and one upstairs. The upstairs phone, in my dad's study, has a monitor button that, when pressed, plays phone calls through a small built-in speaker. You can hear the conversation but the conversation cannot hear you. I can't think of any other reason for this button than to help families with poor communication skills.

I go upstairs into the study and pull the swivel chair from under my dad's desk. I sit down and scoot across to the phone, next to the PC, and press the monitor button.

"...bin seeing this wonderful fella called Koo-free; he's from Nigeria," Martha says.

"Oh, very nice, Marth," Mum says, laughing. "Is there any continent that you haven't sampled?"

Pause.

"Oh please," Mum says, "if it takes that long to work it out then you should probably just say yes."

Pause.

"Fuck you," Martha says, three-quarters friendly.

"Sorry."

Pause.

"Are you okay?"

"Sorry," Mum says.

"You're not okay."

"Shit."

"What's up?"

"Ah, just the usual blah."

"What's the usual blah?"

Mum lowers her voice: "Just Oliver being Oliver."

I spin around on the swivel chair and look up at the ceiling; Oliver being Oliver being Oliver being Oliver. I am suddenly aware of the separation between my-actual-self and myself-as-seen-by-others. Who would win an arm wrestle? Who is better-looking? Who has the higher IQ?

"Is that it?" Martha asks.

"Yeah, I'm fine," Mum says.

"Is Lloyd still taking the, uh—?"

"Did I tell you that?"

"Yeah, 'course you did."

"Oh."

"I thought you said Lloyd'd been on the up, anyways."

"Yeah, but when he feels well, he blames it on the drugs."

"Aw."

"He says, 'I'd rather just be happy or sad.' "

Either my mother or Martha accidentally presses one of the buttons, I think it is the star key, and it makes a short *meeep*, like a wrong-answer sound in a game show.

"Oop. Hello?" Martha says.

"Still here," Mum says.

"So then . . ." Martha starts.

"Come on," Mum says, "tell us about this Coffee."

"Koo-free," Martha says.

"Dish the dirt," Mum says, trying to sound enthusiastic.

Pause.

"Before I forget," Martha says, "I read an article yesterday in the paper that said antidepressants, more than most drugs, rely on a patient's expectations about whether they will work."

"Mmm."

"Have you spoken to that homeopathic doctor who was at the PTA meeting?"

"Who?"

"You can't of missed him. Dafydd. The Silver Fox. He asked a question about school dinners for children with lactose intolerance."

"Oh yeah."

"Love you sound shattered."

"I am," Mum says.

Pause.

"Have you had any more word from Graham?"

I don't know who Graham is.

"Yeah, he's down next month. House hunting in Gower."

"Oh, wow."

"We're going for lunch at Vrindavan."

"Ah ha," Martha says. "He's still into all that stuff then?"

Vrindavan is a café run by the Hare Krishnas.

"Oh yes," Mum says.

I write the words *Who is Graham? (Never Trust a Hippie)* on a piece of scrap paper and stow it in the condom pocket of my jeans.

"What does Lloyd think?" Martha says.

"He says I should go and see him."

"Oh good."

"Yup."

I hear the door to the study creak open. I spin round.

Dad is standing in the doorway. His glasses are in his shirt pocket.

Mum speaks through the phone monitor: "Graham's staying in a barn in the Brecon Beacons, apparently."

Dad squints, as if it might be me speaking.

I reach quickly to punch off the monitor button, but I press the redial button by accident. There's a string of fast, almost melodic tones. I hammer away at the keypad until the monitor clicks off.

Dad has the interested, relaxed face he gets when he listens to classical music.

"Hi Dad," I say.

He doesn't look angry.

"Hi, Oli," he says.

I stand up.

His eyes don't seem to focus on anything. I need to say something.

"Dad, you know, the fair is in town. There's a Skyliner, a waltzer, and all sorts of other fun and amusing attractions. Maybe we could go?"

"Yeah, sounds good." He nods. "Shall we go now?"

"Yes," I say.

"Okay, I'll just get my shoes on."

I look down. He is barefoot. There are badges of hair on his big toes.

I run upstairs to my bedroom. In the name of research and family I take four of his pills. I chug them down with the remnants of last night's mug of Ribena.

I come downstairs. Mum is still on the phone. Dad writes a note and leaves it on the phone table in the hall.

J,
Taken Oli to the fair ☺
Ll x

It's getting dark as we park up on the gravel. I can hear screams and screamy laughter from the Terminator ride. The music is happy hardcore.

Abby King is really into happy hardcore. She tells me that hardcore occurs between 160 and 180 beats per minute. When I hear it leaking from her headphones at the bus stop, it sounds like the first jitterings of an insect invasion. She has a box set of ten tapes— eighteen hours of it—titled *Dreamscape 21*. She also owns a highly sought after black puffer jacket that says *Dreamscape* in textured lettering on the back. Some Mondays, when the bags under her eyes are the color of clay, she wears her *Dreamscape* jacket in every class, refuses to take it off.

As Dad strolls toward the stalls, the lights from the rides make his skin look green and red intermittently.

The recreation ground is right next to Mumbles Road. The cars speeding past add to the feeling of excitement.

First off, we stop to watch the dodgems. The music is straining through tinny speakers: bass drum thuds nestled in static.

"The music is called happy hardcore," I say encouragingly.

Dad watches the long sparks fall from the meshed metal ceiling. Two cars have a head-on collision. The young men jolt in their seats and throw their heads back, laughing.

"Do you want a go?" he says, leaning down to my ear.

"Nah, I want to go on the Skyliner."

I point to the far end of the fair. The Skyliner is moving slowly as they load people into each cage.

"Come on then," he says, walking ahead.

"Care to join me, Dad?"

"Mmm, I'll let you safety-test it first."

I am pleased. That was almost a joke.

We approach the booth where a pale man has coins piled in stacks of ten. Dad offers me a handful of change. I pluck out a pound and slide it through the mouse hole in the plastic window. The man adds my pound to a pile without saying anything.

I look up at the multicolored lightbulbs on the spokes of the wheel; they flash in swirls, spiderwebs, windmills, like the gambling machines in the arcade.

I walk up a textured steel ramp.

A man with a short, straight fringe and uneven stubble steadies an empty red cage.

"Right?" he asks.

"Yup," I say.

He signals me to get in.

He pulls a safety bar down over my head. It is not very safety, positioned at the same distance from my forehead as bicycle handlebars. I imagine a dotted line displaying the arced trajectory of my skull as it crashes, teeth-first, into the metal bar. There is a small metal panel on the roof that says *TriForm Construction Co.*

The wheel rotates one notch; there is still one empty cage.

A couple of girls walk up the ramp, drinking from matching cans of Cherry Coke. They look about sixteen. I turn in my seat to watch them. One of them has Nike tick earrings and is wearing a white coat with a fur-lined collar. The other is wearing white jogging bottoms that reveal the contours of her crotch.

"You can't take 'em on with you," the man says, nodding to their drinks.

They look coldly at him with their mouths slightly open, eyes tightened.

He doesn't say anything.

"I promise, *promise* that I won't spill any." She speaks in a singsong, her head slightly cocked.

"Sorry, love," he says.

"Tsuh," the other one makes a sucking sound, "but we'll be *really* careful."

"Sorry, girls, naw drinks," he says.

"'ckin 'ell," the one with the Nike earrings says before necking the whole can; I watch her throat pulse. She finishes. Her eyes glaze over. And then she burps; her mouth is wide open but the sound comes from her chest; little specks of fizz-froth jump off her tongue and catch in the light.

She throws her empty can at the bin on a small patch of grass below us. It clatters straight in. She lets out another, smaller echo of her first burp and smiles at the man.

Her friend is laughing. She throws her can too. It misses, bouncing and spluttering Coke, turning the gravel dark.

"Oops," she says.

I look over my shoulder to watch them jump into the cage behind me. They lean into each other as he pulls the safety bar down.

Dad watches me from the ground as I slowly gain height. I wave. He waves back.

As I move up from seven o'clock, past the watershed, I can see right across the fair. The generators look like squat toads, chain-smoking in the shaded corners behind each ride. In the cage behind me—below me—the two girls are pretending to be scared even though the ride is not going properly yet. One of them shouts, "Aaaah, fuckin' 'ell, *slow down!*"

As I reach the apogee I can see the word *DAVIS'S*, written in strobing lightbulbs on the roof of the dodgems.

I wave at Dad. He waves back.

The guy in the booth speaks into a police-style walkie-talkie.

"Are you ready?" His voice distorts through the Tannoy. He has a cockney accent.

"Yes!" I say.

"I can't 'ear you," he says. He is standing behind a thin plastic window. "Are. You. Ready?"

"Yeeesss!" I yell.

The man presses a button.

There is a cheer as the wheel starts to speed up.

As I reach the lowest point, I wave at Dad. He exaggeratedly pretends to bite his nails, as if he is terrified.

The wheel gains more speed. My cage starts to swing on its own axis, like a cot. They are playing "Rhythm Is a Dancer."

The girls start to scream.

I notice my dad has already been distracted by a game where you fish for plastic hoops.

The wheel accelerates. My cabin begins to pivot and roll. I think about the pills I have eaten bouncing around in my stomach like the balls in a lottery machine. I think of all the serotonin backing up in my brain. I think of the five different lottery machines: Arthur, Guinevere, Lancelot, Merlin, and Galahad. I start grinning like a mental.

"Woop!" I shout.

Centrifugal forces press my back against the seat. As I reach the apex, I see the floodlights have been turned on in St. Helens Rugby and Cricket Ground, squares of white light suspended in the air like open portals into the next dimension. I stare into the lights. Squares burn on my retinas as I plunge downward, my bum slipping forward on the cool metal seat, my chest against the safety bar.

I close my eyes. There are melting marshmallow shapes on the backs of my eyelids. My stomach does one. I concentrate on the pickling sensation, my happy synapses. I open my eyes.

"Yaaaaaaaaaaarrr!" I scream as I whip past the man with the wacky stubble. He is staring at nothing, looking bored, a cloth sack of change in his fist.

As I start to rocket upward, the bliss becomes overwhelming.

Rising, I have the floodlights in my peripheral vision like dizziness stars. I feel as though my head is growing. I have quite a large head anyway. I feel it swell as though someone is pulling all my hair at once.

There are some serious happy-screams coming from the other cages: girls, boys, men.

As I come over the apex and start to plunge, my neck becomes too weak to hold my head up straight. I feel like an alcoholic. I rest my head on the safety bar.

Everyone is screaming. I imagine that, like me, they believe the screws that hold their cage to the wheel are loosening. They foresee their red cage being tossed like a cricket ball, leg spinning over the fair, lit briefly in the floodlights. And just before visualizing their impact—crushing the roast pork caravan—they realize that the worst of it is over and they have survived one rotation. And for the few seconds while they are in the bottom third of the wheel, on their way up, they feel safe. That's when they laugh and scream simultaneously.

I rip past six o'clock and start to climb again; I am so happy that I can think about death without getting on a downer. My stomach is at Tumble Tots: forward rolls, cartwheels, rolypolys. I am close to ecstasy.

My cage turns briefly upside down as I reach the summit and start to plummet.

My mouth lolls open, my tongue is zero G. My IQ is in free fall. I can't think of the word.

Until I sweep upward again.

Prolapse. It means to fall or slip out of place, especially an organ.

Chips once showed me a photo on the Internet of a prolapsing rectum: a protrusion of the rectal mucous membrane through the anus. It looks like a monkey's brain. One of the ways I can tell that I am unhappy is if I get squeamish about looking up Internet photos of STDs, footballers' broken legs, napalm babies.

I reach the zenith and start to sink. The girls in the cage above are still laughing.

One of them yells, "Shut up, I'm bustin' for a slash!"

My ears go out of focus. There's the taste of blood in my mouth. I grip the safety bar weakly.

I start to lose touch with ups and downs. I scream, but only out of habit. The screams from the other cages start to become less frequent, less convincing. I try to focus on something stationary: two men are crammed into the control booth, speaking to each other.

I hear a man with a deep voice being sick.

I focus on my body. My temples feel swollen. I am aware of the shape of my own brain in my skull—I could draw its outline.

"Oh my God!" says one of the girls, again. After a few more rotations, they are the only ones still enjoying themselves. They are laughing hysterically.

Drops of liquid fall through the ceiling of my cage—landing on the vacant seat and splashing onto my hand and forearm. There are two smells: petrol and ammonia. I look up through the mesh toward the cage above me. I make out two colorless ovals, pressed together. Liquid is coming through the bottom of their cage. Some of it gets whipped away by the wind, some of it lands on my cage. They are more than mere ovals, they are bare buttocks.

As my cage tips forward the fluid runs off the seat and down onto the cage below.

"Oh my God!" says the one.

Paruresis is the fear of peeing in public places.

The Skyliner begins to resemble the water feature in the botanic gardens.

I rest my forehead on the safety bar and wait for the ride to stop.

I concentrate on visualizing my various internal bits. My lungs are rolled-up cereal packets. My heart's a wet tennis ball. My gut's a stolen purse. My spine is Jenga.

Eventually, they turn the Skyliner off: lights, music, the lot. There are two shrill screams as we freewheel to a stop.

They turn it back on; the lights disco and stutter at first. They slowly bring us down to the ground, a cage at a time.

As I get off the man with the short, straight fringe presses a pound into my hand. The ground feels like a water bed. So this is happiness. I have no idea what it will be like to be normal again.

Sitting on the gravel, I watch the two girls get out. One has splatter marks down the back of her trousers.

"This aim is out," Dad says, speaking to himself.

I find him bending his knees to look through the sight of a small rifle next to a sign that says: EVERYONE WINS! He takes a step back for perspective and notices me standing behind him.

"Ah, there you are. Was it fun?"

"It was good," I say.

He turns back to the gun and looks down the barrel with his right eye.

"A man was sick, but only on himself," I say.

"That's lucky," he says, squinting.

"Lucky," I say, sounding cryptic. I warm the pound coin in my fist.

He must think that it is normal for a Skyliner to spin for five minutes. He probably thinks it is good value for money.

My dad fires the gun; he hits the paper target mostly in the red zone and only partly on the thick black line that separates the red zone, where you win a prize, from the white zone, where you win nothing, or to be more precise, you win a badge.

"Yes!" my dad says.

The stall owner, who has been hidden from view, sitting on a stool, stands up to examine the paper target.

"Still got it," my father says, turning to me.

The stall owner is wearing a comfy-looking zip-up puffer jacket.

"Sorry—it didn't land entirely within the red zone. It has to be entirely within the red. Hard luck."

As my dad leans forward to look closely at the target he lets his mouth fall slightly open.

"Oh," he says, nodding gently, "not to worry."

The man holds out a bucket with the words EVERYONE WINS! in gold paint on the side. He rattles it at my dad. It is full of pin-on badges showing red and white targets. I think they are designed to let the other stall owners know who the suckers are.

Dad smiles to the stall owner and turns to me.

"Do you want one of these?" he asks me.

"No thanks," I say.

My father looks as though he might shatter.

"Thank you. We're okay," he tells the stall owner.

I try to think of what he would say if this had happened to me.

"Funfair? Unfair, more like," I say.

He laughs. It is not one of his normal laughs but it is a laugh all the same.

He bends down and picks up a furry whale off the gravel.

"I won this on the fishing game," he says, holding it out to me. "I'm sorry. It was either this or a crab."

The arcade is a low-ceilinged temporary construction, a bit like a demountable classroom. The walls and ceiling are black.

With my dad in tow, I ignore *Ridge Racer*, *Streetfighter II Turbo*, *Mortal Kombat*, and *Pac-Man* and walk straight up to *Shocker*, the authentic electric chair replica, which takes up the entire back wall.

The seat is an oversized oak throne. Above the back rest is a genuine volt-o-meter that records your progress toward the ultimate goal: 13,200 volts.

"Here we go, Dad. I want to pay for you to have a go on this," I say. "You've got to hold on until the end of the ride otherwise it's a waste of my money."

There are warning signs all around it. HIGH VOLTAGE and OVERHEAD POWER LINES. They have a Welsh-language one with a picture of a man being electrocuted: DANGER/PERYGL.

"How much are you paying to kill me?"

"Enough," I say.

I remember the time Dad gave me thirty quid to go to the therapist.

Dad sits down in the chair. He straightens his spine.

I help him do up the leather limb restraints. I make sure that his fingers are making secure contact with the electrodes on the armrests.

I put the warm pound in the coin slot.

"I didn't do it!" he says.

"Repent! Repent!" I say.

"My wife made me do it!" he says.

"Any last words?"

He opens his mouth while he thinks of something.

"If you gotta go, you gotta go!"

Dad says this on long car journeys when I tell him I need a piss.

"Any *better* last words?" I say.

"And now for the mystery!" he says.

A few of the kids in the arcade look across from their games. Two boys glance from the sunken seats of Formula One cars.

My dad is wearing a green short-sleeved shirt and khaki shorts.

"I sentence you to death by electrocution," I say, hitting the *High Power* button.

There is the sound of a heavy steel door being slammed shut and bolted. Then we hear his heartbeat beneath the hum of an electric generator warming up. The volt-o-meter twitches.

He raises his eyebrows and does a "this is scary" face. He has no idea.

The execution begins. The chair vibrates violently. I can tell that he was expecting something more serene. His sandals flap against his feet. There is the sharp fizzing of static.

Two boys in caps stand next to me, watching.

Dad holds on.

"Go on, Dad," I yell.

His best glasses slip off his nose, onto his knee briefly, before falling to the floor.

One of the boys laughs and points.

"You can do it!" I tell him, scampering forward to pick up his specs. I look up at him. He is blinking wildly.

The needle on the volt-o-meter waggles past the halfway point.

The woman who hands out change is watching from outside, smoking a cigarette. She looks bored.

Wisps of steam unfurl from behind his head.

His face has gone red, but to my surprise, he is beaming, his teeth chattering with the force of his grin. His laughter sounds choppy as he bounces on the seat.

I can see the shape of his knuckles, white against the skin.

One of the boys yells, "Bang!"

A shaft of smoke bursts out the top of Dad's head. There is the sound of frying and sizzling.

As the sound of the electric current fades, all that remains is the monotone of my father's flatlining heart monitor.

"Yes!" I shout.

The two boys nod approvingly, and saunter away.

The smoke rolls along the low ceiling and pours up into the night—a reverse waterfall—like when the kettle boils beneath the plate cupboard.

The seat slowly stops shaking.

Dad's eyes look glazed. His grip loosens on the electrodes.

His head slumps onto his shoulder. His tongue lolls. His limbs go limp.

I step up to the throne and take his hand in mine, as though I'm about to propose.

"You're not dead," I say.

His eyes roll back into his head. He groans, long and throaty. His arms rise slowly, his wrists are limp. The experiment has worked. It's been months, maybe longer since Dad pretended to be a reanimated corpse. His zombie hands wrap around my neck. They draw me into a hug.

"You're not dead," I say.

devolution

It's Wednesday. We're sat round the dinner table. Since my treatment, Dad's returned to work and has become far more communicative at mealtimes. I'm thinking of becoming a psychiatric doctor.

We had honeydew melon with Parma ham for a starter and now we're eating Moroccan lamb with couscous and sultanas. For the first time in weeks Dad has cooked our evening meal.

I am thinking about the name Graham. Over the years, I've heard my parents talk about all their friends. I've heard every kind of name, nickname, and surname—Maya, Salmon, Porko, Chessy, Morwen, Dyllis, Silent, Colleen—and yet I can't remember them ever mentioning Graham. On the phone, Mum's friend Martha was talking about Graham as if he was a major character, needing no introduction.

My parents are discussing public transport.

"It's almost cheaper to fly," Dad says.

I think it's important that all my parents' secrets are out in the open.

"Stop this," I say, raising my fork into the air. "I have a new topic of conversation."

They both look at me.

"Oliver, in polite society we change the direction of a conversation by pretending that the thing we want to talk about is in some way linked to the topic at hand," Dad says.

"Very important skill," Mum agrees. "Your granny is an absolute master."

"Let me try," I say.

"Okay," says Mum. "We were talking about the price of trains."

"Think of yourself as a TV presenter moving between segments," Dad says.

"Trains you say . . ." I allow a pregnant pause. "How incredibly dull, let's talk about what I want to talk about. *Who . . .* is Graham?"

My parents share a look.

"He's an old friend of ours," Mum says.

Dad whispers to me with a hand hiding his mouth, "He's the bloke I stole your mother from."

He chuckles like a gremlin, his shoulders jiggling.

Mum looks at him as if he is a child. His lips shape the word *oops* then he straightens up—back to adult mode.

"How old a friend is he?" I ask.

"Old, old," Mum says.

She sips her wine.

"Why haven't I heard of him before?" I ask.

"Well, because we haven't seen him in a long time. Lloyd, could you pass me the plum chutney please?"

"Why are we going to see him now?"

"What?" Mum says, although my question was clearly audible.

Dad pushes the chutney across the tablecloth.

"You're going for lunch with him," I say.

"Yes, *you* are," Dad says.

"That's right, Lloyd. *I'm* going for lunch with him because he's moving to Port Eynon."

"And he's an old friend," I say.

"Right," she says. There is a popping sound as Mum breaks the seal on the chutney jar.

"How can he afford to buy a place in Port Eynon anyway?" Dad asks.

Mum scoops out a forkful of the chunky, blood-red gloop, and shakes it onto the edge of her plate. Dad picks his napkin off the floor.

"Don't tell me he's actually got a job?" Dad says.

"Lloyd, the man has spent the best part of a decade setting up capoeira schools all over the States. He can afford a cottage in Port Eynon."

The man. She calls him *the man*. This worries me.

"I never knew there was so much dollar in dancing."

"It's not a dance, Lloyd."

"Oop. Beg your pardon," he says, throwing me a wink.

She raises her eyebrows at him before going on: "Anyway, he's very kindly invited *us* out to dinner."

"Hang on, let me just check my diary." Dad mimes turning the pages of a notebook, shakes his head and clicks his tongue. "Shame, I think I've got ballet class all weekend . . ."

I laugh.

"Lloyd—don't be a twat."

Don't be a twat—brilliant.

"No, seriously, I've actually got tons of work."

"Come on, you haven't seen the man in ten years."

Again—*the man*.

"You haven't seen my pile of marking."

"I'll do your marking, Dad," I say, thinking that it would be good for him to get out once in a while.

"There you go, Oliver'll do my marking. How's your knowledge of Welsh devolution, Ol?"

"Is that about how people from Cardiff are closer to apes?"

"Ba-dum," says Dad, hitting an imaginary cymbal. He hates Cardiff too.

"I'm not letting you change the topic of conversation," I say.

"Oh."

"So tell me: How did you steal Mum and did it involve tearing off your vest?"

Dad opens his mouth to speak but Mum looks at him sharply with her jaw cocked to the side and her tongue pressed against her bottom teeth.

"Your father did not steal me, Oliver."

"Is that when you tore your vest off, Dad?"

Whenever I tell Dad that he is boring, he claims he once tore his vest off. He never puts the story in context.

"Graham's an old, old boyfriend of mine but now he has a very nice girlfriend—"

"Whom he mentions at every opportun—"

"Whom he loves very much please Lloyd grow up."

All one sentence. Great.

"So why is he back in Swansea?" I ask.

"A very pertinent question, Oliver," Dad concurs, turning to my mother like a news reader going live to a reporter at the scene of the crime.

Mum balances a perfect mouthful on her fork (a speared nugget from the eye of the lamb chop with couscous—two sultanas included—balanced in a pile around it). The fork jitters; a few yellow grains tumble.

"You're a prick," she says to Dad before yomping the whole lot, chewing vigorously. When Mum says "prick" it scratches like a bramble.

I am still doing the face that says: *Hey-lo-oh? I have asked a question.*

My dad turns to me. "Oh, he must be moving back to Swansea for the cuisine, Oliver."

"Is he going to come round here for tea, then?" I ask.

Mum increases the speed of her chomping.

"Mmm, only if Jill cooks nut roast. Graham thinks I don't know my pulse from my elbow."

Dad laughs at this on his own.

Mum swallows. She gets up from the table, scrapes the rest of her food into the compost bin, and can be heard loudly putting her plate in the dishwasher.

Me and Dad keep eating. We stop talking about Graham. I expect Dad to wink at me or something but he doesn't.

canicide

"...I found out yesterday—it's called a medulloblastoma." I am shaken up; this is the first time Jordana has used a word I don't understand or told me that her mother, Jude, has a brain tumor.

We are on the footbridge on the way home from school. We stop and lean over the side, watching the cars disappear beneath us.

"That's a very long word," I say.

"Oliver, she's not on *Countdown*—she might die." Jordana lets a cable of spit hang from her lips.

I think about telling her that the maximum length of a word in *Countdown* is nine letters.

"Here comes Mrs. Riley's car," I say, pointing at the approaching Vauxhall, but Jordana has already spotted it. She bites her sputum loose. It misses; Jordana is not well.

"Unlucky," I say.

She is staring down at the road; her hair hides her face.

"The operation's in three weeks. The doctor said it is a very dangerous procedure; even if she doesn't die then, she may never be the same."

"Oh."

"They're going away just the two of them this weekend." Jordana doesn't look at me. "You should come round."

20.6.97

Word of the day: Exungulate—to trim or cut nails or hoofs

Dear JorDiary,
I've never met Jordana's parents. I don't think Jordana wants me to. I am content to imagine them from hearing about what they eat for tea and from seeing the inside of their house when they are out. They have a dresser with plates behind lightly frosted glass. They have a watercolor painting of Three Cliffs beach. They have a disconnected gas heater.

I imagine her father's nose is sturdy like a handhold on a climbing wall. I imagine the skin on her mother's neck, like boiled ham, mottled from holidays in Spain, in the days before it was bad to sunburn.

Fred cannot bark properly. He has a white goatee and a black body. Sometimes he opens his mouth and nothing comes out.

Pets mimic their owners; Fred is very protective. A few days after me and Jordana had done the dirty for the first time he swiped me across the ear. I would like to exungulate Fred.

He is ninety-six in dog years. He has a birthday every sixty days. In the book *Parenting Teens with Love and Logic*, it says that pets are important because they die. They allow children to adjust to death and mourning. It is in Jordana's interest that Fred should die before her mother does.

Jordana says there's been talk of putting Fred down—which is a way of phrasing nonvoluntary euthanasia. He's been shitting halfway up the stairs—I think this is because he is old and frail and gets vertigo on the way up. Fred also has arthritis. This means he runs in the manner of a rocking horse.

Because I am an excellent and attentive boyfriend, I take an active interest in Jordana's physical health. According to my Internet research, pets can encourage eczema. The problem is twofold. Firstly, eczematics—a word I have invented—are often allergic to pet hair. Secondly, microscopic dust mites feast on the dead skin and hairs which pets distribute.

On an unrelated note, I went to the hardware store on Sketty Road today. They had snap traps called Lucifer and The Big Cheese. I settled for Ratak, which is a tube full of pellets. Kills rats and mice including those resistant to warfarin. I will never forget the day I saw a tremendous rat, checking out the bin bags outside number thirty.

I like the word warfarin.

Howl,

O

Saturday morning.

I am in Jordana's kitchen. I arrived at ten o'clock knowing that Jordana would still be in her pajamas. They are not sexy pajamas; they have pictures of clouds and rainbows on them. She is upstairs getting changed.

In the cupboard below the sink there are tins of dog food and a big bag of Canine Crunch balls. I take a handful of Canine Crunch and then a handful of Ratak and drop them in Fred's bowl. The rat poison looks convincing enough, if slightly off-color and too small, among the Crunch.

Fred stumbles in, pushing the kitchen door open with his head.

Ratak is actually made of *cholecalciferol.* I put this word into Yahoo and discovered more about its effects. As luck would have it the Web site—an online scientific journal called *Isis*—warned that this chemical is specifically dangerous to dogs.

As a matter of respect, I tell Fred what will happen, although, of course, he does not understand human words.

"First off, your lungs, stomach, and kidney will calcify."

He looks at me dumbly.

"Then a few hours, maybe days later: internal bleeding, heart problems, kidney failure."

Fred's on his last legs anyway. I am sure that, on balance, he would be willing to put up with some discomfort and a slightly curtailed life-span in order to safeguard Jordana's long-term emotional stability.

Fred opens his mouth but no sound comes out.

I wash my hands and go upstairs to tend to Jordana.

Later, when I come downstairs to see how he is getting on— Jordana is worn out—only the rat pellets remain, huddled together in the center of his bowl. Fred is sat in his basket with his eyes wide. He opens his mouth but no sound comes out.

I take the rat pellets out of the bowl and put them onto a chopping board. I use the handle of a carving knife to mash each ball individually, like my dad crushing garlic. Fred jumps stiffly up onto the wooden stool by the counter to watch. I look at his black lips.

I take the can of Pedigree Chum, Heart, Liver & Paunch flavor, from the fridge and sprinkle in the death dust, mixing it with a fork.

"You are very noble," I say, putting the tin back in the fridge.

He stares at the fridge door.

Monday afternoon, walking Jordana home from school, I ask, "How's Fred?"

Jordana cocks her head toward me and narrows her eyes.

"I'm just curious," I say. "I like him."

She opens her mouth to say something but then closes it.

Then opens it again. "He's stopped eating actually." Jordana looks suspiciously at me. "I think he knows that something's wrong."

She is suspicious because I am taking an interest, not because she thinks I am planning an assassination.

"Oh. Dogs are very intelligent," I say.

We walk in silence down the middle of Watkin Street. I have a Tesco bag for my P.E. kit, which I am prepared to wrap around Fred's muzzle.

"Shit," Jordana says, stopping, as if she's remembered something important. She bares her teeth guiltily.

"Poor old Mrs. Riley," she says.

Mrs. Riley is our religious education teacher.

"I really think we went too far," she says.

Since Jordana has known about her mum's tumor she has changed in two ways. First, she's more sympathetic. She calls people by their first names instead of their nicknames: Scab and Rid are now Joseph and Rhydian. When a teacher has clearly made a special effort, like when Mr. Linton brought in his electric guitar, she pays attention and looks interested. She hasn't slagged off Janet Smuts in days.

Second, she values her own life. She waits for the beeps before crossing the main road. She has bought a cycle helmet although she hardly ever rides her bike. She puts her bag on her lap to hide the fact that she wears her seat belt on the school bus.

Mrs. Riley has a large mole above her right eyebrow. While she was out photocopying we stole her BluTack. On Chips's command, all eighteen of us molded our own attachable moles. Chips even went to the trouble of plucking one of his pubes—he has them to spare—to give his some decoration. Jordana seemed reluctant, but knowing the rules, she still conformed. We wore our benign accessories above the right eyebrow. Mrs. Riley must have been surprised that our heads were down, working hard, when she came back in.

"What's wrong with you lot?" she asked, as if she'd finally made a breakthrough with her problem class.

We looked up from our work. It took about four seconds before she started to cry.

Her classroom has one of those doors that you have to lock or it keeps swinging open; it took about twelve seconds of jiggling with the key before she could run out into the corridor.

We keep walking. Jordana is biting her bottom lip.

"Shit," Jordana says again, stopping in the road.

"Well, nobody expected her to cry," I say, remembering Chips's exact words: *I bet she weeps.*

I stop and look back; her eyes are wide, staring past me into the road. Jordana needs to control her empathy.

"It was probably symptomatic of deeper emotional turmoil," I say.

"Shut up," she says; her eyes are fixed on something.

I follow her gaze to the middle of the road a few meters ahead. A black dog is laid out, its legs twitching.

"It's Fred," she says.

I step a bit closer and see that his gut is split, tiny intestines spilling out, spag bol on the tarmac. His eyes are straining at their sockets like zits ready to pop. His jaw is slack. His teeth are mostly yellow but the tips are white—snowcapped. Just beyond him, there is a gory comet-shaped splat of blood on the road.

"Fred's dead," I say, trying not to enjoy the rhyme.

And then, for the first time in his sixteen years, Fred makes a noise to be proud of. He sounds like a failing hedge trimmer: half gargling, half squealing.

"He's still alive," Jordana says, and I wonder whether she is going to try to save him: press his eyes back in, sew him up with her shoelaces. I think of the old guy from Saint John's Ambulance who came to morning assembly and showed us how to snog a plastic twelve-year-old girl whose heart had stopped. One of the things I like—liked—about Fred was that he didn't have bad breath.

Jordana disappears. I assume that she's gone to get help, that she can't handle the horror of it. I kind of know what she means. It's the way his legs are twitching that's really making me unhappy.

I ought to put him out of his misery. That would be the humane thing. There's a skip just down the road that I could get a brick or a plank from. I wonder how Fred would prefer to go. Brick or plank? Which carries more dignity? But I don't do anything because I can't stop staring at him. The hair on his back is spiked up—punky—in tufts of gore. A trail of blood leaks toward the gutter. I turn away from Fred so I can think more clearly.

I'm surprised he can manage it but Fred makes the sound again—a caterwaul.

I think that at least Fred is dying with an obscure word.

Jordana returns carrying a cinder block.

The look on her face is focused and sad. It's the same face she puts on when she's doing a maths test.

"You're joking," I say.

"We can't just leave him."

"I don't think the cinder block is the way forward."

"We've got to do something."

"Maybe we should just wait for another car?"

"Oh God," she says.

"How long do you think he'll last?"

"Poor Fred," she says.

His mouth isn't even open but he makes a noise again. The sound comes from his throat. It is closer to gargling.

"Oh Fred!" Jordana's face has gone red. She stands over him with the cinder block. "I've got to."

"You can't," I say.

"It's for his own good," she says.

"But."

"Help me hold it."

"He'll be dead soon."

"Help me hold it."

Her eyebrows are scrunched low over her eyes.

We stand either side of Fred's skull and hold the edges of the cinder block. Patches of dried skin run up Jordana's wrists where she's been scratching. It looks like when you scuff carpet the wrong way.

I think that if Jordana's mum was in Fred's situation we would not have this option unless they flew her to Switzerland, where there are no rules.

"Hitler did this to disabled people," I tell her.

"Shut up, Oli."

"The word is *euthanasia*," I say.

"Shut up!"

It used to be one of my favorite words.

"Right, after three," she says. She's blinking furiously.

"I can't," I say.

"Three."

"Stop."

"Two."

"Please."

"One."

"God."

"Go."

Neither of us let go.

"Shit," she says.

"Sorry," I say.

"Shit."

His legs stop spazzing after four and a half minutes. I help Jordana slide a sheet of cardboard under Fred's remains. The smell, I can only assume, is of half-digested feces. We stretcher him into the skip, tossing him beneath a mattress, among a load of coat hangers.

We hug in the middle of the road. I spare a thought for Fred the martyr. At least he died under his own steam. His death will be a huge help in the event of Jordana's mum's death; and it may help reduce the dust mite population. I feel Jordana crying against my shoulder.

I am happy because I see the bigger picture. She has passed the mock exam for losing a loved one.

Two days later. Two weeks before the operation. We are sitting on the swings. It is nice to be able to sit here and not have to worry about Fred running off or shitting in obscure places.

"My parents asked me to thank you for helping me with Fred. I told them that you liked Fred. That you worried about him."

Jordana's face is fixed in the expression that means she thinks she understands me, knows my good side, sees how caring I am, even if I do not. She does this face more often nowadays.

"Jude said she wants to meet you," Jordana says, looking across at me. Since her mother's illness, Jordana has started referring to her mother by her first name, Jude. This is unfortunate: she now sees her mother as a fellow human being. "They've invited you round for dinner."

Again she is making the face. She thinks that I am endearingly nervous because I want to make a good impression. I try not to think that this may be the one time I get to meet Jude before she dies.

"Don't look so worried. They won't kill you."

I look away. I'm thinking about the rat poison on the chopping board.

trojans

Last Sunday, Mum went for lunch with Graham at Vrindavan—the Hare Krishna café. Dad stayed home.

I once had the misfortune to be taken to Vrindavan. Vegan chocolate cake was the safe option. Their menu is partly a manifesto. Vegans claim that beekeepers are slave owners, that honey is theft.

I believe in market forces and I think that if bees had the power of rational thought they would be willing to exchange their surplus honey for clean, freestanding, man-made hives that are reminiscent of up-market beach huts. Bees already work in a pleasant environment—flowers, et cetera—and they would want the classy living arrangements to match.

When my mother came back from the luncheon she went straight upstairs and had a long conversation with Dad. Then she came to speak to me. She sat with me on the floor of my bedroom. She explained that their friend Graham volunteers at a meditation retreat in Powys and that he offered her a spare place. I said congratulations. She said that she'd always wanted to try something like this.

She said it was a good opportunity because these courses are normally booked up for months in advance. I asked her if she felt indebted to Graham. She said that the introductory course was going to take ten days. I said she should be careful not to believe everything she hears in Vrindavan café. She said, It starts next Saturday. She told me that Dad would look after me while she was away.

Dad thinks that rice pudding is my favorite dessert. I think it looks like fly pupae.

Mum left yesterday morning to go to Powys. My father and I have been spending some quality time together.

"This used to be my favorite too," he says, portioning his spoon through the wrinkled skin. A swollen rice grain has attached itself to his mustache. Dad will eat leftover rice pudding—cold—for breakfast, lunch, and dinner.

"More?"

"No thanks, I'm stuffed," I say.

He nods, swallows.

"Dad. About Graham?"

"Yup."

"What's he like?"

"He's a decent-enough chap. Why do you ask?"

I feel like saying: I wouldn't let my girlfriend go away for ten days with a decent-enough chap. Chips is a decent enough chap.

"What's Graham's surname?"

"Why?"

"I'm just thinking about Mum."

"Mum'll be fine."

"Will she?" I say cryptically.

"Yes, she will."

"Right."

I stare at the painting on the wall behind my dad's head. My parents actually paid money for it. It is of a shrunken old woman in front of a terraced house.

"Anyway, how's Jordana?"

"Improving," I say.

"Do you think you'll ever let us meet her properly?"

"No. Not until you're terminally ill."

"Oh, nice."

"I'm meeting Jordana's parents for dinner."

He puts another spoonful in his mouth and chews. The sound reminds me of two fingers: a courtesy, according to Chips's rule of thumb. There is a kind of white tidal foam at the corners of his mouth.

I try and imagine what would actually happen if my father and Jordana had a lengthy conversation. I visualize them sat around a table in a French restaurant with a red and white checkered tablecloth. I visualize my father ordering the snails in garlic. I visualize Jordana's lips retreating inside her mouth. I visualize her asking for half chips, half rice. I visualize my dad's ears turning red. The universe might actually end. When two immovable objects collide.

"I hope you're using condoms," he says.

I clink my spoon around the sides of the glass bowl.

"I use Trojans, America's number one," I say.

My dad is a historian. Albeit in Welsh history. I expect him to say that I should be wary of trusting a condom brand named after a moment in history when the Greeks snuck their army—or penis—into a Trojan fort—or vagina—by hiding in a giant wooden horse—or condom—that they pretended was a gift. When the Trojans got drunk, the condom split and all the Greek soldiers wriggled out and got down to some serious pillaging.

"Oh well, right," he says.

I Ask Jeeves to "tell me about the meditation retreat in Powys where Graham volunteers."

Jeeves knows exactly what I am talking about. The first Web site he comes up with is for the Anicca meditation retreat. There is a person named Graham Whiteland who is one of the volunteers. The Web site has some information about the style of meditation as well as directions for an address in Powys.

Then I Ask Jeeves, "Who the heck is Graham Whiteland?" Jeeves shows me a Graham Whiteland who is an antique jewelry dealer from Islington. And a Graham Whiteland who has a gallery of underwater photos from his honeymoon to the Great Barrier Reef; he and his wife look very in love beneath their goggles, surrounded by marlin like confetti.

"I'll need to get on that machine in a minute," Dad yells from downstairs. My dad thinks that anything with a plug is a machine.

My father shouts for my mother, even though she is in Powys: "Tell Oliver to get off that bloody thing," he says.

There is no reply.

"Oliver!" He yells, although I can hear him perfectly.

I disconnect from the Internet.

"I'll need to get on that thing soon. You shouldn't be on the Internet at this time of night anyway."

My dad thinks that the Internet gets more filthy after the watershed.

We only have one phone line in our house—we use it for both the modem and the phone—so I have to disconnect from the Internet to allow incoming calls. When the phone rings, it is proof that I am not downloading child porn.

Chips once brought in a black-and-white printout of a girl, about my age, with her legs spread. He said that he hates his father so much that he downloads child pornography onto his dad's computer and puts it in folders marked things like *Private* and *Carl's Stuff*. He says he likes to wank off to proper porn, that child porn is like being in the bath with your sister. Chips's sister lives with his mum.

The phone rings.

My dad answers halfway through the second ring.

"Helloo?"

He is never depressed when he answers the phone.

I switch on the monitor button. It's my dad's oldest friend, Geraint. They grew up together. Geraint's accent is melodic, mellifluous and deep.

"I'm good, Butt, battling on," Geraint says. The bass from his voice is too much for the crappy in-built speaker. He distorts. " 'Ow-er you, boy bach?"

"Very well, ta. Just pootling along, as per. You sound well."

"Pootling? Yew getting old, mush. 'Ow-zoo lady-wife?"

"She's away at the moment, not far from you actually."

"Oh yeah?"

"Up in darkest Powys. She's on a *meditation retreat*." Dad says the words *meditation retreat* as if he were saying the words *colored person*.

"Oh, a meditation retreat, is 'at what she told you?"

Geraint does his big valleys laugh; the speaker fizzes.

Dad laughs too, after a pause.

"You want to be careful, Butt. She might run off with a monk."

"Hahahaha," Dad says.

Dad stops laughing.

"So, how long she there for?"

"Ten days."

"*Ten days?*" Geraint says.

Ten days is too long. Ten days is basically a honeymoon. According to Chips's seduction time scale, Graham will have brokered the deal by Thursday next week.

"I know. But apparently that's the minimum time it takes for someone to *feel the benefits*."

"Well, I'm sure she'll be in touch with something by the end of that."

Geraint does his big laugh.

"Oh yes, I should think so."

"Well, Butty, since you lady-wife is off enjoying herself, this brings me to the important matter of a certain rugby tournament disguised as five weekends of binge drinking."

Part of the deal with being friends with Geraint is that my dad has to pretend he loves rugby. Every year, they go with an old school friend, Bill, stay in a hotel in Cardiff, and watch Wales play in the Five Nations tournament.

"I've got us three tickets for Wales–England; Bill's booked the hotel. All we need now is you and your liver."

"Well, let's 'ope we do better than last year. We owe those bastards a beating."

After a weekend spent with Geraint, my dad's *h*'s disappear. Like me, he knows how important it is to sound the same as everybody else. Dad's parents are Welsh, and he was born in Mount Pleasant Hospital, but he spent the first ten years of his life in London, where my gramps—who is dead—worked in insurance. My grandad is commonly known as the man who invented the no-claims bonus. Growing up in England, the schoolkids used to call Dad "Taff" even though, by age ten, he had an English accent. Then his parents settled in Newport, Pembrokeshire, which is where Dad went to secondary school and they called him "Toff." It was at this point that he met Geraint and learned to play rugby.

Dad only sounds properly Welsh when he's been drinking with Geraint and Bill. I only sound properly Welsh when I am trying to impress someone.

"Oh God, now don't get me started," Geraint says. "Those cheap bastards."

"We should 'ave let France win."

I can't stand to hear my dad pretend to know about rugby. I switch off the monitor button. I think about Chips. I wonder whether we will get together when we are forty and go through his porn magazines, just like old times, and I'll have to keep saying, "Oh my fuck!" and "Look at her minge!" and so on, just like I do at the moment. It's a show of affection, I suppose.

I hear my dad say, "Byeee," and put the phone down.

I think that if Dad can pretend to like rugby, he can pretend to be happily married.

I reconnect to the Internet and go back to the Anicca Web site.

The nearest train station is Llandrindod Wells. I start to print out the map and directions. The Epson 610 mumbles, struggling with the various colors.

I search train times from Swansea. The screen shows a clock while it checks availability.

"Oliver! You can put these dishes in the machine too," Dad shouts.

There's a train that leaves at eleven tomorrow morning. I can hear him noisily putting the dishes away.

The printer heaves and groans—halfway done; I can see that the retreat is next to a river, couched in contours. Cutlery clatters. I close all the windows and clear the cookies just in case. The dining room door slams shut. Dad stomps down the hallway. He clops loudly upstairs, two steps at a time.

"I'll put a brick through that fucking machine!"

I remember when my dad said that we could not afford a new computer. But then he went to Hertec Computing in town and came back with a top-of-the-range Pentium 90. The man had told him it was an investment.

The door swings back. I yank the A4 tongue from the printer's mouth, crumple it awkwardly at my side.

"Now what are you doing?"

His hands are red and wet; the top of his forehead is reflective. He smells of fake lemons.

"Hey?" he says. I can see the cartilage at the bridge of his nose, straining at the skin.

I think about a story Chips once told me about his dad finding him with a porn magazine. I remember what Chips said.

"It's porn, Dad. Sorry." It helps that I look guilty.

In Chips's story his dad asks to have a look.

"Oh well, right," he says.

26.6.97

Dear diary,

- I have decided to stage an intervention. I've promised Jordana I'll go for dinner with her parents tomorrow so I'll have to leave on Monday morning. I only hope it's not too late.

- Anicca meditation is mostly about the total eradication of mental impurities and the resultant highest happiness of full liberation.

    The site claims Mum will undergo "a process of self-purification by self-observation." For ten days, she will not be talking, writing, reading, listening to Radio Four, drinking alcohol, killing any living creature, or making eye contact. The site seems designed to throw a worried spouse off the scent; it claims there will be "no physical contact whatsoever between persons of the same or opposite sex."

- The Web site says: "No charges are made, not even to cover the cost of food and accommodation. Neither the teacher nor the assistant teachers receive remuneration; they and others who serve on the course volunteer their time and efforts." The word *volunteer* arouses my suspicion. Graham "volunteered" to spend ten days in a room with my mother, eyes closed, breathing deeply—there are many different kinds of foreplay.

- Volunteering also gives Graham a chance to cook meals, make beds, bleach the showers, pull slugs of hair from the plug holes; he knows my mum is modern and likes a man who can perform domestic tasks.

- Earlier, I found Dad not playing a thing at the upright piano, not even D minor which is easy and sad. I also caught him at his desk: flossing. He ignored two phone calls and, ever since Mum went away, he has regressed to drinking hot water and lemon—using the same mug over and over—never washing it. The mug is decorated with a variety of cartoon penguins: Emperor, Little Blue, rockhopper, Adélie, and King.

- I told Dad that while Mum was away I was going to spend a few days with my friend Dave. He said: "That's fine." I don't know anybody called Dave.

A feeling of unease,
Oli

decollation

"Now here's a riddle for you, Oliver."

Jordana's dad's name is Bryn.

We are seated at a dark varnished wood table. There are six seats but dinner was only set for four. Jordana is opposite me, next to her dad. I'm sat next to Jude. We ate roast beef that, although tasty, did not respond to chewing. I was forced to swallow large gristly fur balls. The carrots had been boiled until they looked out of focus. The broccoli was delish and the roast potatoes were crispy balls of molten salty goo. There are cork mats laid out at each place and two in the center.

Jordana groans and lets her head drop: "Dad!"

"Now I know Jor has heard this before but it's a good one, right."

I nod.

Bryn has exactly the nose I'd expected. Sturdy and thick. Nostrils I could fit my thumb into.

He leans onto the table with his meaty forearm, turning to me.

"Right. The king wants to find a suitable man to marry his daughter, the beautiful princess."

"Okay," I say. Basically, this is it. This is the moment when I am going to be found out.

I can smell perfume, remnants of dog hair and onions.

"Now, as you can imagine, every man across the land wants to marry the beautiful princess so the king devises a test for any potential suitors. If they pass the test then they can have his daughter's hand in marriage; if they fail, then they will be beheaded."

Bryn's smile is enormous. Jude is smiling too.

Decollation is another word for beheading.

I'm glad that I thought about my outfit. I am wearing my darkest jeans and a navy blue shirt made by L.L. Bean that my mum brought me back from New Orleans.

"It's a very simple test to make sure that the man who wants to marry his daughter is really committed to her. The king has a bag with two grapes in it. One white, one black. Okay?"

"Right," I say, thinking about my half-Welsh half-Bangladeshi friend Rayhan.

"All you have to do to marry the princess is pick the white grape out of the bag, not the black."

"Okay," I say, starting to get into it, "fifty-fifty chance of survival."

They are both smiling. Bryn is nodding slightly. I don't look at Jordana.

"Right, yeah, exactly." He looks down at the table for a moment, at his dirty plate, a rainbow swoosh of clean plate where he had mopped through gravy with a roast potato.

"So the first suitor comes to take the test. He reaches inside the bag and pulls out a black grape."

"Oh no," I say.

"Oh yes. So he's for the chop."

I raise my eyebrows as if to say, phew, life can be tough.

"But what he didn't know was that the king, who loved his

daughter just a little too much," he laughs at this and glances to Jordana, who looks exasperated, "had put two black grapes in the bag."

I open my mouth a little. Bryn takes a sip of his wine. Jude's fingertips rub the stem of her glass: it is still full.

"So many suitors came to try their luck but unsurprisingly they all failed and were beheaded.

"So the question is: How do you pass the king's test?"

I look to Jordana and then Jude. Jude's hair is her best feature. She has the hair of an air hostess.

"No clues," Bryn says, "his life is on the line."

I try not to think that the impression I make now is the one that Jude will take to her grave.

At first I think of peeling the grape so that it would be a kind of greeny red color; perhaps that would be enough to get away with my life—how much can one girl really be worth?

Then I think of having Tipp-Ex all over the palm of my hand so that, whichever one I grab, the grape will turn white. But I don't think Bryn is a Tipp-Ex sort of guy.

I think of fighting the king, rugby tackling him and legging it with the princess under my arm.

I could pull out both the grapes and expose the king for the fraud that he is.

I look around me for clues. I look at the video on top of the TV: *Carreras, Domingo, Pavarotti—The Three Tenors: The Greatest Concert of the Century.*

I look at Jude. Her tumor is the size of a grape. She is lightly madeup, her thin lips painted pink. She has light blue eyes and, I am surprised to see, a conspicuous zit near her temple.

"Don't look at me, you're on your own." She laughs.

"Um, I don't know—he could pull out both grapes and then everyone would see that the king is a cheat."

"No, good try, though. And you can't peel the grape either. That was Jordana's idea."

He is still looking at me, waiting for a better answer. I want to say, *Chemotherapy?*

"Uuuuuh," I say.

He lets me flounder.

"No? Well, here's what the future prince did. He pulled a grape from the bag and immediately popped it into his mouth and swallowed."

Bryn mimes the gulping back of a grape like a pill.

"Then he says, 'You can see which color I've chosen by the grape that remains,' which was, of course, black."

"Ahh, I see. Brilliant," I say.

"So now you know," he says, "next time you're looking to marry a princess."

We've been sitting for a while. I've drunk a glass of wine. Jordana is very relaxed with her parents.

"God, do you remember how Jordana was conceived?"

"Come on now, Bryn, you're embarrassing the poor boy. Oh, go on then."

They gaze into each other's eyes as they talk.

"Jordana was conceived in the cleavage of the Three Cliffs."

Jordana looks very young; her mouth is agape, she scratches her forehead. Her eyes are searching for something to distract them.

"She's heard this a hundred times but it was a beautiful night. We found a spot out of the wind, made a fire, and put a couple of jacket potatoes in. It was a big moon—"

"And there were bats." Jude interrupts, suddenly interested. Her voice kind of fluttery, excited. "They flew out of the cliff face and spun around us like a tornado."

This is the first time I think I have heard her speak like this: all imagey. She leans forward to put her hand on Bryn's.

"We always thought you'd be able to see in the dark or something," Jude says, looking at Jordana.

Then she turns to me and whispers in my ear, "Jordana probably doesn't want you to know this," her breath is warm on my eardrum, "but when she was born her ears were curled up like autumn leaves."

Impressive: She uses another simile.

"You can still see it on her right ear, can't you, my little bat girl?" Bryn says.

"Dad!" Jordana complains.

Jordana's right ear does have a hint of pixie about it.

Jude and Bryn are chuckling, smiling at each other. I wonder whether it is the tumor or the wine that has made them go schmaltzy.

"God," Jordana says.

"By the time we were finished the jacket potatoes were perfect. Best jacket potato I ever had," Bryn says.

A jacket potato can take up to forty-five minutes to cook. I think I could learn a lot from Bryn.

I expect Bryn to bring out grapes for dessert. Instead, he offers me a choc ice. Which I accept. Choc ices are black on the outside but white in the middle. I don't think this means anything.

When I say goodbye, I don't tell Jordana that I am going away to save my parents' marriage. Having not read my diary since before Fred's untimely death, she's not up to speed. Which is probably for the best. A small tumor is enough on her plate.

apostasy

I was the only person to alight at Llandrindod Wells station. Then I got a bus to Llanwrthwl. It was a two-mile walk up a gravel track to get to the retreat. It gave me time to reflect and plan, to meditate.

I set up my headquarters around a large dead log in a clearing among the trees. The rotten trunk feels soft beneath my pelvic bones. It is the sort of day where you would like not to be wearing any clothes. My perineum, in particular, is sweaty. There is the musky smell of spores and fungi.

On the chapped ground next to the log, I notice the word *help* has been laid out in lowercase twigs and leaves. It has no exclamation mark. I stare at the *help*. Either someone wants help or they're telling me I've found it.

Downhill, within screaming distance, stands a hall with floor-to-ceiling windows on three sides. It is somewhere between a demountable classroom and a pagoda. I count ten people, sitting cross-legged on stiff cushions, straight-backed, equidistant as skittles: meditating. None of them is my mother. The hall is encircled by a grassy area, the size of a rounders court, in the center of which a few baby trees are looking immature.

Beyond the pagoda lies a barn, a stable, a series of redbrick buildings, and a gravel car park. The meditation retreat looks very similar to a farm. *Anicca* means "to see things as they really are."

The light fades; the clouds have dark seams. I hear a droning sound, a chanting male voice coming from the pagoda. It sounds like Chips's impression of any religious person in prayer.

Chips says that on horsebang.com they hardly ever do it inside the stables; Estelle, eighteen, from Missouri—who says she will never go back to man-cock—does it in the meadow and they use a mail-order harness to hold her in place. I will keep my eyes out for any such specialist equipment.

As the sound trails away they stand up to stretch their backs and legs, the still room suddenly bustling with semaphore.

I walk down along the line of the trees to get a closer look. I figure that, since it is bright inside the pagoda and dark outside, they probably can't see much. I get close enough to make out their faces. One of the women looks young, like a student teacher. Her yellow hair has not been properly brushed; she looks in touch with her emotions. The hall slowly empties; men leave from one exit, women from another.

I scamper back up to base camp.

From my bag (for the time that I am on the road it shall be known as my knapsack) I take out a pack of blueberry Pop-Tarts. Removing one from its foil bag, I eat it quickly—chewing five or six times for each mouthful before swallowing. My mother tells me I do not chew my food enough; she says I am making it harder for my body to get the essential nutrients it needs. If she were here I would remind her that I am eating a blueberry Pop-Tart. If she were here—which, now I think about it, she is—I would posit my theory of healthy eating.

It is fine to scoff unhealthy food: Pop-Tart, Battenberg cake, custard slice, blueberry Danish, pain au chocolat, but you *must* scoff; do not chew more than necessary to swallow. However, when eating wholesome foods like broccoli, haddock, or red cabbage, chew to liquid—*be a smoothie maker*—upward of forty jaw rotations.

At ten, the sky blackens. The pagoda's glow cuts out, sending the surrounding area into darkness. It is a warm overcast night with a moderate northeasterly. I don't bother with my tent. I just get into my sleeping bag and lie on the dry ground with the smell of the slowly mulching log. I grab my knapsack, pull out my torch, diary, pen.

Monday 30.6.97

Word of the day: Retreat—a place affording peace, quiet, privacy, or security.

Checklist of useful items

• Map of the local area printed from the Web site

• A Trangia meths-burning stove borrowed from school

• Methylated spirit—purple

• Spare shoes—"Hi-Tec"

• T-shirt: Brunsfield Sports

• Dad's Durham University hoodie

• A two-man tent—orange

• A sleeping bag—purple

• A golf monocular (still boxed as new)

- Two packs Pop-Tarts, one blueberry, one chocolate

- A bottle of undiluted Ribena—not to be mistaken for meths

- An instant camera

- Reading material printed off from ramameditation.com and treefields.net

- A pad of Post-it notes

- A Dictaphone

- My logbook

- A black biro

- A four-pack of choc muffins

- A packet of Q's Pork Scratchings

- Sausages—38% pork

- A twenty-pound note stolen from my father's wallet

- I also have a single Trojan condom; if the worst comes to the worst I will give this to Graham.

I wake to shapes; ghosts fatten and melt. Either there is torchlight shining in my eyes or I am "seeing things as they really are." I wriggle around like a worm in the dirt, turning onto my side, my eyes tight shut.

Someone leans over me; I can smell that they are vegetarian.

"Excuse me? I'm sorry but this is private property."

"Mmm," I say.

"I'm sorry, but this area is closed off to the public."

I open one eye. His sandals, spotlit by the torch, are muddy.

"Mmmgh."

"Are you okay?" He has a slight American accent.

He points the light at my face. I feel like a specimen.

He switches the torch off. It is getting light but I can't make out the man's face because of my scalded retinas.

"What are you doing here?" he says, crouching down beside me.

The top two buttons of his collarless hemp shirt are undone.

I look at the ground for a while then say, "I have some problems in my home life." I have learned this approach from Chips.

"Oh," he says.

"Sometimes I just need to be somewhere quiet, to get away from the screaming rows, the thrown crockery."

Crockery is the wrong word. Boys with nearly broken homes have no time for words like *crockery*.

He shows his teeth then leans closer to my ear, conspiratorially. "Look, I shouldn't do this, but I could bring you out a bowl of soup, would you like that?"

"What kind of soup?"

"Oh, um . . . I think it's lentil and vegetable. Look, I'll go get you some. I'll just be a tick."

A tick is an arachnid, parasitic upon cattle, sheep, and humans.

"I'm all right, ta. I got some Pop-Tarts in my knapsack."

I use poor English in order to seem more endearing.

"Look, this is private property. If it were up to me . . ."

He trails off.

I insert the blade: "No, it's okay. Don't worry. I'll go."

I do some blinking.

"Look, I don't mind you staying here for now. The thing is— this is a meditation center, it's very important our guests are not distracted."

The only other person I know who makes this much eye contact is Mr. Thomas, the headmaster.

As my eyes adjust, I can see he has a dry goatee beard and an outdoor person's tan.

"Do your parents live far away?"

"Not far enough," I say.

Oh, he likes that.

"Look, if you need anything, to make a phone call or to get a lift somewhere?"

There is a silence that he thinks means we have made a connection. I examine his face. He has a slender, ridged purple scar on his forehead like a ladder in tights.

"Where d'you get that scar?"

"Oh this?" he says, running his forefinger down the dark tissue. "I cut my head in an abseiling accident and had eight stitches; then I went surfing and the stitches burst—that's why."

"Wow." I do the brave little soldier face—smiling with closed lips—that makes him think he's cheered me up. "Thank you, mister," I say, playing Victorian.

"Please," he puts his hand on my shoulder, "call me Graham."

He smiles, displaying rows of large, plentiful teeth. A black seed is caught in the overlap between two incisors.

"Thanks, Graham. You can call me Dean."

I hate the name Dean.

"I check the grounds every morning about this time so maybe I'll see you tomorrow. But please don't get spotted."

I blink at him.

"That's very important," he says.

I keep blinking.

The gong rings out; Graham does not even break eye contact.

"Well, that's breakfast," he says. "I've got to go now, my friend."

He is quite, but not entirely, convincing in the role of caring older person. I close my eyes and sleep.

———

I am woken again by a sound that I am only aware of as it fades. It's still only seven-thirty. I count fifteen men enter the hall single file, each carrying a blanket and a hard cushion; their heads are slightly bowed. An Asian man is already sitting cross-legged. The sky is light at the edges.

I kick off my sleeping bag and get up. Still wearing yesterday's clothes—blue jeans, turquoise socks, and a yellow Park Ridge Soccer T-shirt—I stealth my way along the treeline to get a look at the rest of the farm buildings.

I spy two men holding a secretive conversation by a pair of green wheelie bins behind the barn. The one carrying a bucket and old-style mop nods and points toward the stables as if to say: *I've washed off all the cum and blood.*

When the coast is clear I sneak toward the back of the stables where I am hidden from view. I quickly glance about the yard before stepping through the open stable door. Inside it gleams with white tiles, evenly spaced shower heads adorn the walls, and the drains are hair-free. No Web cam, no specialist equine sex strap.

Disappointed, I step back out into the yard and, careful to tread on the grass, not the gravel, I walk silently toward a side door to the pagoda. I slip inside to a cloakroom that contains coats, not cloaks. Rough blankets are piled up on the floor plus fifteen pairs of shoes all spattered with mud: boots, sandals, and a pair of espadrilles. I recognize one pair of sandals in particular; they are well cushioned around the ankle with a small white label on the tongue: *Vegetarian Shoes.* These, I fear, are Graham's.

I hear the man chanting again, singing a song with no chorus. The door into the main room has a strip of glass down its center. I peek through at the backs of their meditating heads, their textbook spines. After a while the chanting becomes speech. I look but I can't see the man who is speaking.

"... slightly better than yesterday ... slightly better ... the difficulties are still there . . . what a wandering mind . . . a fleeting mind . . ."

He pauses often and no one seems to mind. He does not care for finishing sentences.

"A flickering mind . . . so instable, so unstable, so infirm . . . no peace, no tranquillity . . . so wild, like a wild animal . . ."

The words rise and fade.

"A monkey mind . . . grasping one branch after the other . . . one object after the other . . . highly agitated, certainly very wild, like a wild bull, a wild elephant . . . when it comes in the midst of society it creates havoc . . ."

With all the people sitting cross-legged on floorboards, I am reminded of story time in primary school except here no one fidgets, no one fights.

"Once this animal is tamed . . . it comes to serve the human society . . ."

I think of horses.

". . . untamed is very dangerous, very harmful . . . but if we train it, tame it, its enormous strength starts helping us . . ."

In a moment of instinct—I swear my brain is empty—I pick up the Vegetarian sandals. Checking both ways, I scurry out of the cloakroom and dart across the yard to the safety and darkness beyond the overweight trees. To meditate means to plan or scheme, to hatch a plot, to machinate.

Back at base camp, I use the monocular to watch the men and women in the pagoda stretch their necks, backs, and arms. So many different ways to look ridiculous.

After unpacking my camping stove, I drink Ribena, diluted with fresh mountain water, sipping it from the dented pan. The Duke of Edinburgh would disapprove. I eat two chocolate muffins.

I change the *help* to an uppercase *HELP!* with an exclamation mark made from a pinecone and a branch.

I cannot get back to sleep so I decide to explore up the hill, away from the retreat. It is the sort of woodland that you cannot tell the depth of, except sometimes, at a certain angle, glimpsed like my father's baldness when he looks down to carve a joint of lamb.

I climb onto the uppermost branch of the uppermost oak, one arm hooked around its trunk. I hang Graham's sandals as decorations from nearby branches. I look out toward the knuckles of interlocking hills, the dented valley: a fist punch into a doughy landscape.

I feel like a pirate, holding on with one hand, the other hand holding up my golf monocular. It is from this vantage point that I espy my mother.

She treads a circular path mown out of the grassy clearing; the path follows the edge of the woods. I track her with the monocular. She wears her brown thick-ribbed corduroy trousers that she uses for gardening and an unfamiliar blanket around her shoulders. A pale blue hospital blanket for the ill, the tricked.

She scratches her skull through her dark, greasy hair. I can see a crooked path of pale scalp. She never glances upward, concentrating only on what's directly ahead of her.

I am impressed by my monocular skills. I am Lee Harvey Oswald. I do not lose her, even when she disappears behind a tree.

Having completed five orbits she strolls down past the stables and disappears inside an L-shaped redbrick building. No rest for the wicked.

It is only just gone midday and I have been up for five hours. For lunch, I eat the pork scratchings and two chocolate Pop-Tarts. I spend a couple of hours walking upriver trying to balance on rocks and not get my feet wet. After getting my feet wet, I go back to base camp, take my shoes and socks off, and get into my sleeping bag. I lie on my front reading about all the different kinds of meditation from the information that I printed off. I read about reconnecting to nature. I read about the way modern society has disconnected me from any sense of understanding my innate bond with the earth and my surroundings. I learn about receiving intuitive information about myself. If I knew myself better I would have known that I was bound to keep walking upriver until I got my shoes wet. Even my mother would have known this. I would like to learn to intuitively receive information about myself. I think this would be a good one for my CV too. *Am a proactive intuiter of self-knowledge.*

We've been learning how to write CVs in school. It has introduced me to the word *proactive*, which is like the word *active*, but more so. Employers also like the words *challenging, interpersonal,* and words with dashes, like *self-directed.*

I read about expanding my consciousness. I discover a new word: *egregore.* An egregore is a kind of group mind that is created when people consciously come together for a common purpose. Which is what is happening at this retreat, I suppose. It is more than just a brain orgy, so the Web site claims. An egregore is the "psychic and astral entity of a group."

It goes on to say: "They are somewhat like angels, except that they are relatively mindless and quite willing to follow orders. They may take any number of physical forms. Some UFOs may be egregores."

Since the egregore is an amalgamation of the group's minds, it will contain knowledge about both Graham's intentions and my mother's feelings toward those intentions. I may not even need to interrogate the entity. If, for example, the egregore takes the physical form of a ghostly divorce lawyer then I will just assume the worst.

The forest is warm and musty. It reminds me of my bedroom when I haven't opened the window in weeks and I've been wearing my shoes without socks and there's a damp towel balled up beneath my desk. It is a good smell for napping.

My stomach wakes me up. It is still light but gray and starting to fade. I kick off my sleeping bag and find the least flammable-looking spot within which to set up my camping stove.

I boil up some river water for an aperitif of hot Ribena. I dry-fry four Lincolnshire sausages. They take forever to cook. Jordana would hate them—the skin is either burned black or transparent.

After dinner, I make plans: the unveiling of Graham.

At nine-thirty, I hear the man chanting again. It catches in my skull like a radio jingle.

I climb into my sleeping bag for an early night. I've got a big day tomorrow. Camping makes me remember the first time I was attracted to Jordana. It was during Bronze Award Duke of Edinburgh; she showed me what an aerosol can of Mango Madness Foamburst Shower Gel sounds like in a campfire. It whistles at first before cracking like a dropped dinner plate.

I was camped at the same site as her: Broughton farm. She came over to my tent and showed me her blisters. She asked me whether I knew the reason why a blister can keep on producing fluid ad infinitum. I said that I had always wondered the same thing about mucus. One of the reasons we are together is because we have similar interests.

I wake up at first light. I add a twig arrow to the *HELP!*, pointing uphill. Then I stick a trail of Post-it notes on trees, fluorescent markers leading Graham deeper into the woods:

GRAHAM!

YOU'RE A
VERY GOOD
ACTOR

THIS WHOLE
SETUP IS
REALLY VERY
CONVINCING

I UNDERSTAND
WHY WOMEN
FALL FOR YOU

I RESPECT
YOU, IN
A WAY

BUT THIS
HAS GONE
FAR ENOUGH

I stick the last Post-it to a smooth-barked beech in front of a coarse stretch of brambles. A few blackberries are out but they're not black yet, they're green and tight as acorns.

I find a break in the brambles and squeeze through; they act as a protective barrier between me and the soon-to-be-raging Graham. I hide behind a swollen, blistered yew tree, waiting.

In South Wales, people say "yew" instead of "you."

The birds are waking up. I listen for the chanting.

Eventually, I hear slow footsteps coming through the woods, twigs snapping. I don't trust people who walk slowly: headmasters and priests.

"Dean?" The voice is far away but I can tell it's Graham—a hint of Yank in his accent.

"You shouldn't litter the woods like this."

I've already got him riled.

"Dean?"

He's getting closer.

"What is this all about?" he says and then, trying to stay in character: "Are you okay?"

"Graham!" I shout at the beech tree opposite, imagining my voice reverberating off its trunk, coming from all directions: omniscient.

"You do the sort of group meditation when you are in a room full of cushions and you are discovering each other's bodies and the women say yes with their eyes!"

I wait. It sounds like laughter.

"I'd think we'd be a lot more oversubscribed if we did," he says. He is close; he does not shout.

"What's going on, Dean?" he says.

This will break him: "I hung your sandals from the highest branch of the highest tree!"

"Really?" he says.

"I hung them from branches that will not hold your weight!"

He says nothing. I get ready to sprint.

"Dean, Anicca meditation is about getting to understand your own mental and physical processes. It helps you observe the way your mind and body work so that you don't just react to things, so you don't just function on autopilot."

He doesn't sound angry.

"Is it good for getting laid?"

"Please, come out. I can see you're behind that tree."

I peek. Graham is standing on the other side of the brambles looking nonaggressive.

"Hi," he says.

His arms are passive, at his sides, his clothing neutral-colored, his hands covered with Post-it notes.

We talked about meditation and I asked him some tricky questions about equine sex straps and wild animals. I told him I had jumped to the wrong conclusion. He asked me again whether I needed anything. I said I was fine and that I'd leave by the afternoon.

I decide that, in order to empathize with my mother, I ought to try a spot of self-purification.

In my research I read that some people use trees for meditation. It explained the importance of finding the right tree. The trunk represents the spine so I look for one with bad posture.

The amount of sunlight the tree gets relates to spiritual nourishment.

I find a dark, hunch-backed oak. At its base, two large roots protrude in a V shape, creating a kind of throne with armrests. Cross-legged, I nestle between the roots with my back against its trunk. Its eczematous bark reminds me of Jordana.

According to the Web site you have to ask the tree's permission to contact it. I try a formal approach, thinking: *Dear Tree, my name is Oliver Tate. I would like to be intuitive with you, to learn about myself through your deep connection with nature. The details are on www.forestsangha.org.* The tree says nothing. *I don't think it'll take too long—I know myself pretty well.* Still, no reply. I understand the tree's indifference. *If you don't say anything then I'll just assume it's okay?*

Okay. First, I have to close my eyes and clear my mind. I think of my mind as my attic bedroom. I throw out the bed, the desk, the books, the annuals, the wardrobe, the Super Nintendo; I tear down the postcards, posters, shelves; I sledgehammer the blue, sponge-painted walls; I crash a wrecking ball through my parents' bay windows; I authorize an air strike that reduces my street to rubble; I fold Swansea bay like an enormous omelet and scoff it all in one giant bite . . .

. . . the nothingness doesn't last long. The emptiness unwraps to reveal a memory, a new memory, a memory about a dream.

When I was ten years old, I was in love with our German au pair, Hilde. She studied theology at the university and cooked an excellent chocolate bread and butter pudding. She had boy-short yellow hair. Her eyebrows were so blond they were almost invisible, making it difficult for her to look angry, apologetic, or quizzical. She used to call me "Olifer." We used to walk to the supermarket and she would tease me about having a girlfriend, which I didn't, but I liked to be teased. She stayed in the spare room, next door to my bedroom. I used to put my ear against the wall and listen to her singing along to the Stone Roses.

She was always very polite around my parents and cleared the table after every meal. They sometimes discussed religion and ethics at the dinner table. It was a Sunday, the night before she was due to go back to Germany. I had spent the day writing her a comic book as a leaving present. It was called *Warp*, and was about time travel. It used multiple choice endings to good effect. And I remember, when I went to bed that night, I was very upset, plus we had eaten mushroom lasagne for tea. And so I would not have been surprised to have dreamed of my tongue becoming a rat or that everything I touched turned to salt. I remember the dream I had.

I dreamed that I woke up in the middle of the night and got out of bed. My room was the usual version of my room. I was wearing the same pajamas I went to bed in. Everything was normal. There was a smell of burning plastic like when Jordana put a ruler in the Bunsen flame. I put on my slippers—who puts on slippers in a dream?—and went across the corridor into Hilde's room. Her stuff was already gone. Which was also normal because her flight was very early in the morning and Dad was going to drive her to Heathrow.

The door to my parents' room was open. The bed was unmade and empty. I could hear some noise from downstairs. I went down to the living room. It was not a particularly cold night but Mum had made a fire. She sat on the edge of the coffee table, blowing her nose into the sleeve of her white cotton nightie, the one that makes her look like a ghost.

I knew it was a dream because she had the bay windows fully open. The smell from the fire was tarry and sharp. The fire was spitting and the smoke was black. Presented neatly along the mantelpiece was a series of five of my father's classical record sleeves. The sleeves of classical records are designed to look worthless. Dad has some records that are worth over two hundred pounds.

She looked up from her hands. She looked at me and she stopped sniveling although she was still evidently unhappy. Classical music is about these sorts of topics: death, sadness, loss.

I was only ten years old and I was not yet familiar with Jerry

Springer or Vanessa Feltz but I had played football for my primary school so I said, "Chin up, Mum, get stuck in."

Then I went upstairs, got into bed and in my dream, I had a little trouble sleeping but I soon dozed off.

I woke up in the real world and my mum had pulled back the curtains and it was a school day. Dad had already arrived back from Heathrow. He was in bed.

Before heading off to school, I went in to say hello. His tiny head was the only thing showing above the bedsheet. He was not asleep. I asked him who he would save first in a house fire given the hypothetical situation that both me and my mother were of exactly equal difficulty and risk to save. He did not hesitate: "I would save your mother first so that we could have a better chance of working together to save you."

I wondered whether he had prepared the answer in advance.

I may have slept. The tree smells like my mother's Faith in Nature shampoo. The bark feels rough as a loofah. I am cleansed. This surprises me. To meditate also means to think deeply, to reflect. I am aware of the river trickling. Meditation is like a long bath.

I polish off the rest of the muffins in the first rays of sun. My teeth feel furry as moss.

At mealtimes, the pagoda is deserted.

I break cover and sprint out across the grass. I run up the grassy incline, along the side of the pagoda, and straight in through the open cloakroom door. Monks do not believe in locked doors. Nor do they believe in possessions. The two may be linked.

The door leading to the main hall opens without a creak. Sunlight beams through the wall of windows, heating the room. My trainers squeal on the floorboards, leaving black scuff marks.

A Sony CD player squats in the corner of the room. I turn the volume down and press *play*; the sound of the man chanting rises to fill the space. I am disappointed by the thought of the spectacled

Asian man chanting in a recording studio. I thought they would have a real, live chanter. Taking my Dictaphone off my waistband and pressing *record*, I hold it close to the speaker. The chant will never go platinum but it stays with me like a splinter. I want to keep this as a reminder. The man chants to an empty hall. I am on my knees in sunlight.

I pack once the sun is up but I am not leaving yet. Before pulling on my backpack I kick and trample the *HELP!*

I wait for breakfast to finish: the pagoda fills up—a full thirty people—the chant is played, and the meditators settle down. I give them time to get spiritually involved.

Crossing the lawned area, I pass the waist-high baby trees that have little plastic labels on—pear, cherry, apple—and I approach the windows of the pagoda. Their eyes are all closed. Mum faces out, cross-legged, her palms on her thighs. She has her hair pushed back with a purple band and she is not wearing a bra. Her chest and shoulders rise, fall. Graham sits on the other side of the room, with the men, totally still.

This was going to be the moment. I was going to bang on the windows and reveal my mother's illicit affair. I was going to point at Graham then at my mother, then I would have simulated sex with my fingers. I planned to scream into their peaceful, empty minds.

Nobody blinks. Everything is fine.

I put my forehead gently against the cool glass. Mum is no farther away than a forward roll, a hop-skip-jump. I watch her breasts gently swell and droop. I see the simple, unfussy wrinkles around her eyes, her faultless neck. Chips calls her a yummy mummy; I made him promise not to fantasize about her.

I breathe in and out, in and out. The glass starts to mist up. My mother disappears. With my forefinger, I write the word *Lloyd* into the condensation and draw a heart around it. The glass squeaks. No one opens their eyes.

I feel like a schoolteacher whose pupils have fallen asleep.

I stand back from the window. The condensation fades, nothing permanent. I think of cartwheeling, of stripping, of wanking. They wouldn't notice.

One man's head bobs in tiny circles. His hair is half dreadlocks, half normal.

I stand in Graham's line of sight and concentrate on the dull scar on his forehead. I imagine pressing my thumbnail into the brawny skin. He doesn't open his eyes.

I start to feel hot. I rub my hands on my face. I look at my mother. I would do anything she told me to. I would throw myself off a cliff if she took the time to suggest it.

It's a strange kind of pressure—so many grown men and women in a room together, empty-headed. I just don't believe them. They must be thinking about something. At the least, they're thinking about not thinking about anything.

Then my legs have an idea. They are doing it by themselves.

The word *retreat* also refers to the act of withdrawing, especially from something hazardous, unpleasant, or formidable.

I swing round the corner of the pagoda, onto the track that leads down through the farm. The weight of my knapsack propels me. I kick and scuff. The gravel makes maracas but it is not nearly loud enough. I stomp past the stable-cum-shower block; it is innocent and clean.

In the middle of the yard, the gong—dark bronze-colored, not gold, as I expected—hangs from a wooden post. I pick up the beater that lies beneath it. I think I might be on autopilot. I concentrate on a physical process.

The noise will fill their empty heads. This is not the worst thing I could have done.

The only word is *gong*.

fastigium

On 5.7.97 <Jordanabanana@yahoomail.com> wrote:

Hellooooo!
Where have you been, mystery man? I rang you and your Dad said
you were at Dave's? Who is Dave? You're not allowed to make any
new friends!

   Mam's in Morriston hospital at the moment. The operation is
next Friday. I'm going to be off school to stay at the hospital with
her. You better miss me. I got a new word for you: fastigium. It's the
part of the brain where the tumor is growing. On top of the fourth
ventricle. After spending three days at the hospital, I feel like I
know as much about brain tumors as the doctors do.

   You could come and visit her after the operation if that's not
too weird? Maybe it is too weird . . .

   Anyway, I'll be in the hospital some of tomorrow but I might
be at home for a bit so anyway............call me! (Who said that?) Call
me............!

Jo xxx

12.7.97

Word of the day: Monologophobia—fear of using the same word
twice.

Dear Diary,
I've decided not to reply to Jordana's e-mail. The operation will
have either been a success, in which case she will be too happy to
care whether I e-mail her, or her mother is dead, in which case she
will be beyond comfort and, as such, my well-worded commisera-
tions would be a waste of time and talent.

Because I have been away on business, I have not had a chance
to do any revision for my forthcoming mock GCSEs. To make up
for lost time I will, therefore, undertake a short comprehension exercise:

The use of the colloquial hellooooo and the playful banter of the
opening paragraph immediately sets this piece up as a communiqué
between two friends.

The narrator mentions the word hospital four times. This is
stylistically poor. She could have spiced things up a bit with words
like infirmary and clinic. The repetition does, I think, highlight her
worries about her mother; she is understandably fearful that her
mother might die.

As a symbol of affection towards the recipient, she offers a
"new word": fastigium. Sadly, she only lists one of its definitions.
Fastigium also means the acme or period of full development of a
disease.

It is worth noting that the narrator uses the rhetorical device
of pretending to have a split personality. She uses the line—who
said that? This is used to make light of her underlying despera-
tion.

She suggests that the recipient might visit her Mum in hospital;
the implication is that, by seeing her mother full of wires and tubes

and morphine, the recipient will gain a better idea of what the narrator is going through. She wisely preempts the possibility that the visit might be weird.

The overriding tone of this piece is neediness. It strikes me that the recipient of the e-mail is the one in a position of power in the relationship. Perhaps he is thinking of the phrase—treat 'em mean, keep 'em keen.
Later alligator,
Oliver

P.S. The truth often rhymes.

euthenics

Tonight, for the first time in over a month, my parents are going out together. They're going to see the Welsh Philharmonic performing Bartók at the Brangwyn Hall. My dad has been looking forward to it; the tickets came months ago, pinned to the corkboard in the kitchen. He wears a corduroy suit jacket and a cloth tie. He has a handkerchief in his breast pocket.

Mum is still in the shower. Dad wanders around the house, putting things in their places. I follow him from room to room, just watching. He positions the remote control on top of the TV. He moves the unopened letters off the dining room table and lays them on the third stair. Pulling a towel off the radiator, he folds it carefully into a square, places it in the airing cupboard. He washes out an empty cat food tin, removes the label, scrubs off the glue, and stands it on the windowsill above the sink. After doing each thing he glances at his wristwatch. Whenever he walks past the bathroom he looks at the steam curling from under the door.

My mum comes out of the shower. Her towel, tucked into itself above her breasts, hangs down to the middle of her thighs. With short wet hair and her cheeks and forehead flushed, she looks like a boy. She goes into their bedroom, shuts the door. The hair dryer hums. Dad examines his watch.

He goes and gets the car keys from the hook, puts them in his pocket. Then he disappears into the cellar and brings out a tray of frozen pork chops. He puts them in the fridge.

"Dad's special lemongrass pork tomorrow," he says, smiling at me.

I don't say anything.

The hair dryer stops.

My dad shouts up from the hallway, "We need to go now."

He puts on his long navy coat although it is a mild evening.

There's no reply. He goes upstairs and stands in their bedroom doorway. I follow at a distance, hanging back on the landing, watching through the spaces in the banisters. I watch Mum in her pants, filing through the clothes in her wardrobe. I am careful not to focus on anything in particular.

"We're going to be late," he says.

She is so white and the tops of her thighs bulge out from her knickers.

She pulls out a black dress and considers it. Dad backs out of the room and closes the door quite loudly.

He walks away then stops. He turns around and shouts at the closed door, "Every. Fucking. Time."

Dad clomps past me on the landing, down the stairs, and out the front door, which he also slams. My mum opens the door to her bedroom. She smiles at me and raises her eyebrows. She is wearing the black dress; it stops just above her knees. Her red kneecaps protrude like swellings.

"Are you going to be all right on your own tonight?" she asks.

"Yeah, there's some things I need to do," I say, expecting her not to take an interest.

"What things are they then, mystery man?"

I must be losing my touch.

I buy myself some time by walking into her bedroom and looking out the window. Dad is conducting a three-point turn in the road. I try to think of things.

"Hatch some plots. Plan some coups," I say.

"Oh well," she says, hopping as she puts on her posh shoes, "good luck."

Dad has turned the car so that it faces the right direction. He is an excellent getaway driver. She takes a pair of silver earrings out of a felt-lined box and holds them to her ears. She is a useless jewel thief.

"Yes or no?" she asks.

I hesitate, but I'm thinking no.

"No?" she says before I can speak. "No, you're right."

She drops the earrings in their box, which, in turn, she puts back in her chest of drawers. Dad beeps the car horn for three seconds. Mum picks up her towel from the floor and hangs it on the radiator in the hallway.

"We won't be back too late," she says, wandering downstairs, her feet moving deliberately, each step a distinct action. On the third stair from last she picks up a letter; it has a picture of an aquamarine-colored credit card with cartoon fish swimming around it. Standing on the bottom step, she rips open the envelope and glances over its contents. She tosses the free biro into her brown leather handbag hanging from the newel and dumps the rest of the letter in the wastepaper basket. She walks, without hurry, to the front door. She opens it, steps outside, closes it. I don't know how much my mother likes classical music.

Over the last few weeks, the dimmer switch in my parents' bedroom has remained at full: showing no sign of an increase in bedroom activity. I've been thinking about ways to ignite the bonfire of their passion.

thefengshuicastle.co.uk has been very helpful. Peach-colored walls and furnishings are said to encourage affairs. I can see why; peach is the worst color. Luckily, my mother despises it.

Shades of red, however, encourage romance. Yesterday, I bought balloons from the Party Shop. I had to buy fifty, of which only six are red.

I blow them up and Sellotape two above their bedroom door, two to the legs of the ironing board and two to the light shade above the dining table. I swap all the white candles on the living room mantelpiece with the festive red ones.

The mirror on the dressing table opposite my parents' bed "drains them of vital chi and may attract a third party to the relationship." I spin the mirror round to face the wall. Apparently, it is important to wake up and see an image that inspires you, one that is "tranquil and uplifting—epitomizing your journey in life." I scan a photo of myself as a baby—ugly as Play-Doh—blow it up to A4 size, and stick it to the back of the mirror. I am their greatest achievement.

The finishing touch will come from the back garden. Because our street is on a steep hill, all the gardens are terraced with shallow steps joining each zone. Zone one is the yard, zone two has grass and a picnic table, zone three contains flowers, herbs, and a feeble-looking apple tree. At zone two, I jump over the stone wall into the next-door neighbor's garden. They're on holiday in Spain, so we're looking after their house. "A heavy statue or figurine at floor level at the base of the stairs could act to bring stability to the situation." Next to their tiny pond sits a statue of an overweight monk, meditating on a beanbag, his palms flat together. With my hands round his neck, I tip the monk back so I can get a grip underneath him. Beneath the statue, in the mud, an earthworm gets nowhere.

I hear the key in the door. I am sitting at the top of the stairs in my black Lands' End pajamas waiting for them.

"Hello?" Mum calls, entering the porch.

"Hello!" I reply.

She walks into the hallway, flicking the light switch on.

"Why are you in the dark?"

I hadn't noticed. Dad follows behind, not slamming the front door.

They stop to gawp at the monk.

"Oliver—what's this?"

"He's feng shui, Mum."

She takes a couple of steps closer, looks down.

"And what's all this muck?" she says, pointing to the trail of footprints on the linoleum.

"Looks like muddy shui to me."

Holiday Dad appears for a few hours after a successful concert. Mum almost laughs. I think a little less of her.

"Where on earth did you get him?" she asks me.

I had hoped she would ask this question.

I speak slow and Buddha-serene: "Do not question the how, simply enjoy the now."

She looks up sharply, one eyebrow kinked. "What have you done with Oliver?"

I imagine a dead-eyed Oliver clone chopping me into pieces.

My dad is wearing his coat and flat cap; he pretends to be puffing on a pipe, tracking my footprints into the dining room.

"By Jove, I think I have it." His voice grows more distant as he heads toward the kitchen. "The perpetrator 'alf-inched the figurine from our neighbor's backyard!"

"Oh God, Oliver," she crouches down next to the monk, looks him in the eye, "you have to take him back."

She strokes the monk's bald bronze head. She is wasting valuable affection on an inanimate object.

Dad returns from the kitchen with a dustpan and brush. He holds them up toward me. "Oi, boy; back to work." He is still pretending to be Victorian. " 'Em chimneys wunt sweep 'emselves."

My mother, against expectation, finds this genuinely funny.

They stand side by side at the bottom of the stairs, gazing up at me, blinking. They both look small. I am the grown-up and they are my hideous children.

"We're waiting," Mum says.

Dad nods.

They look perfectly happy.

So that's that then. Job done.

I expected to feel more euphoric, having salvaged my parents' marriage.

15.7.97

Word: Euthenics—the science of improving the condition of humans by improving their surroundings.

Dear Diary,

Close, but no cigar. They seemed happy in the evening but the next day they made me take down the photo of myself on the mirror. They allowed the balloons but within a couple of days even they'd started to sag and wrinkle in the style of Grampa's neck so I took them down too.

Every night, I listen until two for the sound of fucking. I check each morning but the dimmer switch is always turned up as high as it can go.

Mum sat on the end of my bed this morning. She was smiling and her eyes and mouth were a little puffy because she'd only just woken up. We had a chat that could never have happened in the afternoon or evening; she caught me while I was sleepy. Here are some of the things we said:

Her: "Oli, thank you so much for the balloons."

Me: "S'okay. Your chi was blocked."

Her: "You know that me and your dad are going through a rough patch?"

Me: "Yah."

I say yah instead of yes sometimes.

Her: "Well, I want you to know that we really appreciate your trying to help..."

Me: "Yup."

Yup is chirpier than yes.

Her: "...but that you really needn't worry—your dad and I are both adults and although we may not always act like it, we can sort out these problems ourselves."

I asked her how she was hoping to do this, if she had considered writing a step-by-step plan. She said that she was going to talk to my dad about it. I told her that I was going to check up on their progress.

All important conversations should take place before breakfast.

They have a number of options:

1) Seek "help." My mother used to use this tactic with me—leaving leaflets around the house. But it did not work with me and would not work with her. She would tidy them away.

2) A romantic long weekend. We often go to La Rochelle, France, by car. Even if the trip is a success and my parents are blissfully in love, all the good work will inevitably be undone by the travel. (Car journeys are the frowning parentheses at the start and end of any good holiday.)

3) Spending quality time together—this is a good option. If only there were classical concerts every night.

There is one option that they must avoid at all costs: a baby. Couples say this: "We're staying together for the baby" so, logically, the reverse is also true: "A baby will glue us back together." The last thing any of us want is to go through childbirth. A placenta is terrible; it looks worse than jellied eels. A third-degree tear is a rip that may occur during labor—two holes become one.

I do not trust them to take the appropriate action to fix their relationship. I will count the number of tampons my mother has left each month. There are currently eight. If she is not using them, I will intervene and suggest an abortion, more feng shui, and self-help books.

I am running low on solutions.

Peace,

O

botanical

Jordana ought to be keen enough by now. I've let her hang on for long enough. She's not been in school since her mum went into hospital.

I called her up and her dad answered. He seemed very pleased to hear from me. Without prompting, he mentioned his emotions.

"Alright, Butt," he said. "We haven't seen you in a bit. Don't worry though. Jordana's had so much on her plate at the moment. We've all been having a hard time.

"The first operation went okay but the doctors have said that she'll need to have one more operation just to make sure they get rid of all of it."

"Oh, I understand," I said.

We arranged to meet up in Singleton Park to retrace the route we used to walk with Fred. Habit can be reassuring in difficult times. I get there early and wait on the bench by the north entrance. As a gift, I have brought a pack of her favorite matches—Swan Extra-Long.

I see her coming down through the gates; she spots me and smiles. She keeps smiling as she walks; her eyes are half closed. She's wearing khaki combats and pink trainers. She's wearing her crop top with the smiley-rave-face on it. Her hair is up on top of her head like a samurai's.

"Helloo," she says.

"Hiya," I say.

I feel something uncomfortable and tight in my chest, like I'm filling with insulation foam. I realize that I have not seen Jordana for a long time. If she's calling you all the time and trying to meet up and saying that she needs you, then the only thing to do is ignore her. This was the right thing to do; I talked it through with Chips. The foam is filling my lungs.

I stand up. I look over Jordana's shoulder. We hug.

"I've missed you," she says.

The foam is hardening, working its way up my throat.

I put my lips against the downy hair on the back of her neck. Her skin is smooth and pale and less dry than usual.

"I'm saw sorry. I've bin nowhere," she says.

She sounds more Welshy today.

"Oh God," she says, squeezing me, "I've needed a cwtch."

Normally, I would tell her about the other words that have no vowels. *Syzygy* means the alignment of three celestial objects.

I feel my mouth and jaw seizing up.

We stand back to look at each other. I take in her midriff and her arms and her neck and her feet.

"I sen' you an e-mail," she says.

"Yes," I say.

We hold hands in silence as we walk. We pass the lake, then the Swiss cottage, then the stone circle. We walk up toward the botanical gardens, dipping in and out of sunlight, silhouettes of treetops mapped across the path. There are birds wolf-whistling.

"I know I've been a bit out of it recently," she says.

We walk. I am a little bit faster than her so every eight paces I stop and say the word *medulloblastoma*, to allow her to catch up.

"My dad's a mess. And my brother got brought home by the police the other day. Him and his mates were riding horses down Kingsway."

There are wild horses on the scrags of grass on Mayhill. Some young men use them as public transport.

Medulloblastoma.

I once saw a topless boy riding a horse into Castle Square. The poppers on his trousers were undone to the knee. He was armed. Nobody had the guts to stop him spraying beams of lime green Fairy Liquid into the brand-new civic fountain.

"Mam seems younger. She's getting so quiet and gentle, turning into a baby, or a hippie. And she's totally changed her diet."

Medulloblastoma.

We approach the black gates to the botanical gardens. Jordana always used to say she hated the botanics: *Why call a sunflower a yellowy tallicus?* I wonder whether all this trauma has softened her up. She must have bought a fair few bouquets in the last week. Good job I've been treating her so badly. Keeping her tough.

There's a boy in school, Gruff Vaughan, whose parents died of two different kinds of cancer. Our P.E. teacher never forces him to play rugby. Even if Gruff plays, nobody is willing to tackle him.

"Let's go through here," she says, pointing to the gates. "Now that we don't have a dog, we may as well."

Medulloblastoma.

There's a sign on the gate showing a black dog with a fat red X across its body.

Jordana slows down as we enter. She walks at the pace of a funeral train. I now have to stop every three steps.

Medulloblastoma.

"The second operation is on Sunday."

"Your dad said."

There are tall thin plants, holding up strips of pale blue flowers.

Medulloblastoma.

"You could come along and see her?"

She grabs hold of my hand.

Medulloblastoma.

I think that I have already made a positive impression on Jordana's parents and it would be foolish to risk undoing my good work. I would be the sort of contestant on *Bullseye* who ignores the studio audience shouting gamble and takes home two hundred pounds and a washer-drier.

Medulloblastoma.

"My brother will be there but you don't have to speak to him."

"Why would I not speak to him?"

"Okay," she says.

Medulloblastoma.

"Sunday?"

"No, the operation is on Sunday, but we're going to see her on Saturday."

I stop.

Medulloblastoma.

I nod.

"What have you been doing anyway?"

"I've been very busy."

Medulloblastoma.

"Revising?"

"A kind of revision, yes."

"Oliver, please, I can't ..."

Medul-

She stops walking.

"What's going on?" she says.

I turn around and look at her eyes. Some of her lashes are tangled, like stamped-on spider's legs.

"My mother might die. . . ."

She gets caught up in the moment. There are dark spots on the tarmac path where her tears have landed.

"I just can't take . . . all . . . what's going on?"

Problems are like top trumps. I have a pretty good card: *Adulterous Mum*. But Jordana's is still better: *Tumor Mother*.

I imagine that if I say it out loud—My mum is having an affair—then it becomes more true. So I say something else: "Vectors, quadratic equations, and the respiratory system."

"Oh fuck," she says.

"They're only mocks," I say.

"Fuck you," she says.

She is dripping.

"It's not the real thing," I say.

"Fuck you," she says.

She is sodden.

"They're fake."

"Fuck you."

Her head is bowed as she steps toward me. She puts her forehead on my shoulder.

"Fuck you," she says, wiping her face over my collarbone and cwtching into my neck.

I put my arms around her. Her arms stay at her sides. I pull her in toward me but she resists.

I think that paying her a compliment would be a good idea.

"You have good skin today."

She doesn't say fuck you.

"I did some research. You may well have been allergic to Fred," I say.

"I've been following Mam's special diet—that's probably why."

"You look more attractive," I say.

"We eat loads of Chinese—for the ginger," she says.

"Lemon chicken?"

"Sometimes."

I take hold of her hand and place it on the rectangular bump in my back jeans pocket.

"I brought you some matches," I say.

She pulls the matchbox out.

I pull her toward me again. She rests her chin on my shoulder. Her arms link around my waist. I listen to the sound of scratching. I feel a faint heat on the back of my neck.

The next thing Jordana says makes me realize that it's too late to save her.

"I've noticed that when you light a match, the flame is the same shape as a falling tear."

She's been sensitized, turned gooey in the middle.

I saw it happening and I didn't do anything to stop it. From now on, she'll be writing diaries and sometimes including little poems and she'll buy gifts for her favorite teachers and she'll admire the scenery and she'll watch the news and she'll buy soup for homeless people and she'll never burn my leg hair again.

nonage

"And you'd get to show off those arms."

Mum reaches across and squeezes Dad's bicep.

"Hoh," she says, trying to look impressed.

We are sat round one end of the dinner table: me, then my dad, then my mum. Mum's put two candles out and we're eating on the square plates: baked trout with field mushrooms and boiled new potatoes with parsley butter. She wants to convince my father to start capoeira. The tone of her voice flutters as she attempts to convey excitement.

"And they play the most wonderful music, Lloyd." She tries to catch his eye.

Dad doesn't look up; he slides his knife into the upturned field mushroom's gills.

"I think you'd like it—two drummers and a guy twanging this kind of one-stringed guitar," she says.

It sounds awful.

"It sounds awful," I say.

"It's not awful, Oliver. Your dad would like it. It's really quite hypnotic."

I remember: Graham makes eye contact like a hypnotist.

"And Graham's putting me in for grading on Saturday," she says.

Why would she mention his name? I can hear the squeak of grilled mushroom against Dad's teeth.

"To try for my yellow belt," she continues. "You could come along and see what you think?"

Dad pinches the top of the headless trout's spine, he pulls it upward, carefully; small bones unsheath from the pinkish flesh, the tail fin comes away still in its skin. He lays it out solemnly on the blue tablecloth.

"Will you be fighting?" I ask.

"Playing—we call it playing," she says, still looking at Dad for an answer.

"Why is it called playing?" I ask; we are talking across him. He concentrates on his plate. He pulls a small bone from between his teeth. He will finish his dinner before us.

"Because we don't try and hurt each other."

"Well, I don't want to watch unless it's fighting," I say.

"Think of it like break dancing," she says, trying to help me understand.

I imagine her spinning on her head, wearing baggy jeans, listening to Cypress Hill. I feel unwell.

"But you could accidentally hit each other?" I ask, thinking of a reason why Dad might want to join in.

"No, not really. You're allowed to head butt each other sometimes," she says.

Dad chews.

"Just come along to the grading?"

He doesn't look convinced; in fact, he doesn't look anything— he could be running through his tenses: *je mange, tu manges, il mange.*

"If we both learnt it then we could practice together." She looks at me and nods. "How cool would it be if both your parents did capoeira?"

"On a scale of one to terrible, I would say—"

"Graham will be there but you don't have to talk to him," she says.

Dad speaks; I sometimes forget how deep his voice is: "Why would I not talk to him?"

Mum's turn to watch her plate.

"Yep," he says, hardly opening his mouth, "I'll watch."

"It's on Saturday morning."

He deposits half a boiled potato into his mouth, rotates his jaw.

"Mm hm," he says. It is a positive sound.

Saturday morning. Mum's been excited for days. She is practicing on the grass level, zone two, in the back garden—half crab, half ape, bounding and twirling in bare feet. She wears loose cotton trousers and a yellow vest that clings to her chest. She pretends she has an opponent: dodging, swerving, ducking.

I've already delivered my excuse for why I can't go to watch and it was not: Graham will be there and he thinks my name is Dean. Instead, I exploited my mother's faith in human nature. I explained that Jordana's mother is in Morriston hospital, which is true, and Jordana needs my support, which is true, and visiting hours sadly coincide with her grading, which is also true. I never actually said: "I am going to visit her." Mum assumes I am thoughtful.

Dad has a foot-high pile of marking on his desk. He stacks his papers in a heap just so we know.

"Lloyd, I'm going to walk down to St. James's now," she calls up the stairs.

There is no reply.

She walks up a few steps.

"Lloyd?" she says, on tiptoes.

She notices me watching her and goes upstairs into the study.

"Lloyd?" She lowers her voice but I have better hearing than she can imagine.

"Mm, sorry, what was that?"

"I was just saying: I'm going to walk down to the grading now, if you'd care to join . . ."

"Okay, I'll just finish this—"

"Could you not do it after?"

"It won't take a minute; when's your big moment?"

"Well, my bit won't be until the end of the class but you can see how the lessons work and there are some really amazing people. . . ."

"I'll follow you down in ten minutes or so."

Or so.

"Okay, it's St. James's Church."

"Got it."

"Okay."

"Good luck."

Mum comes downstairs, kisses me on the forehead and says, "Give my best wishes to Mrs. Bevan."

"Bust some ass, Mom," I say, Americanized.

She nods, pauses, gives me a second, unnecessary squeak-kiss on the cheek, grabs her towel from the banister, and closes the front door quietly.

I let exactly ten minutes pass before going upstairs. He is reading the dictionary when I step into his study.

"Dad, aren't you going to watch Mum?"

"Mm?"

"Mum's grading?"

"I thought you're going out," he says, his head down, an index finger descending the page.

"I'm going to Morriston hospital; you're going to St. James's Church."

We both have responsibilities.

"Yes, you'd better get along then," he says.

"I'm going now."

"Time doesn't wait for the terminally ill."

It is the sort of thing that I would say. I try to think of a reply.

"Well, I'm off to do my duty," I say.

"Good chap."

I shout, "Bye!" and close the front door loudly. I run along to the end of my street and turn left up Constitution Hill. Constitution Hill is cobbled, very steep, and famously good for joyriding. My legs start to ache but I keep on running.

I turn left again, coming back on myself along Montpellier Terrace, the street behind our house. I sprint until I recognize the tall frog green gate that opens onto the upper level of our back garden. My parents usually bolt the gate closed and, as a further security measure, the high back garden wall has been topped with broken glass embedded in concrete. From so many days of forgetting my house keys, I have learned that there is a certain spot on the wall where I can get a decent handhold without opening my wrists.

I stick my toes into gaps in the masonry and heave my head above the lip of the wall. I can see into the kitchen, the music room, the study, and the frosted glass of the bathroom.

Dad is standing in his study. His right hand is on his belly through an undone button on his shirt. His left hand is a fist; he rubs his knuckles on his lips. He looks around at the things in his room: the inset bookshelves, the crane-neck lamp, the letter holder, the expensive painting of navy and yellow squares, the off-white filing cabinets that prop up the slab of hardwood that he uses for a desk. He is thinking: *Just look at all this shit. What is any of it for? Lloyd! This is the moment to save your marriage.* He puts a hand out for balance onto his pile of markings. He's thinking: *Fuck Graham! I love that woman—yes, that woman—and I'm going to show her how much.*

There's a whole soap opera monologue going on in that freckled, pinkish skull. He's gone; he's walked out the door and left it open.

I jump down off the wall and stand in the road, feeling conspicuous, like a burglar scoping out a property.

I think about Dad busting through the double doors of St. James's Church, tearing his vest off, karate chopping and elbow dropping his way past twenty or thirty sweating henchmen. Mum's in the pulpit, tied up at the hands and feet, a capoeira cord stuffed in her mouth. Dad rips off her restraints.

"Welcome to the advanced class," comes Graham's voice from the rafters.

Dad spins round, looks up. Graham's in full capoeira costume, standing on a ceiling crossbeam.

With Mum clinging to his back like a shell, Dad defies gravity, leaping up onto a rafter.

"First lesson: the cuckold kick," Graham says.

The world slips into slow motion. Graham launches a flying kick. Mum whispers something into Dad's ear as she slides off his back; Dad sidesteps to the left and Mum to the right. They reach out and hold hands to create a formidable, romantic clothesline that catches Graham on his Adam's apple, sending him coughing to the floorboards.

There's a sound from the garden, in the top terrace. Someone treading, the rustling of leaves. I wait for the sound to subside before clambering up to have a peek. I see Dad walking down the steps with a fistful of rosemary. I watch him go back into the kitchen. The chopping board is out. There's a lemon, a pestle, and a mortar, and I think I can make out a bulb of garlic.

With his back to me, he has headlock control over the pestle and mortar. He lines up clove after clove under the knife handle, smushing each one with a swift chop. The lemon squeezer is a torture device—he crushes two citric skulls.

So this is it. Marinating. If *Die Hard 2* had ended like this I would have felt utterly cheated.

27.7.97—Summer holidays are go.

Dear Diary,
My mother tried. I saw that she tried.

Who can blame her for coming home after her grading, showering quickly and heading straight out again to a beach party celebration with her capoeira mates. I managed to speak to her for a moment while she was looking for a beach towel.

She told me that she had passed the grading and they named her O Mar—the sea in Portuguese—which is also what I yell when she refuses to give me a lift to school.

Her note said:

L,
have gone to 'Gennith
for a party, back tom,
J x

Abbreviations say it all. Dad spent much longer staring at the note than it took him to read it.

Since Dad missed the grading, Mum has been with Graham at capoeira on Wednesdays and Sundays, and Graham is teaching her to surf whenever the waves are good. On one occasion, she even went abseiling. She makes a point of being full of energy.

This evening, we all had Sunday dinner together and, as per usual, nobody argued. She cut up her broccoli and I noticed the dried sea-salt crystals on her elbows. These are the equivalent of another man giving your wife jewelry.

One of the things about the sea around Swansea is that it's a dark, bluey-gray color and nobody can see what your hands and legs are up to.

From my attic room, I have watched Graham's Volvo pull up when he drops Mum off or picks her up. If I have my window open I can sometimes hear the slide guitar music he listens to. I imagine he is the sort of guy who only has two tapes in his car. Mum leans across to the driver seat and they have a one-armed hug and cheek kiss, sometimes the one arm rubs her shoulder.

When she goes out, Dad spends his time reading the *Radio Times* without listening to the radio. Also, the fridge is bursting with marinated lamb chops, sea bass, mackerel. When she is in, he goes up to his study and does marking which, by the way, he has almost finished.

Somehow, they never go to bed at the same time.

Stay calm,

Oliver

(Baby Watch: Tampons Remaining: 8)

12.8.97

Word of the day: Swell—a word used by surfers to refer to a series of waves. Also, a word relating to a building up of emotion.

Dear Diary,

Jordana rang today. She tried to break up with me. I made things clear.

I said: "No. Now is not the time. I know it must be frustrating."

I used very controlled language and did not raise my voice.

She said: "What are you talking about? You can't say no."

I said: "Listen, I understand where you're coming from but this will have to wait."

She said: "Oliver—I'm breaking up with you."

I said: "No, you're not. Look, trust me, you're just having a nonage." A nonage is a period of immaturity.

"What?"

I put down the receiver calmly.

She was only angry because I had not inquired about her mother's second potentially lethal operation.

I have had a realization: my father may be unattractive. He has these fine hairs on the end of his nose that, in sunshine, can look like dew. The whites of his eyes are often a yellowy white—like seashells. He has one of those dark patches, a melanoma, on his forearm. It is not cancerous, merely repulsive.

I have bought him some Soltan self-tanning mousse, a pair of tweezers, and VitalEyes eye drops.

He has finally finished his marking.

No more excuses,

O

(Baby Watch: Tampons Remaining: 8)

llangennith

I woke up early this morning because a tile came off the roof and shattered in the backyard. Mum is standing in the front room, still in her dressing gown, looking out at the bay. The sea looks frilly with breaking waves. Just visible above the beach, rainbow-striped kites strain in the wind.

"Surfing today, Mum?"

"The waves are too big—I'd get squished."

"What about Graham?"

"Oh yes, he'll be down 'Gennith probably."

This is my chance. Graham's off being heroic. Dad's in Sainsbury's—he goes at six on Saturday mornings to miss the rush.

I draft a short note in the mind-set of my father. My dad's handwriting is impossible to imitate so I print the note on the computer—using Garamond, the romantic font—seal it in an envelope, and stand it on their dressing table.

Jill, now that I've finished marking essays and done the

shopping, I'm all yours. I've turned the dimmer switch down to halfway. Why go out for rump steak when there's marinated chateaubriand at home?

LX

I hang around on the landing halfway up the stairs between her first-floor bedroom and my attic room. I wait for her to come and get dressed.

She walks into her bedroom. I listen to the ripping paper. She must be opening it. There is a pause.

"Oliver?" is the word she says.

I wonder whether she is going to ask me to leave the house for a few hours so that she and Dad can get clandestine.

"Oliver?" she says, sharper this time, the 'Ohl' sounding like the beginnings of a phlegmy cough.

I tread downstairs and stand in her doorway.

"Oliver," she says, in her ghost dressing gown, "what is this?"

She holds the note up, held between the tips of her extended fingers; her hand makes the shape of a gun.

"I don't know. What is it?"

"I think you do know."

Her hair is flat against her head.

I scroll through some responses: *Oh, is that the note from Dad? Yeah, I was involved, but only in an editorial capacity.*

Yes, it was me. I was only trying to save your marriage.

Dad's been so busy, but he does want to make love to you—think of me as his attractive secretary.

"Okay, okay, I admit it. I wrote it. But I spoke to Dad and this is what he wants."

She frowns; lines of a dying person's handwriting appear on her forehead. She lets the gun fall to her side; it opens into a hand.

"You spoke to Dad. About what?"

"I spoke to Dad. He knows he's been imperfect. And he wants to make it up to you."

"Oliver, what did you talk about?"

"Jill, listen," I take a step toward her. "He still finds you attractive."

She blinks. Her jaw juts, pulses.

"Oliver, are you making this up? Don't lie to me."

I don't answer so quickly that it sounds like I'm panicking, and I don't wait so long that it sounds like I'm thinking about it. I get it just right: "I swear to you, Mum."

Plus, I do my truth-eyes.

She is about to say something important like how come he'll speak to you but not to me, but she stops herself.

Her mouth falls slightly open and I see her tongue tap against her teeth. She pulls open her wardrobe. There is a full-length mirror on the inside of the door. Half of me is reflected, split down the middle. I realize that my truth-eyes just make me look a bit psycho. The collar of my Crocodile polo shirt is curling up.

Mum obscures my view of myself as she yanks out some clothes.

"Oliver, I'm going for a surf," she says, turning to me.

"Right. Don't get squished," I say.

She keeps looking at me.

"I'm going to get changed," she says.

"Oh," I say. She wants me out of her room. She normally changes with the door open. I have seen her nondescript white underwear many times. Until now, it has never been a problem.

I step out of the room backward, like a butler, closing the door as I leave.

I go downstairs and sit in the lounge. I hear her stomping around. I wait for her to do something.

Outside, Dad pulls up with the shopping.

"Here he is," I call. "You can speak to him now."

She waits in the hall, watching through the stained glass of our inner front door.

When Dad is halfway across the road with three bags in each

hand she flies out the door, down the steps. His mouth moves but she doesn't wait; leaning into the wind, she stomps up to the car, pulls the keys out of the boot, slams it shut, gets in, drives off. Dad stands still in the middle of the road, fists full of shopping, shoulders sloping, looking alone.

I go upstairs, open the cupboard in the bathroom, and start to count and recount the tampons.

This is something I never thought I would know about my mother: she is super-plus. This means that, during her menstruation, she expels between twelve and fifteen grams of menses, the equivalent of twelve to fifteen raisins.

My mother uses Natracare tampons. In the instruction manual, an illustration shows a slim, blank-faced lady wearing a very short dress, one leg propped up on a chair. In a second illustration—close up—the woman is naked with transparent skin. She is inserting the tampon; her womb does not contain anything that resembles a fetus.

There are eight tampons remaining. I quickly run through my scientific findings. Week two—eight tampons remained. Week four—eight tampons remained. Week six—eight tampons remained. I won't bother with a graph.

In my research, I've discovered that there are other reasons a woman can miss her period: stress, sport, hormonal imbalance. My mother is a strong candidate for all of these.

But still, I need to take action now.

I decide to ring Jordana; I figure it is possible to save two relationships in one evening. I know we haven't been spending enough time together recently.

"Oh, hello?"

"Hello, it's Oliver."

"Oh, 'ello, my love, wonderful to 'ear your voice, 'ow are yew?" It's Jordana's mum, Jude; her favorite way to start a sentence is with the exclamation *Oh*.

"I'm good, thanks. I didn't realize you were out of hospital."

"Oh yes, I came out last week, didn't Jo tell 'ew?"

"No, she must've forgotten. Well, I hope you're feeling better."

"Oh, much improved, thank you. I'm afraid Jo's in the bath at the moment."

"Well, I was going to ask Jordana if she wanted to come camping down the beach."

"Aw, how romantic—I'm sure she'd love that. Where to?"

"Llangennith."

"Woh, 'at's a bit of a trek—why don't I give you a lift down?"

"That'd be great."

"Who you going down with?"

"Oh, we're meeting some people down there," I say. If you are trying to impress someone, I find it is useful to copy their speech habits. A subtle form of flattery.

"Well, we wun't have dinner till half-five so I'll come pick you up about half-six, all right, love?"

"Oh, brill."

"T'ra now."

"T'ra."

I am waiting with my rucksack on the bench in our front garden. I have packed my sleeping bag, my diary, a Bic biro, my swimming trunks, my toothbrush, and a Trojan condom. I see their sky blue Vauxhall cruising slowly down the street. I wave at them but still, Jude overshoots and parks outside number eighteen.

I run down the steps and up the road to meet them. I notice their car has two bumper stickers: one of a Welsh dragon and the other for Penscynor Wildlife Park.

I climb into the backseat. Jude says, "Oh, hello, love!" as if it's a surprise to see me, and Jordana doesn't say anything; she is in the passenger seat, flicking through the radio stations: Swansea Sound, Red Dragon FM, the Wave, Radio 1. I see Jude blinking, the corner of her eye tightening at each blast of static.

"Choose one station now, Jo-Jo," says Jude, as we drive off.

I choose the middle seat; it allows me to observe both their necks through the headrests. I examine the portion of Jude's head that has been shaved and the S-shaped scar amid the downy hair.

"So how have you been, Miss-is Bevan?"

"Not too bad, Oliver. Thanks for asking." Keeping her eyes on the road, she rubs Jordana's thigh. "My girl's been looking after me."

We turn a corner and bright sunshine beams through the windscreen. Jordana and Jude simultaneously pull down their sun guards; on Jordana's side there is a mirror that she does not check herself in. She is wearing her least favorite jumper and black jeans.

I examine the back of Jordana's neck. There are no striation marks, no flaking skin behind her ears, no flecks of scalp caught in the strain of her tied-back hair. She is getting more attractive while I am staying the same amount of attractive. This is not healthy. I can tell she is getting complacent because she is wearing her least favorite jumper.

"So, how ya parents then?" Jude asks.

"Dad's got a lot of work on at the moment; Mum's been on holiday."

"They didn't go together?"

"No, Mum went on a meditation retreat where they don't speak to each other or look each other in the eye."

"Oh, a bit like some of our holidays eh Jordana?"

Jude laughs loudly. Jordana breathes out.

I watch Jude's scar for a bit; I imagine pulling the flesh back and peering inside at the throbbing golf ball tumor.

"So I bet you're happy that the doctors did such a good job?"

"Oh God, hasn't Jo told yew? They removed as much as they could but they didn't want to risk doing any damage so there's still a little bit left over. I might have problems in the future but right now it's not causing any trouble."

"Congratulations," I say, thinking about the tumor taking stock, then growing slowly.

We come over the brow of the hill into Llangennith campsite. On the left side, semi-permanent caravans on breeze blocks, on the right, two large fields speckled with VW Beetles, Ford Kas, and tents of various sizes. There's also a red and white VW camper van with its accordion roof raised.

"My God, it's like the sixties down yer, Jo."

In the distance, surfers trail through the dunes, some with their wet suits unzipped to the waist, waddling and stumbling in the wind. We slow for a cattle grid—it sounds like flatulence—then Jude pulls into the gravel and sand car park.

A man kneels next to his board, scrubbing it with surf wax. A couple in a Morris Minor smoke with the windows closed.

"Have fun now," Jude says, staring through the windscreen at the rack of cardboard gray clouds.

Having spotted the brickish shape of Graham's gray-silver Volvo at the bottom of the field, I set up our tent at the top, claiming that "in the event of rain, we will be better off."

We walk down to the sea in silence. I keep my hood up for camouflage. A low, gunky mist coming off the sea obscures the far ends of the beach so that it could go on forever.

Jordana marches on ahead, looking increasingly romantic in the thick mist.

I track her fuzzy silhouette, listening to the sea lap and crash. The sand grows darker. I quicken my pace and catch her up.

"Your skin's looking good," I tell her.

She pretends not to hear me. I try a more proactive phrasing.

"Woof—your skin looks snazzy," I say.

She quickens her pace. I try to show her that I am an attentive boyfriend by displaying my knowledge of the subject area.

"Is it environmental factors or your new diet or maybe you are using a different brand of steroid cream for your atopic eczema?"

"Just fuck off, Oliver," she says.

Which is the first thing she's said to me today.

As we get closer to the sea, I see the mishmash of large, rowdy waves. They are uneven, moving at different speeds, some swallowing those in front of them. Amid the rumpus, a surfer abandons his board as the wave behind him puffs up and spits like a bursting zit.

Out of the water directly ahead of us, a torso is emerging: bowed head, hunched shoulders. From the wet suit's silhouette, I notice the figure has breasts. She tiredly clings to her long board as if it were the floating remnants of a torpedoed U-boat.

Once the water is too shallow for her to lean on the board she heaves it from the water, tucks it under her arm. She tilts through the battery of smaller, bullying waves. Her board catches in a crosswind and she stumbles drunkenly, splashing to her knees. As she wipes the froth from her face, I realize it is my mother. I grab Jordana's hand and pull her along the beach; she resists.

"What are you doing?" she says.

"Come on—this is what couples do," I say.

"What?!"

"We've got to run along the beach hand in hand—trust me!"

"Seriously: fuck off!"

She digs her heels into the sand as I yank at her arm.

"Please!" I say, seeing my mother wading through the shallows behind her.

She thumps me on my wrists, breaking my grip. Then she comes toward me and hits me again on my shoulder. It hurts. I start to run and, thankfully, she follows, kicking at my heels. This is what couples do.

From a safe distance, I glance back: my mum—just a blur through the mist—kneeling, unleashing her calf.

Jordana kicks me in the shin.

I wonder whether Mum and Jordana would recognize each other outside of the context of my front porch. I've been careful to ensure that their meetings have been brief and impersonal. At the last school parents' evening, Jordana and I planned our routes meticulously so that our elders would not bump into each other. I told her to be careful because my parents would be quick with the sciences but would take forever in humanities. She started at maths, I started at art, and we went round the hall clockwise.

It's dark. Since we arrived, the fields have filled up. Campfires lick and whip in the wind; tents huddle in groups. In the caravan windows, thin curtains are backlit, glowing.

I bought dinner from Beano's Fast Food Caravan, ordering Britain's favorite pie: chicken and mushroom. Jordana used her perfect skin to buy a bottle of blackcurrant Mad Dog 20/20 from the campsite shop.

We are standing by our tent. She shines the torch under her chin. I glimpse the purple crust around her lips from the Mad Dog. I am not drinking because I want to remain in control.

At the bottom of the field, near Graham's Volvo, a large campfire swirls into the dark.

"Who am I?"

She starts running in circles around me, her arms out, aeroplaning.

"I'm so free and in love!" She laughs.

She dive-bombs and swoops.

"Who am I?" she says.

She is hysterical. I start walking.

"I'm you."

She does a flyby, skimming my nose with the tips of her fingers.

"I'm you."

The wind briefly pushes the sound of a badly played guitar in our direction.

Jordana has nearly finished her Mad Dog. Unexpectedly, she offers me some. I swig and she pulls the bottle from my lips.

"Oi, that's enough," she says.

She sniffs at the air. I think she is going to tell me that I smell.

"I can smell hash," she says.

She looks around and, spotting Graham's campfire, she lopes off down the field.

I follow her at a distance, careful to stay well back from the firelight. Graham and four other pink-faced men are sitting on camping chairs in a circle. They have three slabs of Biere d'Alsace.

I wonder where my mum is. There's a light on in one of the nearby tents.

"Give us a drag on 'at spliff." Jordana's voice is unreasonably loud.

"There's manners," one of the men says. "Say please."

"Pretty please with hippies on top."

I watch Jordana's shoulders rise as she inhales. She hands the spliff back to the man then turns around and runs toward me. She kisses me—the first time in weeks—open-mouthed, and blows smoke down my throat.

I cough; she laughs.

"Whoa, trippy, man," she says.

I feel my bronchials tingle.

The wind carries with it a brief blast of trance music, a deep, thumping bass topped with a burglar alarm melody. Jordana looks around, trying to locate the source of the music. She spins a full three-sixty then stops and gazes off toward the car park, which is deserted, apart from two small cars parked side by side.

"I'm going over there," she says, pointing to the cars.

"Right."

"You go do what couples do," she says, and as she runs off she does an impression of a plane, her arms out wide.

I make my way up the field, weaving around the guy ropes by the light from the campfires, and climb into the porch of our tent. I try to formulate a plan to save two relationships in one evening.

After a while I hear the sound of a woman wailing. I know it's my mum because whenever she gets drunk she performs the greatest hits of Kate Bush. It's coming from nearby—I peek out through the unzipped tent flap. She's singing "This Woman's Work." I can't see her face, only her torchlight discoing as she lurches toward the toilet block at the top of the field. Rows of porthole-type windows—brightly lit from within—make the building look like a recently landed spacecraft.

Once she's disappeared inside, I step out of the tent and walk into the center of the field, careful to stand well back from the perimeter of light emanating from the toilet block. I can see through the open door into the Merched/Ladies. There are six sinks, each with a mirror above it. I am careful to stay at a safe distance. Mum pulls out her toothbrush. She is the only person I know who brushes her tongue, retching all the while.

Sometimes I don't brush my teeth for days and they feel like the mossy boulders on top of a stone wall. Mum used to time me, to check that I was cleaning my teeth properly, standing by the sink tapping her wristwatch. Out of a kind of defiance, I used to brush only my bottom teeth. Just for a sense of independence. As I fell asleep I licked my furry upper molars and knew that I was not a mummy's boy.

She gargles and shoves her toothbrush into the pouch of her gray hoodie.

She wears loose black linen trousers and Reebok running shoes. I wonder if Graham will brush his teeth. I think about the ash black seeds in the yellow tide between his large, overlapping incisors.

She leans into the mirror. With an index finger, she pulls at the skin beneath her right eye, like someone about to put in a contact lens.

She brings her face up close to her own reflection and then huffs on the mirror with her boozy breath.

Her Biere d'Alsace stands lopsided in the soap dish. She swigs it.

Wiping away the condensation with her sleeve, she examines herself, runs her hand from her chin down her neck. Then she picks up the beer and finishes it in one admirable glug. She turns toward the exit, toward me. I quickly jog to a hedge and pretend to piss.

I hear the clank of her bottle tossed into a bin.

"Oi, excuse me," she says.

I don't know who she is talking to. She is quite close.

"You know you're pissing right next to the toilets?" she says.

She's talking to me. I pretend to be holding my penis.

"Spare a fucking thought," she says. I didn't know my mother could do swearing. She sounds genuinely outraged.

I wait for her footsteps to grow quiet before turning around. In the distance, I see her weak torchlight sweep erratically as she dances over guy ropes.

I walk along the edge of the field, staying in the shadows next to the hedges.

I see her disappear into a well-lit tent: a lantern, I assume, rather than a torch, swinging from the apex of the dome.

I quietly pad to within a few paces of the side of the tent, close enough to be able to interrupt calmly, without raising my voice.

"Check out the fluoride stink on you," he says. It's Graham—there's still a fleck of Yank in his resurgent Welsh accent.

"Yum, chemicals," she says.

He laughs.

"You should try my fennel toothpaste. Do you know how much fluoride they put in tap water?"

"Too much?" she says.

"Fluoride's a carcinogen and a mutagen and even in small quantities it can be harmful."

"Unlike beer?" she says.

"Exactly," he says.

There is the *fss-tok* of a bottle being opened.

"Thanks."

Fss-tok.

"Cheers." They say it at the same time. There is the sound of glass on glass.

"Do you remember the last time we were in a tent together?" he says.

The lantern swings; their silhouettes morph and warp.

As I take a step closer, the heel of my shoe clips a guy rope, twanging it like one of the instruments they use in capoeira.

"Hello?" Mum asks.

I stay still.

"Who's that?" she says.

"Some piss-head," he says.

"Hello-o?" she says.

I turn quickly, pull my hood up, and walk back toward the darkness of the hedge at the edge of the field.

I try to think of my father's take on this. I worry that he would say in the modern age, there's nothing wrong with a man's wife being in a tent with another man. Dad is full of childlike naivete.

Chips says that if a girl gets inside a sleeping bag with you then she's already said yes.

I realize that if I want to catch them at it I'm going to have to be far more stealthy. I wish I had brought my disposable camera and Dictaphone.

I imagine that the guy ropes are laser beams linked up to an alarm system. I take on the mind-set of a light-footed cat burglar. My mother's clitoris is a valuable diamond. I reapproach Graham's tent quietly and crouch within pouncing distance of the porch.

"How do you turn this thing off?" she says.

"You've got to twist it," he says. "Let me. It's got a dimmer."

The lantern dims to candlelight. Their silhouettes fade.

"Thanks," she says.

"Right," he says.

"Where's the mood music or whale song?" she says.

"Shut up," he says. "Take your T-shirt off."

Women find confidence sexy. Too often, Dad lets Mum drive.

There is the crumpling of a single sleeping bag.

"Comfortable?" he asks, playing sensitive.

"Yah," she says. *Yah* is my word.

"Right," he says.

There's a quiet slapping sound.

"Relax," he says.

"Mmm."

I get that feeling again. Insulation foam expands in my skull, my lungs, my gut.

"Oh," she says.

Then there's the sound of an exhalation, a release. There's none of the usual clumsy, carpentry noises like when Mum and Dad do it.

I knew this would be tantric. The whole thing is virtually noiseless.

"I can feel that you're tight," he says.

He just said those words. He actually said them.

I think of pulling out the pegs and rolling them into a ditch or jumping off the Volvo's bonnet and body-slamming the tent.

"Here?" he says.

"Ow," she says.

Her breathing goes jerky.

I never wanted to hate her this much.

"Right?"

"Mm."

"Too hard?"

"No, s'good, thanks," she says.

I could kill her.

"Nada," he says.

I quietly step backward.

"Aah," she says. And again: "Aah." Like Bisto.

My heart is a cold, hard stone.

"Ngh," she says.

My body is a shell.

I stand up and turn to walk away but I am having trouble communicating with my body. I am seriously disabled. I need round-the-clock care.

Somehow I start walking. My legs are doing it by themselves.

I walk down past the embers of the campfire to the bottom of the field. I step over the stile into the car park. I check the time—1:17—and I mentally chart their trajectory toward tantrigasm: multiple is too restrained a word for the oodles of cumming that starts at her toes, throbs up through her gut, inflating her, transforming her into gas. Orange moths will gather on the fly sheet. Worms will rise to the surface and cavort in the dirt.

My father wouldn't understand. He is the sort of man who has spectacle marks on either side of his nose bridge. He has memorized the phone number for Swansea Council's Pothole Hotline.

I look at my watch—1:18. Dad lasted ten minutes.

I can hear techno. It sounds like someone rhythmically clearing their throat.

The two cars are still parked tightly side by side. The smaller of the two cars has its courtesy lights turned on. The best gift that Dad brought back from his trip to Boston was a selection of cheesy—corny—words for everyday things. I already knew the obvious ones—*sidewalk, trunk, restroom*—but we both fell in love with *courtesy light*. There are two boys, older than me, sitting in the front seats; one rests his head on the steering wheel.

As I walk across the gravel, I watch the tip of a spliff, occasionally flaring in the dark, being passed from one car to the other. It bobs up and down like a red dot from a laser-targeting sniper rifle.

As I get within a few meters, I am suddenly blind or dead or back in the womb or comatose or undergoing shock therapy or they've just turned their headlights on. There is the sound of semi-sympathetic laughter beneath the euphoric trance. They dim their full beams; four TV screens of static light remain burned onto my sight line.

I walk up to the driver's side window of the small Fiat. They turn their courtesy light off. I stand there for a while, unable to see anything through the glass.

The window lowers slightly; a pair of half-closed eyes appear.

"Wha's the password?" he shouts above the music.

The question is too open and the thought of my mother rutting Graham comes rushing in to fill the empty space. I imagine the smell in their tent, like when you sneeze in your hand and then sniff your palm.

I try to focus. I make out empty packets of Monster Munch and an unopened Petit Filous on the dashboard. I can't see Jordana.

"Monster munch," I say into the gap.

They laugh. I have no idea why. The window lowers jerkily. He passes me out a crooked spliff.

"I'd get in the back of the other car if I were you. Miffy's trying to cop on to your girlfriend."

I walk around the back of the cars, carrying the joint aloft— Olympic-torch style. The bass churns from the boot of the Fiat. Next to it is a red Mazda; I make out two stickers on the rear windscreen: *Surfers Against Sewage* and *No Fear.*

I pull open the back passenger-seat door and peer in. It's dark inside but I can make out Jordana, sitting in the front passenger seat. She's talking intently to the driver. She doesn't stop to introduce me.

I wait for a little while to be invited to sit down—it doesn't happen—so I slide along to the middle of the sand-gritty seat and shut the door gently. There are no seat belts. The smell is of drying towels, burned plastic, and tobacco.

"... and when she woke up she kept tasting metal," Jordana says. "It was so weird."

"Fuck," the boy-man says, nodding his head slowly.

Eventually, he turns to me. "'Right? I'm Lewis."

He has short strawberry blond hair and a pancake-freckled face.

"Hi, I'm Oli."

"Are you gonna smoke that spliff?" he asks.

I'm still holding it upright, not casual. I am a lawyer.

"Oh yeah, yeah," I say and put it in the corner of my mouth. I am careful not to pull too hard. I have seen enough films where choking on a spliff automatically loses you your girlfriend. My lungs strain like a microwave popcorn bag. I breathe out quickly, my nostrils burn. I tense my gut and take it.

I pass to Jordana as a kind of reconciliation. She looks at me briefly as she grips it between all five fingertips. She seems subdued. She pulls hard, before exhaling a Superman ice-wind of smoke.

In the adjacent car they are nodding to the music: two lads in the front and one in the backseat

"So, was she different afterwards?" Lewis asks.

Jordana takes a moment to consider the question, which, in my experience, is an unusual thing for her to do.

"I mean, a bit," she says. "Mam said some stuff, like she thought that they had left a pair of scissors in her brain from the operation. She actually believed that."

"Wee-ud," Lewis says.

"You never told me that," I say, leaning forward between them.

She looks at me for a moment and then carries on speaking.

"But the worst thing is that I felt sorry for her, like I was the grown-up. I hated that."

I watch Jordana talk and it feels like she might be acting, like she has just invented a whole new persona. This is not to say that she is unconvincing, just that I've never seen her speak in so many full sentences. Then I remember that she's drunk a bottle of black-currant Mad Dog.

"Yeah, bad one," Lewis says.

I nod. "Yeah," I say.

"Nobody wants to think that their mother is vulnerable," she says. As she speaks, I notice her tongue is stained violet.

I want her to keep talking. Because even if Jordana is pretend-ing—this brand-new personality—I still reckon we could get on, me and the new her. After that time in the botanical gardens when she compared flames to teardrops, I thought that was it—game over—she would soon be arranging flowers, noticing the elderly, and working Saturdays in Oxfam. But this is different.

I realize that Jordana and I have never got drunk together. And I realize that there are questions I want to ask her.

I start speaking: "I've been wondering, do you think your parents get on better since the op—"

"Oi, fuck sake!" The boy in the front passenger seat of the adjacent car leans in and interrupts. "Nuff fuckin' sorp op'ra, right. Talk 'appy."

Jordana stiffens in her seat.

"There, there, babs," Lewis says to the driver, speaking in a baby voice. Lewis takes the spliff from Jordana—I expect him to take a toke but he doesn't—and then he passes it through the window to the other car.

The clock on the dashboard reads 1:23. My father would already be halfway there by now.

Looking up through the open sunroof, I watch stars blink on and off, gaps in the fast-moving clouds.

"So, Oliver, do you surf?" Lewis asks.

I think of Mum and Graham in the waves, rubbered up in wet suits.

"No," I say. Lewis looks immediately disappointed. I try to save things: "But my mother does."

"Oh. So how come yew down 'Gennith then?"

Jordana turns round to watch me.

I scroll some replies, all of which sound ridiculous:

I am the official adjudicator for my mother's boyfriend's sexual performance.

I am drawn to the ocean; I find solace in its mystery.

We needed to get away from the hustle and bustle of modern Swansea life.

"I wanted to spend some quality time with Jordana," I say.

Jordana cringes.

"Fair dos," he says. "Can't blame you. She's hot."

He says this to Jordana, not to me. He has a little blondish cowlicked fringe, like a breaking wave.

I look to Jordana, expecting her to blush, but she doesn't.

I try to think of a retort, a touché, but the clock flits to 1:24 and I get distracted. Six minutes in. My father would be trying to think of something repulsive by now—old people's genitals—to buy himself some time.

Laughter and shouting rise above the music. The boy in the passenger seat of the adjacent car pokes his head in. He looks ecstatic.

"Oi, boys, Dann-o's whiteying," he says.

I look across at the boy-man in the backseat of the other car; his face is dead—a genuine, blue-white, mortuary corpse color. He looks at me emptily through the glass.

Lewis starts laughing. Jordana laughs too, jiggling in her seat. I sit back in my seat and look around me.

The two boys in the front of the other car turn in their seats to face each other and start to rap. It's the theme song to *The Fresh Prince of Bel-Air.*

"Oh boys, leave it out, is it?" the corpse says, but they don't stop. The cadaver rubs his palms over his ears.

Jordana and Lewis are giggling. I want to join in. I try to think of something funny. The only thought my brain will allow me is of Graham telling a joke to his mates: What's the difference between Jill Tate and a wet suit?

I look at the clock: 1:25.

You're not supposed to piss inside a wet suit.

I think about Tantra.com. Assuming that they're going for the world record, it is about this time that Graham and my mother will totally surrender all mental, emotional, and cultural conditioning, so that universal life energy will flow freely through them.

Jordana and Lewis are still finding something funny. Their heads loll.

I test-drive a laugh. "Hahahaha," I say.

I look at the sky for a gag. I see a drab satellite moving slowly. I think of the things I would look at with a military spy camera.

I remember that tantra is the cosmic union of opposites, to create a polarity charge that connects with the primordial energy from which everything arises in the universe . . . the totality of all.

The boys in the adjacent car are into the second verse.

The basic difference between unenlightened sexuality and tantra is that sex becomes sacred and divine when you approach it from your heart and body, rather than solely from your mind.

I bounce up and down on my seat.

One twenty-six. In two minutes' time, my father's sexual record will be obsolete. That will be it. Once you are enlightened then there is no going back. You can't shut the lid.

Jordana is laughing so much that she's having trouble breathing. Her chest vibrates. Her head seems loose on her shoulders.

Lewis keeps looking over at Jordana and laughing. She wipes her eyes. Technically, she's crying.

I've got about a minute and a half. According to my personal best at last year's Sports Day, it should take me approximately thirteen and a half seconds to run the hundred meters to the stile.

Fuck it.

"You can have her!" I tell Lewis.

He's still laughing. He cups his ear at me, pretending he can't hear me over the noise.

"Go for it! You win!" I say.

He's still smiling.

I slide along the seat, pull the door open, and get out. I slam it, even though I don't mean to, and then I start to run.

My legs feel rubbery. My skull is glowing. I start running in what I hope is the direction of the stile: a dusky plus sign in the dark.

I clear the stile with a hurdler's aplomb.

I stop at the remains of their campfire to catch my breath. A log glows among the ash. The empty beer bottles have been stacked neatly back into their cardboard casing.

There are no wild sounds of adulterous fucking, which does

not surprise me. At this stage in tantra, they do not need the super-ficial affirmations of groans and grunts. They are perfectly silent and perfectly still—a single point of light and focus, a slowly gath-ering offshore swell.

I look at my watch; I wait for the big hand to sign the divorce papers.

It's 1:29. Our home is broken.

I stand in the ashes of the campfire.

I close my eyes and focus on my breathing.

I match my breaths to the distant sound of the tide.

I experience a slowly dawning sense of perspective . . .

I was wrong to think that Mum doesn't understand the decisions she is making. If I weren't so caught up in the details, I would be able to see—at this precise moment—the rare beauty of two au-tonomous beings in perfect alignment, an eclipse by torchlight. It's not so hard to imagine Graham and Jill's nomadic life together, fol-lowing the swell, in tune with the cycles of life and death, mind and body, moon and tide.

And Dad even, maybe this is just the break he needs. To be screwed out of his routine, forced to make a new start. I see him taking up carpentry. He's got the face of a carpenter. He'll be alone but he'll be content, living in the Brecon Beacons, surrounded by his own sculptures. His themes will be rebirth, history, and the body. And when I'm grown up we'll talk wood, meat, and Welsh de-volution.

I am so well adjusted.

I quietly walk closer to their tent.

There are still some sounds: "Ahh," my mother says.

The grass is wet, and since I have the feeling I might be here for some time, I lie on the ground and shuffle underneath Graham's Volvo, where it's dry.

There's the smell of grease and petrol. I stare straight up at some miscellaneous piping. From their tent I hear rustling.

"Well, thank you for that," Mum says. "I feel two stone lighter."

Sex is excellent exercise.

More rustling.

"I need the practice. I want to learn reflexology as well."

"Uh huh."

"It's surprisingly technical—all the different pressure points. I think you can do a course that's about the oils and aromatherapy side of it, but the one I'm on's more practical."

I wonder if that spliff was laced with formaldehyde. My dawning sense of perspective was a trick of the light.

Chips has studied seduction techniques. Massage or other physical contact is one way in which a woman can be made to reach "buying temperature." This means that she has been physically or mentally aroused to make her ripe for the picking.

"It's really interesting the sort of people who are on the course. There's an old gay couple wh—"

He is interrupted by something.

"Jill? My God, what are you do—"

Again, he's plugged.

"Jill, this is not a good idea." Graham sounds like someone reading an autocue.

She sighs, as if the explanation is a chore, then says, "Oh, come on, Graham, it's been there all along." She speaks a little too quick: "We both knew this would happen."

"Right, you're right," he says.

Graham is very trusting.

There is the *popopop* of his button fly jerked open.

"Christ," he says, sounding slightly terrified. "We should talk about this."

He is badly scripted.

"Shh." She makes the sound of the sea.

He inhales sharply.

"Oh fuck, Jill. I don't this is."

She moves him beyond language.

There is the sound of sleeping bags crinkling.

"Oh," he says.

I get that feeling again. Like I'm full of the foamy stuff they pour down sinks.

"Jill, fuck, Jill." He keeps using her name.

In the faint light, I make out the poles of the tent straining against the material. They look like bones in an X-ray slide.

"You want me, you want me," he says, whisperingly, talking in pairs. Dad would never be so presumptuous.

She says nothing, focused.

"Oh, oh," he says.

There is a quiet but steady sound, like someone inflating an air bed. It goes on for some time.

"Uh. Uh. Mm," he says. He said *mm*, not *mum*.

She says nothing.

"You-want-me-you-want-me-you-unh," he says.

And again: "unh."

"There," she says.

He breathes like someone in shock.

"There."

There's the sound of zipping. My breathing stays steady.

"Oh fuck," he says, sounding bereaved. There's the sound of more zipping. They're into bondage. That's fine.

I put my head on its side. A bare arm throws back the outer tent flap. A hand reaches out and wipes itself, knuckles then palm, on the grass. It is Mum's hand. The sleeve on her right arm is pushed up to the elbow. She crawls out on all fours: underevolved. She's wearing a grubby gray T-shirt. She has some trouble standing up. I see that she's not naked, she's now wearing jogging bottoms. She is more or less fully dressed. Except her feet are bare. And she is having some trouble using them. She steps in small wonky circles, trying to keep her balance. She reaches back into the tent porch and yanks out a fleecy jumper. It drags on the ground as she stumbles out of sight.

I wait to see if Graham will follow her. Whether they're going to continue things on the beach.

There's no sound or movement.

I wait and watch, thinking about what has just happened. Chips says that in Studio Masseuse on Walter's Road, for twenty pounds you can get a woman who looks like a dinner lady to get her tits out while she wanks you off. You have to ask for a "maxi-massage."

I can't believe I thought that Mum and Graham were involved in a deep spiritual coupling. This was reminiscent of the hand jobs I have sometimes overheard in the back row of UCI cinemas. Chips says that it should never take more than a week between getting a hand job and stuffing it in. The clock is ticking.

I shuffle out from under the car. I notice that three blades of grass are webbed, glistening with cum.

Mum left the tent open.

I hear breathing. I wonder whether Graham is in a meditative state. The breathing churrs and stutters. I wait and listen. The sound rises and backfires. I peek into the tent. His Vegetarian sandals—he must have bought a new pair—are paired in the porch. Through the netting, I can make out his shape, flat out, asleep.

This had nothing to do with tantra. This was cheap and boozy and Graham didn't even stay awake to talk about emotions. I have sometimes taken longer to reach orgasm than Graham did. I cancel the idea that Mum and Graham are good for each other or that Dad should be a carpenter. Perspective is for astronauts. I pick up Graham's sandals and start off in the same direction as my mother.

As I clear the stile, I can just make out a smudge stumbling into the dunes. I run after her but I don't shout. The two cars are still there; the red dot bobbing in the dark.

As the gravel turns to sand, running suddenly becomes unworkable, the ground scuffs beneath my feet.

Once I'm into the dunes, there is virtually no light, only a dull contrast between dark—the sky—and darker—the sand. Each step is a guess. The wind whips grains across my face; they gather in my ears. I think I hear someone saying, *"Shit-it, Shit-it,"* over and over again, but the wind and the waves are *shh*ing and I have smoked my first-ever spliff.

I traipse until my thighs burn. I'm on the verge of digging myself a hole to snooze in. I give up on finding Mum and settle for burying the sandals in a shallow grave. They are sand-colored sandals. He will never find them.

I manage to drag myself back, away from the sound of the sea, toward the few remaining caravan lights.

In the car park, the two cars have gone. They are probably taking turns with my girlfriend. I am too tired to care. Besides, Lewis seemed nice, and he was a good listener. I liked his freckles. Jordana could do worse.

When I get back, Jordana is on top of her sleeping bag, asleep. The last time I got to see her sleep was during our Bronze Award Duke of Edinburgh expedition. She had her tent flap open. I sat by the fire and watched her rolling from side to side, itching in her sleep.

But now, she sleeps facing away from me, fully clothed, knees up to her chest, hands tucked under her chin. She smells of blackcurrant. I watch her, wait for one of her arms to jerk to her neck and scrape a trail of inflammation. I wait for the sandpaper sound of her nails raking her crotch. But none of this.

She is still.

In the morning, I wake with a dry mouth. The tent is a bright, clay oven. I am alone.

I get out to look for Jordana. The sky is clear; the wind is timid. I see Jordana talking to some boys—a whole new set of boys—around a red VW Golf in the car park.

Even from this distance I can see she wears a thin cotton vest top that shows off her midriff and only her bikini bottoms. It's not hot enough for bare thighs. She sees me coming and quickly walks up the path to meet me, or to cut me off. She smiles with her lips, no teeth.

"Morning," she says. I can hear the sea. I look at her smooth forearms, her milk white neck.

"I saw a woman asleep in the dunes who looked like your mum if she was a tramp," she says.

I am staring at her thighs, her flawless belly. Not a dapple in sight.

"What?" she says.

"What happened to your skin?" I ask.

She looks beautiful.

"You look beautiful."

I should have said that last night.

"Have I not told you? *You* were right," she says. "I'm allergic to dogs."

"I was right."

"You were right. I got tested."

She watches me.

"You'd best go take down the tent. Mam's on her way."

On the drive home, Jordana is almost friendly. She says "Bye!" with a certain longing. When I get up to my room, I prepare to write a cathartic diary entry. Instead, I find Jordana's looping handwriting:

Word of the day: Apothegm—a blunt remark, conveying some important truth. (It took me ages last week, but I found this word for you—though I'm sure you've already heard of it.)

Dear Oliver,
I tried to tell you on the phone but you wouldn't listen. I figure you'll probably only believe me if it's in writing. It is *over.*

I've spent the morning on the beach catching up on your diary. There's so much stuff that I missed. You didn't tell me about any of that weirdness with your parents.

I read what you thought about that e-mail I sent you. I think you will get a good mark in your English GCSEs. You were mostly right, yes, I was worried that my mother might die, yes, I wanted you to understand how I felt. I found the word for you because I thought you might like it.

I had a fun time going out with you but we're just not right for each other. If it makes it any easier, I'm glad you were my first. I've left my Zippo as a gift for you in your wash bag.

Also, I think you should know I've found someone else. (He's not a surfie.) Better you hear this from me, rather than see us walking around the Quadrant. When we are in school together, try not to look upset. I know you are a good actor.

I'm sure there is someone else who will fall in love with you.

Love,
Jordana X

delirium tremens

I have more important things to think about than the end of my first relationship, which, as any adult will tell you, is just one of those things that feels life-shattering at the time but means nothing when you're forty.

I leave my diary, grab the Zippo from my wash bag, and head downstairs. My parents are out. I will make Graham realize what he has done to my family by giving him the impression that I've lost it and am capable of anything. I don't feel threatened by him; capoeira is the art of not hitting each other. I take an empty bottle of Robinsons into the cellar, fill it with one third vodka, one third apple, one third cranberry. It is important to seem genuine.

I grab my Rip Curl backpack and load it with the necessaries for breaking and entering: a coat hanger and a pair of Thinsulate gloves. I throw in the Zippo and the cranapplevod.

I run down to the Quadrant and wait on the red plastic tip-up seats for the Gower Explorer Bus to Port Eynon. The journey will take an hour, following the coast road, dipping into Kittle, Oxwich, Scurlage, Rhossili, and Horton on the way.

My parents and I never went to Port Eynon in summer because there are too many campsites and the local pub—The Smuggler's Tavern—is lit by strip lights hanging from chains. I have heard my father rename Port Eynon "Townhill-sur-mer." Jordana holidays here when her parents can't afford to go abroad.

I drink some of my vodka mix. Delirium tremens are the hallucinations caused by drinking too much alcohol. I take another slug.

In Rhossili village, the driver pulls in to the stop although nobody is waiting or wanting to get off. I look down onto Rhossili beach, eight miles of dark sand and, in the distance, Worm's Head poking its snout into the sea. The driver and the other passengers—two old ladies—get off the bus and stand in the fierce sunlight. The driver lights a cigarette so I get off too. The back of the bus has been opened, the engine steams. I jump up to sit on a red postbox so I can see the beach better. Llangennith campsite huddles at the far end of the beach. The surfers are just specks. I swig my luminous drink.

The driver talks to the two old ladies.

"We're not going to be called Davies's anymore; we're gonna be called Morgan's. There'll be a whole new fleet," the driver says.

"What about the routes? Will you have the same routes?" asks the old lady with two walking sticks and no discernible spine.

"The routes'll still be the same, though—most of the drivers too."

"So what's happened then?"

"New owners is all."

"New uniforms?"

"Purple."

"Oh God."

"What about the timetables?"

"All-new timetables as of next week."

"All-new? But what about the old ones?"

"Bin 'em."

"There's a waste."

I picture hundreds, thousands of useless timetables. What about the people who don't know the bus timetable is changing? Someone could be standing at a bus stop—maybe in hail or drizzle or a fierce wind—and thinking, *I'll be on the nice warm bus soon.* The time of the bus's expected arrival will pass and they will wonder whether they got it wrong so they'll check their timetable. And it might be getting torrential with hailstones the size of brain tumors. And the bus still hasn't arrived and the person is wondering whether it was something they did to deserve no bus. And the person might start weeping and wiping their tears from each cheek and putting their fingers in their mouth because someone once told them a lie: "You can stop crying by eating your tears." Or maybe the bus crashed—in this weather—and everyone died and what a thing to think badly of the dead for being late.

"S'all right, Butt. Do you wanna get back on?"

"Cheer up, my love—what girl's done this to you?"

My saliva is abundant. I have inherited weak tear ducts from my mother.

The old ladies tell me to sit by them and I tell them it's terrible about the bus company and the uniforms and the timetables.

"It's nothing to worry about, love."

"Do you want some cranberry-apple vodka?" I ask.

"That's probably the reason you're upset. How old you, darlin'?"

I look at the blurred lady on the seat next to me. She could almost be young.

"You could almost be young," I say.

"Watch out, Miri, I think we got ourselves a charmer."

"Well, don't keep him all to youself now, Elly."

And they laugh like the buses will just keep on coming. My eyes clear and the ladies are old again. The one in the seat next to me has very long eyelashes.

The road falls away steeply as the bus winds into Port Eynon. The post office window is full of junk: turquoise stone dragons on wooden plinths, daffodil-carrying Eisteddfod dolls, and hand-painted Buddhas. This is my stop.

Graham's whitewashed cottage, "The Kite Hole," is opposite the church graveyard. The house name is carved into a piece of driftwood pinned beneath the doorbell. The blue door looks tiny, as though it has sunk into the ground. The garden is small but pretty, enough grass to make love on, surrounded by a low stone wall and tall bushes on three sides. There is no car in the drive. I take a slug of vodka.

The break-in is surprisingly easy. I climb onto the stone wall and then onto the flat garage roof. The bathroom window is closed but not locked. Much to my surprise, the coat hanger actually has a purpose: I jimmy the window and pull it wide. On the sill are four toothbrushes in a cup, an electric toothbrush, and two tubes of toothpaste: one is fennel, the other is Macleans. Directly below the sill is the sink. I throw my bag in ahead of me.

Climbing in headfirst, I knock the toothbrushes to the floor, handstanding on the taps before awkwardly belly-sliding over the sink to flop onto a green mat.

I stand up, relax, and the first thing I need to do is piss. My wee is clear as springwater. I do not flush, imagining Graham taking a dump and my urine splashing onto his buttocks.

On the wall outside the toilet are photos of Graham with a woman who is not my mum: in ski salopettes, in hiking boots, on a train platform. There is also a photo of the two of them scuba diving, giving the thumbs-up to the camera, shrouded in a glimmering shoal of marlin.

Downstairs, the kitchen and dining area is a long, low-ceilinged room lit by buzzing overhead strip lights. My vodka is nearly empty. In the cupboard beneath the sink I find Ecover washing-up liquid, a dustpan, and a compost bin. The composter is brimming with eggshells, mango skins, and lentil snot.

Next to a clay-colored bread bin in one corner sits a wine rack containing Gordon's gin, whisky still in its cardboard tube, and a Gran Reservas brandy. I pull out the brandy.

In a cupboard next to the cooker I find a bell-bottomed glass. I pour myself way too much expensive brandy. I don't even like brandy.

I flick through Graham's diary, which hangs above the phone. I find yesterday's date, Saturday the 30th, and then I turn forward one week to the following Saturday. I pencil in *Come deep inside Jill Tate.* I count forward twenty-four weeks and write, *last chance saloon for aborting love-child.* I count forward another sixteen weeks: *birth of illegitimate son/daughter. Note to self: Cop a feel of Jill's lactating tits.*

I walk into the utility room then through a door into the garage. There's the smell of paint, surf wax, and drying neoprene. Balanced on top of three wooden ceiling beams, two surfboards lie prone, fins upward. A wet suit is suicidal, hanging from the middle beam. On two walls there are shelves stacked with paint tins, rollers, trowels, methylated spirit, turpentine, white spirit, extra-long safety matches, a hacksaw, plastic bags full of nails and screws, barbecue skewers, jump leads, and a hose, curled up like a python.

I take the meths and the hacksaw from the shelf and walk back into the kitchen. The kitchen is well-equipped. In the cupboard I find a steamer, a poacher, and a complicated-looking cheese grater. On the counter is a knife block containing a selection of twelve blades: six steak, two paring, one carving, one bread, a pair of scissors, and a long, thin knife—almost a sword—for which I cannot determine a purpose.

I take a metal teaspoon from the cutlery drawer and place it surreptitiously at the back of the microwave. His microwave is nine hundred watts, ours is only six hundred.

I sit cross-legged in the large wicker chair in the corner of the room, swirling brandy around the bell-bottomed glass. It's getting dark outside. Graham finishes his class at half nine and will be back here by ten. The last bus home is at half ten.

I top up the brandy and go into the front room. On a windowsill are some tribal masks and dried poppy stalks in a deliberately dented copper vase. He has a very small TV. On the wall are black and red sugar-paper puppets with curved jester's shoes. There's also a gourd that you can imagine being used in a bloodletting ceremony. A wood-burning stove is surrounded by a collection of tribal sculptures: faces carved into dark wood with shells for eyes.

There's a fitted bookcase in a nook in the wall. There are books on diet—*Eating Your Way to Happiness*—one on massage—*Chakra Energy Massage: Spiritual Evolution into the Subconscious Through Activation of the Pressure Points of the Feet*—and the bottom shelf is entirely taken up with photo albums.

I pick up the one labeled *1976*. My parents got married in 1977. The first picture is of a young Graham with long hair and what looks like an elder brother, bearded, up a mountain. They are grinning and wearing rainbow-striped climbing socks. All the pictures have handwritten captions. This one says, *Gorillas in the Mist*. I flick through—seasides, birthdays, statues, tree climbing. The pictures have rounded edges and everything looks honeyed.

About two-thirds of the way through, I find a page of photos from a camping trip. There's one of Graham and a girl who despite her mysterious, nipple-length hair is undoubtedly my mum. They are not holding hands or even looking at each other but Graham is puffing his chest up while Mum pretends to be coy. The tent in the background is an old school orange-canvas affair. The note below says, *The Hunter Becomes the Hunted*. My mum's maiden name is Hunter.

It's quarter to ten.

The word *defenestration*, the act of throwing someone or something out a window, was first coined after a Polish revolution in 1605 when they threw the royal family through the palace windows.

To show Graham I am angry, I decide to sacrifice one of his carvings. To show him that I'm not unreasonable, I avoid the bay windows and, instead, choose a small, porthole-type window. I knock back some brandy; it swells in my throat for a moment before settling. The rectangle of wood, with a black man's face carved into each corner, defenestrates onto the drive.

Graham's bedroom is large, with an en suite bathroom and shower. There is a laptop on a desk by the window with a printer on the floor. He has a cloth-fronted wardrobe and a large double bed with an ornate frame made of dark amber wood. I pull back the covers to find a heart-shaped hot-water bottle; I use the hacksaw to make a number of small incisions in it. The sheets are the light blue color of a maternity ward.

I use Graham's computer to write a note in Impact, font size fourteen. His desktop background photo is of your archetypal hippie sunset.

Hello Gram, I am up in your bedroom, so wet and ready for you. I can't wait to have your hot cock up inside me. Me. You. And an unfertilized egg.

Come get it.

I pin it to the front door. It is five minutes to ten. I check that I can undo the childproof cap on the meths. I squeeze and turn; the smell makes me dizzy. I put the lid back on.

I climb under the covers of the bed with the hacksaw and the Zippo. It smells of herbal shampoo and dried sweat.

I hear the car pull into the drive. Its headlights make diamonds of light scroll and stretch across the ceiling.

I have no particular plan.

There is a pause while he reads the note. I hear the front door open and the slow padding of his feet up the stairs. I pull the duvet over my head.

"Andrea?" he calls from the landing.

He steps into the doorway.

The floorboards creak beneath him.

"Hello? Andrea?"

He can't even remember my mum's name.

"Andy?"

That's a man's name.

He stands beside the bed.

"I thought you get back tomorrow? Whose bag is this?"

I start to make the sound of a woman sobbing—very authentic.

I feel his hand rubbing my side through the duvet.

"I thought you were getting back tomorrow?" He sounds guilty, nervous.

I crawl into a ball. The Zippo and the meths smell like a petrol station forecourt.

The mattress tilts as he climbs onto the bed next to me and hugs me through the duvet. I am shuddering.

"What's up?" he says.

His arm reaches round to my belly. I am getting very hot; my head spins slowly. The mattress rises as he stands up.

He throws the duvet back. I cannot speak for all the saliva. I pull my knees up to my chest.

He watches me. His chest goes up, down, up, down. I see inside his nostrils. I shut my eyes and focus on breathing. I listen to the blood in my ears and think of a river. I instantly reach a higher meditative state.

"I am not Andrea, I am Oliver Tate."

I open my eyes. He is widescreen, filling my vision with pores, teeth, and the smell of his breath like compost.

I think he is on autopilot. His thin hands are on me, pulling at my neck and legs. This is not capoeira. His tongue's going, blabbing away.

I keep my eyes closed and concentrate on guessing the weight of my skull.

Then I have a sense of weightlessness.

He's carrying me somewhere. I'm like a baby in his manly arms. He is going to drown me in the bath.

I am wearing a beauty contest winner's sash like a seat belt. It digs into my collarbone. The roaring sound is a waterfall. I lean into the open window; saliva comets from the corner of my mouth, out into the dark. My tongue is a slice of week-old granary bread. He's taking me somewhere to dump my body. He's going to feed me to the wild horses that live on Gower. I feel my stomach slosh with booze. I hear no slide guitar. I could easily wet myself.

Eyes glint in the headlights. At the roadside, rows of contented sheep know absolutely nothing.

My body spasms. A barrage of vomit moves up my throat and into my mouth. I stick my head out the window. I open my mouth. The vomit has no momentum. It runs down my chin and is whisked off into the night.

The taste in my mouth of batteries.

Graham says something. The car slows then pulls to a stop on the grass at the side of the road. The engine dies. The headlights go off. He's going to dump my body. I feel my seat belt unclipped. I rest my chin against the base of the window. Graham flicks on the courtesy light. There's the sound of a door opening. He's gone to get the shovel. I should really try to run away.

I search for the handle to open my door. I pull the handle but the door is locked. He's locked me in. I'm trapped.

He's standing on the grass outside my window. He tries the door. It doesn't budge. He reaches next to my head and pulls up the lock.

"Watch out," he says.

He pulls the handle again and this time it clicks.

Leaning into the door as it opens, I fall out onto the wet grass at Graham's feet. I am not putting up much of a fight.

He laughs. I think it is an evil laugh.

"Fuck you," I say.

I get on my hands and knees.

"Got any more?" he asks. Which is usually what the good guys say.

I feel another surge from my gut, a clench in my throat, and the gush of soupy goo. My eyes are soaking wet.

Graham takes a step back. I hope I have spattered his shoes.

"There you go," he says.

I wait for the spank of a spade on the back of my skull.

"One more," he says.

My shoulders wince as another roaring, full-body vom pulses up my gullet and out.

"Done?" Graham asks.

I spit into the grass, wipe my mouth on my sleeve. The smell is like Lucozade and cleaning fluids.

"Done," I say.

I push up onto my knees and watch him through watery eyes. He looks like a ghost.

"I've been imagining all the different ways to kill you," I tell him.

He offers me his hand. I hold out my left hand because it has more sicky residue on it. He makes no comment as he helps me to my feet.

By the time my eyes start to clear we are driving past the Murco garage in Upper Killay. My head feels less groggy although the taste in my mouth is still like sucking old pennies.

I look across at Graham; I am being chauffeured by my nemesis.

If he's not going to dump my body then he's definitely taking me to the police station. He seems calm, in charge.

I am unable to form any sophisticated arguments.

"Please God don't take me to the police station," I say, paying him a subliminal compliment.

"It's okay, Oliver, I'm taking you home."

I think this must be a metaphor.

We pass my school, the gates locked, car park empty. I feel some type of emotion.

"I think I would probably have done a similar thing at your age."

Graham is talking to me.

I suddenly remember him carrying me like a baby out to his car. I remember him helping me put my seat belt on.

We wind down past The Range chip shop, Lloyds TSB Bank, Nash Sports.

My mouth is still producing a lot of saliva. I swallow it down.

"Are you still going to fuck my mum?" I ask him.

"I was never going to do that, Oli," he says.

He is driving carefully.

"That is a lie," I tell him.

He doesn't disagree with me. His mouth turns down at the corners.

I cut him a deal. "You can think about doing it," I say, "as long as you don't actually do it."

"Okay," he says. This surprises me.

We drive past St. James's Church, where he teaches capoeira to my mother.

He turns onto my road and parks.

"Okay," he says.

I look at him. He looks at me. Graham and I make the high level of eye contact that you usually see only when a man is proposing to his girlfriend.

"You love your parents a lot," he says.

He is better-looking than my father. His scar is actually a really nice feature. There's a reliability to his body, a sturdiness, like a decent tree.

"You were just protecting them," he says.

I could marry a man like Graham. He's a provider. I am drunk and sentimental. He speaks truth.

"I'm sorry," I say.

"Okay," he says.

He gets out of the car and comes round to my door. He helps me out of the car as though I am the victim of a brutal car crash. My legs are useless and limp.

He puts my arm around his shoulder and helps me walk along the road; I don't know where we're going. He tells me I'm home.

"Come on, son," he says, gripping me under my armpits.

I wish I were his son.

My feet knock against concrete as he puppets me up the steps, props me up against a green door—my green front door. My legs do their best to stay vertical. I rest my head against the wood. I could easily sleep here. I close my eyes.

A hand reaches into my jeans pocket. It fumbles around near my penis. I think of Keiron. I asked for this.

It pulls out my wallet and keys on a chain. It puts the key in the lock but does not turn it. I am chained to my own front door.

He tells me that the matter is finished with. It's all done.

I tell him that he is wrong, the matter is ongoing.

He holds my head up by the jaw. He pulls open one of my eyelids with his thumb. He looks directly into the one eye for a long time.

He says I'm on my last legs. Then he lets go of my skull.

He tells me to wait while he gets my bag from the car. He is my chauffeur and valet. He asks me if I understand.

He disappears.

I turn and look out to sea. There is no Corky.

I see light around the edges of the curtains in the living room.

I turn the key in the lock and lean on the door. It swings open with me attached.

My parents are still up, sitting on the stairs in the half-dark, knees together, each clutching a glass of red wine. The only light comes from a lamp in the living room. They look up, both grinning, as I pull my key from the door and stumble into the hallway.

"There you are," Mum says, not sounding worried, "we've been worried."

I peer into the sitting room: on the coffee table stand four empty bottles of wine and three packets of Walkers crisps.

"We had a few drinks to steady our nerves." Holiday Dad is here, smiling, his face bright red. His face gets this color at weddings and births.

In fact, they are both smiling; they cannot see my expression in the romantic lighting.

"It's been a very difficult Sunday," Mum says. "Me and your dad have been fighting and drinking."

She lolls her head onto his shoulder.

I lean on the wall.

"But we're all sorted out now," Dad says.

"Ask me where I've been," I say.

"We've cleared the air," he says.

"Graham Whiteland's house."

"Oliver?" Dad says.

"I was delivering the good news about his soon-to-be-conceived child."

"Oliver—you're drunk and you're loud," he says angrily, as if I've spoiled the mood.

Three of his shirt buttons are undone.

The grating above the coal cellar creaks, boot steps echo on the porch.

"Graham?" Mum says.

I know that Graham has come in the door behind me because my father is wearing an entirely different face.

"Oliver, what have you done?" Dad says. I am disappointed in my father. There are so many cool things he could say: *Graham, if you ever put your tree-loving hands on my wife again I'll massage your face with my fists.*

"It's okay, it's okay," Graham says. "I found Oliver near my house."

"Oliver! And you've been drinking," my dad yells drunkenly, which I think is a little hypocritical.

Mum straightens up. She is wearing makeup. Her hair is in excellent condition.

"Have you driven him back from Port Eynon?" she asks.

"Listen, look, Oliver's fine. I'm fine. Here's his stuff."

"Oliver, this is not acceptable," Dad says. He sounds outraged but also scripted. "Graham drove you all that way."

"It's nothing," Graham says. He is still behind me. I can feel the draft from the open door.

"I'm making coffee," Dad says. As if this is of any relevance.

"I broke into his house," I say.

"What?" Dad says, standing up. He is quite a small man, really.

"I drank his teenage brandy," I say.

"Graham—did he damage anything?" Mum asks.

"It's fine," Graham says, sounding tired.

"I smashed his hippie statue. And a window. And I made holes in his hot water bottle, which is shaped like a heart."

I spin around to face Graham. He is framed in the doorway, cowboy style, carrying my rucksack in one hand like a severed head. His mouth is slightly open. He does look tired. He is wearing a black fleece, blue jeans, and hiking boots. The hiking boots are also one-inch heels.

"You should buy a new hot water bottle," I say.

"Oliver, what were you thinking?" Dad says.

I think my dad has a list of things that are okay for him to say.

"It's fine," Graham says, holding up my rucksack. "Look, Oliver, here's your stuff."

"I'm making coffee," Dad says. "The kettle's just boiled."

I take my rucksack.

"I looked through your photo albums," I tell Graham.

"There's coffee," Dad says.

"I'm fine," Graham says. "Look, I'm going to, uh . . ." He signals with his thumb pointing over his shoulder.

"I'm getting it," Dad says.

"Lloyd," Mum says. "Graham probably just wants to get off."

Nobody makes a joke.

"I found a photo of you and Mum," I tell Graham.

"Okay then, coffee," Dad says, and I hear him jogging off, almost running, to the kitchen, as if this is an emergency.

"In 1976," I say.

Graham's not looking at me. He's looking past me to my mum.

"Look, I'm gonna go," Graham says.

"Yah," says Mum.

"Oliver's doing fine," he says.

It is like parents' evening.

"I know," she says.

My dad is shouting from the kitchen, "I'm glad we could talk about this."

Me and Graham are doing the eye contact thing again. This is like a date.

"Goodbye, Oliver," he says, rather formally.

"Don't ever, ever come back," I say.

He blinks at this and, okay, I suppose we have a moment.

Graham bows out, closing the front door gently behind him.

I taste the acid in my mouth. I turn to face my mum, who is still sitting on the bottom step, still holding wine. She's watching me.

"Your hair was down to here," I tell her and I point at the center of my chest.

She smiles at me.

Dad comes slowly back from the kitchen carrying a tray. He is really concentrating, head down, watching three mugs intently. He shuffles his feet along the floor. Each step is a distinct movement. He thinks that if he spills the coffee then his marriage may be over.

"We're going to have to settle for instant," he says, and he looks up triumphantly. He blinks a bit. He looks left and right. He is man of the house by default.

I feel another surge.

I bow, twirling my hand, as a fist of vomit moves up my throat, out of my mouth—it is bright red—and onto the linoleum.

14.8.97

Word of the day: nullibiety—the state of being nowhere.
Goodbye, my diary, goodbye.

A Moon Cup is a plastic, nipple-shaped device. It is only available by mail-order from California. A woman puts it in her vagina to catch her menses. When it's full, she empties it. Mum uses one instead of tampons; she showed it to me. There is no baby.

My parents helped me be sick in the toilet—I was lion loud. I felt really good afterwards, like I had achieved something. They put me to bed; they undressed me; I didn't have an erection. They sat at the end of the bed and talked.

My dad said Mum had told him about the little "wee-woo"—he made the wanking signal with his hand—at Llangennith. He said that he had taken it on board. He smiled at my mum; his face was red wine flush.

He rubbed my leg through the duvet as he spoke which I thought was in very bad taste. You can tell that he is in a state of shock. The phrase "wee-woo" signifies his retreat to childhood.

She said: "I'm so sorry, my little pot of clay!"

She hugged me through the duvet. It reminded me of Graham.

Then she sang: "My boy, my boy."

I asked Dad: "Aren't you angry?"

He claimed that worse things have happened at sea.

Then, as if for proof, I vomited for the fifth time that evening. A little string and bubble affair onto my pillow.

I told them that Jordana had broken up with me.

My mum kissed me on my neck, my ear, my temple.

They left a bucket by my bed.

I couldn't sleep at first so I thought about Graham's house and what could have happened if it wasn't for my low tolerance to alcohol: the oven preheated to gas mark eight, Graham with an onion in his mouth on the kitchen tiles, his feet and hands tied with string, and me, walking in circles around him, making a wonderful speech.

It would have gone something like this: "Ever since my mum rolled up her sleeve, I've been wanting to tell you something: my parents are fragile. It must be easy for someone like you to dominate them. My father once tore off his vest but cannot remember why. His weapon is the garlic crusher."

I would have rubbed coarse sea salt over Graham's hairless back and chest while chatting away like a TV chef: "Mum's easy: all it takes is a spliff, a few stubbies, a back rub and she's yours. She practices capoeira despite having the grace of a crustacean. Why? Because she wants to be near you."

Two turns of the pepper mill, one for each eye.

"All that I want to say is, look, Graham, fair-dos, you've proven yourself physically and mentally superior to both my parents but— and this is really just bad luck—it turns out that they quite like each other, not a huge amount, not passionately, not with violence, but enough to make your efforts worthless."

His ears and nose, hairy with rosemary. Garlic under his foreskin.

"And you weren't to know that they would produce such a proactive and resourceful offspring. So this, worthy adversary, is it. Chin up. Stay strong. Drive safe."

Feeding the olive oil bottle's crooked nozzle into Graham's arsehole. Listening to the glugs.

I had a dream last night. I knew everything about everyone.

I understand body language. Chips was there; I noticed he rubs his eyebrow five seconds after telling a lie. Jordana was there too; I learned the difference between the look that actually means love and the look that a person makes when they are trying to look like they are in love.

I can't remember all the things I knew.

POWWOW

I can smell that my parents have made me a special breakfast. My sinuses feel exceptionally clear.

I find a plate of French toast and bacon, with a bottle of maple syrup waiting alongside.

I pour the syrup in a zigzag. The bacon is crispy enough to snap.

Dad asks me if I'm listening.

I watch the syrup absorb into the French toast. I cut off a corner, mop it in some juices, and put it in my mouth. There is still the faint taste of bile.

My mother says something about me not even listening.

I pick up a piece of bacon with my fingers and bite off the thin, fatty end. I chew it five times then swallow.

My stomach muscles feel beefy and tense. Like I spent the evening working out.

I finish my breakfast and retire to the sofa in the front room to digest.

I find my father leaning into the mirror above the mantelpiece, examining his nose, close enough to count the pores. He seems surprisingly calm considering that he has recently had to talk about his emotions.

I am wearing my Lands' End old-man slippers that I was given for Christmas. I tuck my knees up to my chest.

I look at the ridged glass bowl on our coffee table. I try not to think of the time that Chips came round my house after school. He explained that the bowl would easily carry twenty sets of car keys. He said, "I'd love to shag your mum."

My father pulls a pair of tweezers from his shirt pocket. He tests a few different grips in his right hand before settling on the thumb and index finger pincer grip. He air-clips twice in satisfaction. The bay window's curtains are open; he is in full view of the road.

This is not the first time I have seen him harvesting. There was one occasion I found him in the privacy of the music room, using a Dvořák CD as a mirror, trying to grab a nose hair between thumb and forefinger. But I have never seen him engage in such a public display of vanity. This is unprecedented. And shameless. He even moves the Moroccan candelabra off the mantelpiece to allow for an unimpeded examination.

Dad is trying to raise his game.

He starts with the blond hairs lying flat across the tip of his nose, before plucking blacks from his nasal passages and browns from in between his eyebrows. Disturbingly, he tilts his jaw to throw light on the unihaired mole that squats, the size and color of a sultana, on his neck. This is futile; Mum has tried before. I know from experience that his mole's supercharged single tendril can grow a centimeter within hours.

I put on *Songs of Praise* to see if it will make him feel bad. God made facial hair in his own image. Dad reels slightly from uprooting an inch of banjo string from his right ear. After examining it in the light, he holds it toward me with an air of self-congratulation.

The hair is amber at the tip, fading to ginger; the bulbous root is a white match head. I turn back to God and focus on the lyrics:

> Summer and winter and springtime and harvest,
> Sun, moon and stars in their courses above,
> Join with all nature in manifold witness
> To thy great faithfulness, mercy and love.

The camera watches an attractive Christian girl, her straight black hair falling from behind her ears as she sings.

"Ho," says Dad, pointing at her while looking to me for approval, "worth converting for, I'd say."

Where has this virility come from? The jeans—he's wearing jeans. Perhaps corduroy had been restricting his libido.

Mum hoofs open the door, carrying a loaded tray: a bowl of uneven brown sugar cubes, a miniature jug of milk, an unplunged *cafetière*, two small cups, and a teaspoon. Dad moves quickly to hold the door, all chivalrous. He props it open with the antique metal clothes iron that we use as a doorstop but which could just as easily be a murder weapon.

She slides the tray onto the coffee table.

"Oliver's had a religious awakening," he says.

"Are you sure it's not a hangover?" she says.

Where is this coming from? These jokes. They think they are so healthy.

Mum leaves again.

Dad goes back to leaning with his forearm on the mantelpiece—imitating nonchalance. He is planning something.

I wonder if he even thinks Mum has done anything wrong. This may be Leon Festinger's cognitive dissonance at work. He seems too calm, too cocky.

"Dad, you need to come to terms with what happened between Mum and Graham," I tell him.

"Oliver, your mother told me everything. We had it out yesterday."

I start with the small details.

"Did she tell you that, afterwards, she slept out in the dunes?"

They start singing another hymn.

"Oh yes, she was drunk as a bishop," he says, not taking his eyes off the telly.

"Right."

He looks so peaceful, watching the choir.

Because Dad does not watch TV very often, he is susceptible to it. It doesn't matter what's on—adverts, game shows, *Countryfile*—he stares at the moving pictures like an astonished simpleton.

When I watch the telly, I am very savvy. I wonder why *Songs of Praise* has a higher turnover rate of presenters than almost any other program. Today, it is Aled Jones; he is Welsh and, it seems to me, fiercely asexual.

I have one tried and tested way to make my father angry.

I flick through the channels: snooker, a black-and-white film, the news about a factory, *Pobol Y Cwm*, the news, a black-and-white film, snooker, *Songs of Praise*, snooker, *Songs of Praise*.

It's too easy: "Oliver, don't flick."

I keep going: snooker, black-and-white film, the news about hospitals, *Pobol Y Cwm*, the news . . .

"Flick-flick-flick," he says.

Snooker, *Songs of Praise*, snooker, *Songs of Praise*, snooker, ITV advert break . . .

"Oliver, I'll put a brick through that fucking machine!"

He leans down and yanks the adapter plug from the wall: the TV and video die. I have filled his skull with blood. I put down the remote control. He is pinkish. He breathes. He looks a bit confused. Like a man waking up the night after a full moon and finding blood all around his mouth. Dad doesn't have nearly enough body hair to be a werewolf.

He is wearing a light pink shirt, tucked into his beltless jeans. He has two buttons undone and the top of his vest is just visible beneath. I think, again, about the story of my father tearing off his vest. I return to the fact that he has hardly any body hair.

His face regains its normal color. He raises his streamlined eyebrows. I wait for him to say something. But he just turns to gaze out the window. There is no Corky.

I expect he is planning to give me a lecture about the importance of respecting other people's property.

Then I realize that he's waiting for me to talk about the things that I have learned. He doesn't want to lecture me because it is more gratifying if I come to the correct conclusions without being prompted. This will prove that my parents have imbued me with a shiny moral compass.

I clear my throat pointedly.

My dad looks at me.

"I've come to realize that I've done some very bad things. I have learned that my parents are only human beings and, as such, they make mistakes. I cannot expect to wield control over the lives of others. I am full of regret."

My dad's still staring at me. He is frowning slightly.

"*What?*" I say.

There is a lengthy pause.

"Has he really got a *heart-shaped* water bottle?" Dad says.

"Yes, he does."

Dad shakes his head, looks briefly at the ceiling, and then turns back to me and asks, "And you cut holes in it?"

"I'm bad. I know."

There's another pause. Then the hint of something— mischief—at the edges of his mouth.

"What else?" he says.

I'm not sure if this is supposed to be a confession of guilt or an action replay.

"Um. A metal teaspoon in the microwave?"

"Graham's got a microwave?" Dad says. He seems thrilled by this.

"Yes. Nine hundred watts," I tell him.

"Nine hundred watts!" he says.

He's beaming now—I can see his gums.

"That's great," he says.

I don't think I've ever seen him so happy.

"Does he know about the teaspoon?" he asks.

"Nobody knows," I tell him.

Dad bites his bottom lip and nods.

Mum comes in and sits next to me on the sofa.

Dad changes his face into something resembling somber.

She reaches to the cafetière and depresses the plunger with the exactness of someone conducting a controlled explosion. Mum pours a couple of cups, and drops a single sugar cube depth charge into each.

"I was just telling Oliver that, in situations like these . . ."

Dad stops to pick up his coffee. I wonder how many of these situations my father has been in.

". . . it's important to be able to talk things out."

We were talking about wattage.

Dad holds his coffee in pincered fingers. He normally takes milk but New Dad drinks his coffee black.

Milk is literally for babies.

I watch the calm horizon. A distant strip of Devon divides sea and sky.

Mum and Dad exchange slurps.

I look back and forth. I watch them enjoying their coffee.

I look at Mum. She stares into her coffee cup. I look back at Dad.

"I think it's fair to say that we all want to break this self-destructive cycle," he says.

Where has this come from?

Are you mentally ill? I inquire.

"*Oliver,*" Mum says. She doesn't like being reminded of the truth.

"This has been a difficult time for all of us," he says, "but we think it's important that we talk about it as a family."

Dad thinks he lives in California.

"Ha," I say, and I look out to sea.

"Your father wants to talk to you, Oliver," Mum says.

She puts her hand on my leg. It is not sexy. I look at her. She does something with her eyes. I begin to realize that this may be about my father, rather than about the family. I remember that there is a chapter in one of the parenting books titled "The Family Meeting: Can Confrontation Be Healthy?"

"Dad?"

"Yes."

"If I were you I'd be very angry," I say.

"Sometimes things happen. The important thing here is that we're being honest." His vocabulary is virtually nonexistent. I suspect he may still have a list of acceptable phrases in his pocket.

"Okay," I say. "How are you feeling?"

He starts slowly nodding, as if this question has not occurred to him. "I am feeling hurt," he says. "But your mother and I are going to do our best to get through this." Then he nods some more.

"If I were you I'd be furious, I'd be tamping."

"That would be destructive," he says.

"Yes. Yes it would."

"What I think your mother and I need to understand—"

Mum stands up suddenly. Dad stops. We both think she is going to say something important. But she moves quickly to stand in front of the window. She folds her arms.

Dad continues: "We need to understand that you've been going through a hard time."

He is speaking to the large crepe-paper lampshade, hanging in the middle of the room. Nobody is listening to him. His crotch juts. "All that exam stress and then breaking up with Jordana, which is never easy at your age. Your mother and I can see why you got things out of proportion."

Mum spins round with her hands held out in front of her. She looks serious.

"*Lloyd*," she says. "Get a grip."

Her eyes are wide open. She is on the weepy verge.

My dad is baring his teeth and pursing his lips intermittently. He shakes his head.

"Round and round we go," she says.

"Round and round," he says.

They are speaking in the secret code that develops from sharing a bed with someone for longer than a decade. They glare at each other. But their gazes weaken as they realize that I am watching them. This is the disappointing fact of my parents' arguments. They always fizzle out just as I get close enough to see the whites of their eyes. Dad pushes his specs up his nose. Mum blinks repeatedly.

What they need is a really good blowout.

I decide to play my part.

"I can't fucking handle this!" I yell. "You two are wrecking my life!" I run out the door, slamming it shut. The ornamental doorstop is no match for me.

I take a deep breath, and then, one more for luck: "I hate you both!"

I stomp repeatedly on the bottom step so it sounds like I'm running upstairs to my room.

I stealthily tiptoe over the linoleum and stand with my ear to the cool door.

They are not raising their voices.

"Oh dear," Dad says.

"Lloyd—you should be that angry," she says.

"I'm very angry," he says, not sounding angry.

There is a pause.

"I am *very* angry," he says. I almost believe him.

"You know what I did."

"I know. I've taken it on board," he says.

My dad is a cargo vessel.

"I wanted to do it," she says. "I wanted to. I'm still angry with you."

"I'm upset," he says. "I'm angry."

"Round and round," she says.

They stop again, possibly to stare into each other's eyes or kiss or wrestle or take off an item of clothing.

"Remember what I burned?" she asks.

"Bach's violin sonatas and partitas performed by Johanna Martzy."

"You remember," she says, chuffed, like he has remembered an anniversary.

"They're wonderful records."

"I was very angry," she says.

"I know. I deserved it," he says.

"Do you hate me now?" she says.

There is another pause.

"I'm hiding it. The hate," he says.

"I see," she says.

"I'm pretending it's not there."

"You're sweet."

"It's there, though."

"I know."

"It's there."

apotheosis

I leave them to—hopefully—fight then fuck. I go upstairs and
think about how I could rewrite last night's disappointing show-
down. I imagine the meeting as an adventure-wrestling story. Graham plays Cyclops. My parents play toddlers. I play myself. In the
final scene, I elbow-drop Graham in the eye—from my attic window—and it sounds like the time at the beach that I played hop-
squelch on washed-up jellyfish.

Then I imagine last night as a love story but with passion and
illegal Chinese fireworks and a mystery to do with a diamond.

Then I imagine my dad as a werewolf with chest hair like Ryan
Giggs, Wales's greatest footballer.

Then I make a decision.

I stand up and reach over my desk to unscrew the fastener of
my single-glazed sash window. I sit on the desktop to get a decent
angle to push up the window's bottom half. With my shoulder underneath, I shove it fully open; it sticks like a faulty guillotine.

I sit on the windowsill with my feet bouncing against the gray, textured outside of the house. The wind flaps my fringe against my forehead. I look down at the rosebush and wonder if it would cushion my fall. Or if I could aim for the old coal chute and slide safely into a pile of firewood. I reach back into my room and grab my diary from my desk. The first page has been torn out because Jordana took it to distribute around the school.

I start to become nostalgic.

I should have known this would happen. There is another bad thing about diaries: they remind you of how much you can lose in just four months.

The first remaining diary entry begins:

Word of the day: Propaganda. I am Hitler. She is Goebbels.

I think about Mark Pritchard. We might have been friends if it weren't for Jordana. I tear the page out and let it fall from my fingers. It is snatched by the wind and shoved back against the wall of the house; it falls in front of my parents' bedroom window, where it does flips for a while before zipping off down the street. I realize I need a paper shredder. I want birds to have strips of my soppy diary to pad out their nests. I want the mother birds to regurgitate food for their young and little bits of half-chewed sick to accidentally land on my name.

I reach into my desk and grab the paper scissors with the fluorescent green handle. I cut down through the pages in pinstripes, dividing each page into ten lengths. *Blue Peter* should run a feature on destroying the evidence.

Eventually, I have two fistsful—pom-poms. A kind of celebration. I let them go.

The strips flutter and churn in the wind. They move like a flock, up and out, shape-shifting, until they're higher than the house and spreading across the sky, licks of white like hundreds of badly drawn seagulls.

The job's not done yet.

I grab the dictionary from my desk.

I yank out the page with the small picture of disembodied hands appliquéing a daisy onto a napkin. I read that an *apple-pie bed* is a bed in which the sheets are so tightly folded that you cannot stretch your legs. Also *apotheosis*. I let the page slip from my fingers and curlicue around in the sky. I find the page with *curlicue* on it and tear it out. There is a picture of a currycomb. It looks like a medieval weapon but is supposed to be used for rubbing down horses. I look up *knacker* and tear out the page. The other meaning of a knacker is someone who buys and wrecks old houses. I start to tear out chunks. It is quite hard work and I am aware that my buttock muscles are clenching. I shift on the windowsill. I think of my mother coming into my room and seeing me here. The sight of her face would be enough to make me jump. The wind is blowing toward town. Some of the pages have got caught in the oak trees that push up the paving stones on my street. I reach behind me and hold on to the window with one hand as I toss the dictionary's carapace out into the sky. It wheels like a shot bird as it drops into the garden. A carapace is a protective, shell-like covering but, in good time, I will forget this.

I pick up the red thesaurus and shot-put it. It fans above the horizon before plummeting onto the pavement. It lies paralyzed, spine broken, in the gutter.

Next, the encyclopedia—heaviest of all three. I weigh it on my palm, wondering where to aim. I grip the window above my head and heave. As my arm reaches full extension I slip forward a little on the ledge—as a reaction I yank on the window to try to regain my seating; the window unsticks and squeals down with me still gripping it until my knuckles crack on the bottom of the frame. I instinctively pull my hand free, yelping, shaking my fingers at the expanse of air between me and the sea.

I do not fall off. I do not die.

I wedge my hands tightly against the sides of the window frame. I kick my heels against the front of our house.

Reference books twitch on the pavement.

I know what I have to do. It is so simple, it's almost like falling asleep.

They love me. They cannot help it. I swallow.

"Dad!"

"Mum!"

"Pops!"

"Maaaaaaaaaaaa!"

III.

lampoonery

I am sixteen. My mother is forty-three.

I am thinking about yesterday—my mother's birthday. Already, I live in the past.

Dad said that a real surprise party should actually be a surprise and who ever expected a forty-third birthday party? It was part of his carefully planned program of spontaneous affection.

It is well known that men are very poor at using their voices to express their emotions. My father has learned that it is easier to drive, or to organize, or to be inconvenienced. For instance, there is nothing he likes better than picking Mum up from Heathrow airport. If there is bad traffic, all the better. White bread sandwiches, un-Greek yogurt, second-rate coffee: it all adds up. The worse the service station, the deeper his love.

The party provided a good opportunity for weeks of secretive hard work and unnecessary stress. He was having to use his office phone to ring all the prospective guests so that Mum would not catch on. He was getting in touch with friends who they hadn't seen for years. He was feigning interest in the same catch-up chitchat ten times over. He told the same almost-joke again and again—*Well, I thought to myself, a real surprise party should actually be a surprise and who ever heard of a forty-third birthday party?*

I know all this because he told me. That was the other thing that happened. For a few weeks, I was his surrogate wife. *I was my own mother.*

Since he couldn't rant at Mum about the grisly day-to-day life of a surprise party organizer, he was forced to come to me for solace.

He started picking me up from school just so he could soliloquize and drive quickly: "Barry is threatening to stay for a whole week because—*if he's going to come all the way down here*—he wants to make the most of it. And that's not to mention the food: 'I've got lactose intolerance, I've got peanut allergies, I've got a fear—not an allergy, no, a fear—of seafood.' I mean, Jee-zus. And what is this rubbish?"

He actually thumped the steering wheel. My father has a love-hate relationship with Classic FM.

"Please, not the fucking Four Seasons. So Tina and Jake are bringing their young son, Atom—Atom!—and Atom can't come into contact with cat hair, dust, or even those microscopic insects that feed on dead skin. The boy has a molecular sensitivity. It's a fucking joke."

And it was strange being his wife for a while; it was nice that he was being so open and I liked hearing him swear, but I can't say that, after a few weeks of listening to him moan, I didn't see the appeal—theoretically—of running off with the guy who comes once a month to do the garden.

So the surprise party was a joint present, really, from Dad, but also from me, because I sat in the passenger seat, nodding and saying "Uh huh" and "Yup."

Dad arranged for Mum to spend the morning of her birthday having craniosacral therapy—she had to go all the way to Bristol. Craniosacral therapy is brand new and, according to my research, does not involve taking off any clothes. The treatment is about a man placing his hands near to—but not on—her body. There is a corkboard in the cloakroom of the sports hall where they do yoga. It brims with the latest treatments and classes. You can pay to have a man come to your house and test the amount of electromagnetic radiation from microwaves, radios, TVs on standby, and mobile phones.

So Mum spent the morning not being touched and the guests started arriving at about midday. Dad had arranged catering with The Anarkali—one of the Bangladeshi restaurants down on St. Helen's road—so there were four different curries, marinated chicken wings, sweet-and-sour shrimp, and aubergine with yogurt.

When the chef from The Anarkali dropped off the food in the morning, Dad wanted to check its authenticity: "Is this the sort of food that you would eat in Bangladesh?"

"No, it does not taste the same, the ingredients are not equal, this is a"—she shook her head at my father, who was nodding encouragingly, it took her ages—"lampoonery."

I think Dad thought that she had said an Indian word, or the name of a curry. But I understood.

The house really filled up. It went to show that Mum and Dad do have lots of friends although you wouldn't think it from looking at them.

With the front room full of people, Dad took pleasure in showing off his pronunciation: "Oli, could you pass around the *gurer payesh khichuri*, please?"

When I was handing out the samosas, I was asked the same question repeatedly: *So Oli, what are your plans for the future?*

A question for which I had already prepared an answer.

I said, "My future is history," and they smiled because it is a beautiful and rare thing for a teenager to want to be like his father.

I got an A-plus on my mock GCSE history exam. I got a C for art.

Although I no longer own a dictionary, I have not forgotten as many words as I had hoped. I still remember the word *nuance:* a subtle difference, a shade of meaning.

I remember when Mr. Hake tried to scare us away from doing biology A-level by showing us the difference between a single cell at GCSE—a circle with a dot in the middle, a cartoon breast—compared with a single cell at A-level—a wobbly shape with lots of other wobbly, spotty shapes inside it.

Nuance is something that happens at A-level.

I don't know whether Dad had not looked into it properly—he doesn't really believe in any of this holistic stuff—but I don't think craniosacral therapy had put Mum in the right frame of mind for a surprise party.

I was in my attic room—a boy can only distribute so many Koti rolls—when the cry went up: "Here comes the birthday girl!"

The Canes and the Clamps had been drinking wine in the front garden, ogling the view, when they spotted her at the far end of the street.

As word spread, the herd moved. I watched from my window as they bundled into the front garden and lined the steps.

Jack Clamp, who has a four-inch beard and plays banjo in a folk band called the Townhill Billies, lead an a cappella performance of "Happy Birthday," conducting with a chicken leg.

As they sang, Mum smiled, waved, and kept walking smoothly down the street, her upper body remaining still as her legs conveyed her forward.

But as she passed behind the large, thick bush at the front of our garden, she stopped. She was out of sight of the party guests.

From my vantage point, I could see her breathing steadily, gazing into space. She reached up and gently touched her own forehead. She examined her own hand and looked a bit confused. This only took a couple of seconds.

Then she rounded the corner, skipped up the steps with her party face on singing, "Right, well, who's to blame for all this then!"

She did a very good impression of being glad to be there. When people asked about the craniosacral she said it was "oh, *very* relaxing."

Once everyone had gone home, we sat around a table of leftovers: *bhajis,* wood apples, and drifts of untouched white rice. I had drunk some pink wine and was feeling relaxed.

I used my fingers to pick shrimps from among the vegetables. She chewed on some wood apple. Wood apples look like apples but taste like wood. They are a popular fruit in Bangladesh. We had seven left over.

Mum was talking about her craniosacral therapy.

"He put his hands inside my mouth—which was a bit strange at first—and after that, he held my feet." She had red tide marks on her lips from the wine. "I know it doesn't sound like much but I don't think I've ever felt so scrubbed clean, so thoroughly comfortable with being human."

It is strange to hear your mother talk about being human because, honestly, it's too easy to forget.

After that, we had a short conversation about how your body can sometimes seem totally separate. She said her body can feel like a distant bureaucracy controlled by telegrams from her brain and I said my body is sometimes like that of Mario Mario, being controlled with a Nintendo joy pad. Mario's surname is Mario.

I wanted to explain by using an anecdote. Two months ago, I saw Jordana walking down the road with her new boyfriend, who is older than me and may or may not still be in education. It was not Lewis, the boy from down Llangennith, but a different boy whom I have nicknamed Aesop for his miraculous, vaselike esophagus.

Jordana and I spotted each other at the same time and, out of respect or pity, she quickly unthreaded her fingers from his. I immediately crossed over to the other side of the street.

As we got closer together, walking became very complicated. I was heavy machinery. I had to deal with each movement, one after the other: lift left foot off the ground, move left foot forward through the air, maintain balance with right foot in conjunction with right calf, thigh, and arms, reconnect left foot with pavement, look straight ahead, adjust facial expression to imply nonchalance, shift weight to left foot, lift right foot, move it forward through the air.

It was not easy.

Worst of all, Jordana's arms were on display—popping out of a fitted green T-shirt. I gazed into the crooks of her elbows—hoping for eczema—but they were clean and smooth. Although Jordana and I are still in school together, she is excellent at avoiding me and she always wears long-sleeved shirts. It was a thrill for me just to see her forearms.

My brain was pleased to note that Aesop's stride was longer than Jordana's and they struggled to keep in sync.

But I didn't say any of this to my mother, even though it was one of those rare parent-and-child-in-emotional-symmetry moments.

She even asked me outright: "How are you feeling about Jordana now a bit of time has passed?" I could have told her the anecdote but, instead, I did a bit of nodding and saying some things that I have seen on TV: "I'm holding up, living day by day, keeping it together." Then I went to the upright piano and improvised the most instinctive, free-form jazz.

After eating leftovers, we played Scrabble. I used to fantasize about using the work *zzxjoanw*, meaning a Maori drum or a conclusion. A blank would stand in for one of the *z*'s. There'd be a fifty-point bonus for using all seven tiles. But I recently discovered that *zzxjoanw* does not exist. It was some lexicographer's idea of a practical joke. It is not a Maori drum. It is not a conclusion. Instead, I turned *sock* into *cassock*. I won by over sixty points. It was unusual that, at the end of the game, neither of them had fallen asleep. They were chatting to each other and kissing because "the day has come when our son beats us at Scrabble," but I could tell this was just another way of saying: *Leave the house for a few hours, we wanna fuck.*

So I went to see Chips. We shared four bottles of hooch. I came home and they were still in the front room kissing and chatting. I went to bed. Then, an hour later, they had sex, loudly and for quite a long time, long enough that I stopped counting the minutes and, in fact, I put BluTack in my ears.

It is clear from the ghostly fluff on my cheeks that, physically, I am not a man. I am also completely odorless. But ever since Jordana dumped me, I've started feeling like a middle-aged person. I think it is to do with trauma. I just walk around doing an impression of a sixteen-year-old.

Once you've been through certain experiences, you may as well accept that your life from that point on will be one massive Ferris wheel of the same emotional trauma, relived and recycled, over and over.

So you were badly bullied in school? Roll up, roll up. So you got dumped for some giraffe-necked moron? Roll down, roll down.

I will remain a victim, forever, like Zoe, who is probably, right this moment, lounging around, wallowing in her own sorrowful existence. You can change schools as much as you want but if you think of yourself as a victim then you stay a victim. Zoe probably can't get off her sofa. She has bunions in the folds of her voluminous skin.

Chips. Now, he's still a child. He's becoming more like an eight-year-old every day. When I went round his dad's house a few weeks ago, he offered me a drop of acid juice. I said no because I am basically forty-three years old. He nodded and then asked if I minded him having some.

One hour later, in Cwmdonkin Park, he said that he could see fucking in the sky. That the sky was full of fucking. Shortly after that, he ran away from me because he said my face had turned weird.

The aging process.

I am sixteen. I live in the past.

I Ask Jeeves the question: "Whatever happened to Zoe Preece?" There is a lawyer, an international hockey player, a chiropractor. I find my Zoe on the sixth page. She's the lighting and sound engineer for Versive, a local youth theater company. I should imagine that you can still be fat and be a lighting and sound engineer. She probably has violent fantasies about the pretty girls who always get the leading roles.

The show they are putting on is about the most recent world war. It's called *Ghetto*. It runs for two days, four performances, matinee and evening, at the Taliesin Theatre, Swansea. I write down the box office phone number on my hand.

I go downstairs. I open my dad's briefcase, which is hanging from the newel. I pull out his wallet, which he has never kept condoms in. I borrow his Lloyds Platinum Card.

opsimath

I walk down through the botanical gardens in Singleton Park, reading the bench plaques.

> *In dedication to Hal Kalkstein 1930–1995:*
> *Father, son, friend, colleague, cyclist, and hiker.*
> *From his loving family.*

> *In memory of Arthur Jones: Husband, son, godfather.*
> *He loved it here.*

I stop opposite an old bloke on a bench. I stand in his eye line and cup a purple trumpet carefully, delicately, in the manner of the girls from his youth. I know how happy it makes old people to see teenagers seeming to enjoy flowers. He sits with his hands resting on his crotch. He looks quite pleased with himself; it is spring and he has seen off another winter. I pout slightly and cock my hips. I reinforce everything he has learned about certain modern boys.

Once out in the fields, I avoid the paved pathways and stride across the grass toward the gray concrete waffle stacks of the university's halls of residence.

They are starting to mention university in school nowadays. Mr. Linton told me that if I worked hard enough for my GCSEs I could get into the fast lane streaming class for history A-level, which will hydroslide me to a top university, flume me into a top job, turn me into my father.

Old people only say that life happens quickly to make themselves feel better. The truth is that it all happens in tiny increments, like now now now now now now, and it only takes twenty to thirty consecutive nows to realize that you're aimed straight at a bench in Singleton Park. Fair play, though; if I was old and had forgotten to do something worthwhile with my life, I would spend those final few years on a bench in the botanical gardens, convincing myself that time is so quick that even plants—who have no responsibilities whatsoever—hardly get a chance to do anything decent with their lives except, perhaps, produce one or two red or yellow flowers and, with a bit of luck and insects, reproduce. If the old man manages to get the words *father* and *husband* on his bench plaque, then he thinks he can be reasonably proud of himself.

I remember from seeing *King Lear* in the Grand Theatre that some of the seatbacks were dedicated to people or local companies. Maybe that's what Zoe's aiming for. Her big ambition is to have a memorial plaque on one of the wide seats.

It was all down to bad timing. If Zoe'd had the chance to read my pamphlet before she moved schools, there's no telling where she'd be now: she'd probably be one of the girls who gets photographed by the *Evening Post* opening their exam results.

But, as it is, she'll be exactly the same, worse maybe. It says a lot about someone's self-esteem if her major aim in life is to keep other girls well lit.

They probably keep her out of sight in the control booth, hooked up to a gravy drip. The faders and switches of her control desk are the closest she gets to interacting with the outside world. In the dark, Zoe watches the lead actor sing with his eyes gazing up into the lights; she *knows* he is singing to her. She turns up the spotlight, pushing the fader with a clammy finger before reaching under her swollen belly, slipping her hand beneath the elasticated waist band of her jogging bottoms, and groping at the patch of sodden mud that she has come to know as her sex organs.

The Taliesin's café is bustling with proud, healthy-looking parents. I walk downstairs to the box-office-cum-gift-shop-cum-gallery and ask for my reserved ticket, passing my father's credit card to the woman behind the desk.

A capillary has burst on the woman's right eyeball; there's a dash of Tabasco blood in the corner of her cornea. I notice a brushstroke of yellow bruising on the skin beneath the eye. I do not invent a story for how she got this injury.

She reads the envelope and says, "One ticket for tonight's performance: Lloyd Tate," as she passes it to me. I wait for a moment, hoping that she might question my age. She smiles as she hands me the credit card.

I head up to the bar and order a chicken and mushroom pie. The other name we had for Zoe was Pie. The barmaid puts it in the microwave for a minute and a half. As it rotates, I watch its sides distend and sag, its skin crinkle, aging a year for every second.

I sit down at an empty table and use a spork to make an incision in one end of the pie. By prodding the lid of the pie, I create a small pyrotechnic steam effect, puffing out of the pastry geyser.

While waiting for the snotty filling to cool, I flick through one of the programs for *Ghetto*. I find *Zoe Preece: sound and lighting director.* There is no photo. On the back page, there are black-and-white pictures from the dress rehearsal. The girls mostly look identical: pretty and straight haired. I try and remember Zoe's face. I should be able to recognize her but all I can think of is the lid of my chicken and mushroom pie.

The theater is more than half full. I am the youngest person in row L.

The play is about a ghetto in Vilna, Lithuania, where the Jews form a theater company, sing songs, and perform them. The songs are deemed to be so good that their deportation to the concentration camp is put on hold for a while. It is lucky for the Jews that the Nazis did not have my taste in music.

The Nazi, Kittel, appoints a Jew, Gens, as ruler of the ghetto and head of the Jewish police. Gens organizes a ball to get into the Nazi's good books.

During the interval, I stay in my seat. I like watching the people in black jeans carrying the props. As if we can't see them.

They cover the stage with flowers, rugs, cushions. Four of them carry on a long, rectangular dining table. They set the table with bottles of wine, convincing-looking netted salamis, and plastic roast chickens.

As the second half commences, there are twelve performers on stage: a folk band made up of a violinist, trumpeter, guitarist, and accordionist who play an irritating jig, while four Nazis slug wine and watch the Jewish police fuck the pissed-up Jewish prostitutes. They are doing them over the dinner table.

I look across at the parents' faces in the seats on my row. They look stern, focused. One man rubs the underside of his chin; his jaw is tensed, his mouth rigidly ajar. I imagine the fathers of the actresses confronting the realization that their daughters are comfortable—and quite convincing—in the role of girl-pretending-to-enjoy-getting-fucked-by-drunk-teenage-boy-pretending-to-know-how-to-fuck.

As the sound of rutting grows more intense, one of the fathers turns to his wife and, half-smiling, whispers a joke of some sort. He giggles but she does not laugh or even acknowledge him; she is thinking about the poor old Jews. He is trying to make light of a difficult situation; the second time that he let his daughter's boyfriend stay the night, he convinced himself that it could have been the creaky radiators or the wind in the backyard—but he wasn't sure and so stayed up the whole night listening.

At the end of the play I clap my hands twenty-four times.

Now now now now now now now now now now now now now now now now now now now now now now now now.

The actors come out and bow. Then they go offstage for a moment—not nearly long enough for the audience to decide whether or not to stop clapping—before they return for an encore. They open their palms toward Zoe, up in her den, her cage: the sound booth. I imagine that they give her extra portions if she makes no mistakes. They applaud her and stare up into the lights.

I flop onto one of the long sofas that snake along the edges of the foyer. The play was not effective. I feel no particular downturn in my emotions, no sudden sadness. In fact, I feel no worse than when the play began. It was getting hot in the theater and my pie was weighing me down; I may have had a sleep and missed the bit that would have made me care.

I watch sets of parents waiting with flowers. It's a bit like an airport arrival lounge: an element of competitiveness about who will emerge first.

I'm not sure I will recognize Zoe's face so I'm going to have to carefully examine other physical characteristics.

The first girl out skips straight toward her parents, swinging an arm round both; they stoop awkwardly into a brief but warm three-way hug. The other parents hide their resentment well.

The girl shows her teeth at her parents. I recognize her but that may be because she was in the play. Her father says something. She laughs. She is wearing a red shoulder bag with a picture of a manga-style robot making the peace sign on it. Her V-neck jumper is nautically striped red and gray; it is baggy and deceptive although the humps of her boobs are visible. She's wearing long, heavily flared jeans that make her look like she has no feet.

I try to think of how Zoe used to dress: white shirt, tie, shiny shoes. Not helpful. I try to remember her face but all I can think of is this girl's face. Which is like vanilla ice cream. Her cheekbones are single scoops.

Then I remember—Zoe had miraculous skin.

I stand up and take a few steps closer, pretending to be reading the program. The girl is so attentive to her parents that she doesn't notice me in the shadow of her father.

Her skin is pale, pasteurized, and slightly flush at the cheeks.

Her trousers are quite tight around the tops of her thighs but I'm not seeing any signs of obesity. I remember we used to say that Fat was the only fat girl in the world who didn't have big tits and what's the point of a fat girl if she doesn't have big tits?

"Oliver!"

The girl is speaking to me. Her parents step back, opening their triangle for me to join.

"It *is* Oliver, right? What are you doing here?"

"Zoe," I say.

Her mum and dad look pleased that I know their daughter's name.

"Mum and Dad, this is Oliver, he used to be in some of my classes in Derwen Fawr."

Their eyebrows go up as one, they nod in unison.

"Don't worry," Zoe puts a hand on her dad's elbow, "he was one of the good ones."

Her dad laughs. He has a long, tanned face, with a chin that could open letters.

I look at Zoe. She's looking comfortable in her own skin. She has clearly selected all her own clothes. Her face is cheery and full of excitement.

I used to say, *Anger does not come easy to me,* but I don't think that's true anymore.

I look at Zoe's face. I'm smiling. But I feel the space around me darken with malice. Like when Dad's hedge trimmer found the wasps' nest. Zoe was supposed to be the proof that a victim always stays a victim, that there is no such thing as "self-help." Unhappy people have a role in society—and that is to make the rest of us feel better.

If this dumb fatterpillar can become a butterfly, then what does that say about me—destined, as I am, to be perma-dumped, to have all my girlfriends stolen by boys with ridiculous necks? Just thinking about giraffes makes me angry. I even hate those tribal women with the bronze rings round their throats who are always wangling their way into documentaries.

I want to make Fat *fat* again. I want to stick a funnel down her throat and pour in the still-warm runoff from the drip tray under the George Foreman Grill at Chips's house.

"Nice to meet you, Oliver," her mum says, "are you feeling as depressed as we are?"

Zoe's mum has an inch of black at the roots of her hair; the rest is blond and dry, not quite long enough to go behind her ears. Her eyes are chlorine blue.

"Yes," I say, "very depressed."

"How do you think *I* feel?" Zoe asks, her eyes tilting up, her voice unfeasibly expressive as she tries to wrestle the attention back. "Every day—twice a day—my entire friendship group gets mown down in cold blood," she says. "It's not good for your state of mind, I can tell you."

Her dad laughs loudly, proudly.

I want to punch Zoe in the ovaries.

"So are you involved in this at all, Oliver?" her dad asks.

Don't blame me for what your daughter's become.

"No, I just came to watch," I say. "I am interested in history."

"See!" Zoe sticks out her tongue, and cocks her head at her parents. "At least one person is actually interested in seeing the play because it's a good play, not because of their little darlings."

She hugs me playfully, side-on, her boobs squeezing into my upper arm. These boobs must be new.

"Thank you, Oliver," Zoe says, stepping back.

I smile and look her in the eyes. My anger is turning to nausea.

It's sickening. She doesn't even remember who she used to be. I never want to learn.

"We *are* interested in the play," her mother says.

"Yeah, it's not our fault that our talented daughter keeps distracting us," the father says.

I feel seasick.

Her mum and dad look like a TV couple. I can actually imagine them having nondisturbing adult sex.

"I'm just going to pop to the loo," I tell them. They say nothing.

I turn quickly and weave in between waiting parents and empty metal tables, quietly repeating the phrase *pop to the loo*, feeling more ill with each step, appalled by my inability to seem anything other than pleasant.

The bathroom is unnecessarily large. It feels like a performance space. The urinals and sinks are deserted, the cubicle doors are open: it's empty. I elbow the buttons on all three hand driers. I use the palm of my hand to slap down the six time-release taps: hot then cold, hot then cold, hot then cold. It should sound wild, like the sound in your ears if you jump off a waterfall, but it doesn't. It sounds lame. I go into a cubicle and spin the toilet roll out so that it gathers on the floor in wafered layers like a fat person's stomach. I kneel on the tiles and hold my head over the bowl. I inhale the shit and bleach smell. I think of the George Foreman drip tray. I open my mouth. I hear one of the driers turn off, the other two quickly follow suit. One of the taps stops running, the other five dry up in close succession. I close my mouth. My stomach keeps schtum.

It's hard to tell exactly how much weight Zoe's lost. In my memory of her, I get the reputation mixed up with the reality. But even if she has lost weight, that's not the upsetting bit. She's just so chirpy.

I open my mouth. I close my mouth.

I go to a urinal and piss as hard and as loud and as long as I can.

It is not a release.

When I come back out, the café is full of lively young people. Fresh-faced girls with slats of thick theater makeup still on their necks. Roguish boys accepting praise awkwardly. Everyone is laughing. This is theater. It feels like this could be some clever extra scene from the play and in a minute there's going to be a song about how lucky we all are to be young and beautiful and live in Swansea at the end of the less awful half of an absolute bum-out of a century.

I return to Zoe and her parents.

"I designed the whole rig," Zoe's telling her parents. "You know that bit when Gens asks Kittel to shoot him?"

She speaks to her parents as if they're her friends—it's frightening. I watch her mouth move. I try to imagine before-and-after shots of her body.

"Yes," I say.

She acknowledges my return with a pause.

"Well, in the script it says 'blackout' but I wanted to do something different." She's actually boasting. I can't believe this. "So I set up the lights so that they blacked out in sequence—from the back of the stage forwards."

"Oh yeah—that was cool," I say. I have no idea what she's talking about.

"I think that the word you are looking for is *heartbreaking*," she says.

Don't tell me what word I am looking for.

"Can a light be heartbreaking?" I ask, trying to keep up the banter.

"Well, that depends who's in control of it," she says quickly.

Her parents are watching us have this conversation.

They expect me to come back with something sparkly and full of the hopefulness of youth.

"And you're in control," I tell her.

Zoe wins. And just to show her superiority, she has the good grace to change the subject.

"So, who are you hanging out with nowadays?" she says.

I want to say, *Chips. You remember Chips, don't you? Chips was behind you in the dinner hall three years ago when you found strips of bacon rind in your hair.* But, for no good reason, I think better of it.

"Well . . . I've still got some good mates."

She nods like a therapist.

"What's your e-mail address?" she says, pulling an olive green notepad from her bag.

She scribbles *Zoeinthedark@hotty.com* on a blank page, rips it out, and hands it to me. Then she writes, *Oli, my new (old) friend,* at the top of a new page and gives me the pen. I write down my e-mail and feel unimaginative: *Olivertate@btinternet.com.*

As she puts away her pad, a boy with long baggy jeans and a tight green T-shirt comes out of the auditorium. He sneaks up behind Zoe, shushing us with his finger held to his lips.

"I'll e-mail you," Zoe says.

The boy throws his arms round her waist, leans back, and lifts her legs off the ground—he has a very supple spine. Zoe screams a little but doesn't look particularly embarrassed. I see a glimpse of her midriff. She is not fat. Her skin is smooth and pale. I notice the faintest dew of hair.

Lanugo is the downy hair that grows on your face and chest when you are anorexic. It is a bit like cobwebs.

Zoe puts her arm round him.

"Oliver, this is Aaron; Mum and Dad—you know Aaron."

"Hi!" I say, with a full-beam smile.

"We know Aaron," Zoe's mum says.

Aaron's dark fringe dissects his forehead in a sweep. His green T-shirt says *Cape Town* on it. His face handles his large nose well. You could fit a fifty-pence piece inside his nostrils.

"Aaron, Oliver went to," she puts a hand on his shoulder, whispers in his ear, "Derwen Fawr."

Aaron's mouth drops open and his eyes and lips wince in feigned disgust.

"Listen, let's just pretend that we don't hate each other," he says, offering me his hand, "for the sake of Zoe's parents."

Zoe's parents smile entreatingly. Aaron's voice is melodious and very Welsh—it fades in and out like AM radio.

As we shake hands, he asks, "Weren't the lights brilliant?"

"They were," I say.

"Zoe is brilliant," he says.

"Puh-shaw," she says, batting her wrist, mincing.

Aaron puts a hand on my shoulder. He is quite beautiful.

"But I bet you're depressed now, right?" he says.

It's dark as I walk out through the Brynmill exit of Singleton Park, going nowhere near the circular route that me and Jordana used to walk with Fred. I am over Jordana. I pass two other dog walkers and they do not remind me of her.

On 14.4.98 <Zoeinthedark@hotty.com> wrote:
Hey Oli, told you I'd e-mail. It was such a surprise to see you! It's weird—I recognized you straight away. You haven't changed a bit. Why weren't we friends when I was in DF? I suppose I was a bit of a hermit . . . and you were a bit of a loner. And I never realized you liked theater!

Is funny—in this new school I got a new identity. I'm the giggly, flirty one. I love it!

You've got to come again tomorrow! We've got a matinee and an evening performance but it'd probably be better if you come to the matinee because it won't be as busy—easier to sneak you into the control room! Don't worry, you won't be putting me off, I could do the show blindfold and with both arms tied behind my back.

Just so you know—it's customary to bring flowers. Chrysanthemums are my preference, in case you're interested . . . ;-)

See you tom,

Zoe <3 Text hearts are lame <3

Oh, and you made a good impression on my mum. I think she might have a crush on you!

xx

I'm finding it hard to make the connection between Pie, the girl with the iced sugar dust on the crotch of her pleated skirt, and Zoe, an almost-woman with the power in her fingertips to silence an auditorium.

I preferred her when she was pure, untapped potential: a sex kitten stuck in the belly of an orca.

I suppose I should be impressed. She took my advice, without knowing it: she learned how to be someone else, with a little help from the acting community. She used six exclamation marks in her e-mail.

But I can still see the cracks where Fatty is trying to get out. I Internet search the words *Victim loves abuser* and on page sixteen I come across something interesting: *Stockholm syndrome is a psychological response where a victim or captive exhibits seeming loyalty to their captor.*

It makes sense, really. To her, I am still a figure of immense power. I burned her diary, I pushed her in a pond. No wonder she wants me. She knows that I can see through her "new identity" as though she were a paper napkin turning transparent with the grease from a sweaty chicken wing.

fustilarian

It is not yet lunchtime in the botanic gardens. I am surprised to find the old bloke has changed benches. He sits in front of the hothouse for tropical plants.

I stroll up to some soppy-looking flowers. He watches me from across the path. He stands up. He walks toward me. His knees don't make the sound of a football rattle.

He reaches out and squeezes a flower's neck; its mouth pouts and opens.

"*Antirrhinum majus. Anti* means like, *rhinos* means snout."

He looks at me. His eyes are watery.

I add the word *botanist* to his imaginary plaque.

"Like snout," he says.

His nose bridge is thin, delicate, and perfectly straight.

"Wha's a lad your age doing here two days on the trot?"

I watch him. Tiny white hairs poke out from the tip of his nose like stamens.

"If you're going to steal flowers then take 'em from round by yer," he says.

I follow him off the path to a flower bed that is tucked away behind the greenhouse. He walks quite quickly, with a kind of skip-limp.

"Chinese gardenias. If these don't get her, then nothing will."

He snaps off four long-necked whites and a few flowerless greens and holds them out.

Zoe is waiting for me in the café, wearing thick-cut beige cords that droop onto her green plimsolls and a baby blue T-shirt beneath a black zip-up hoodie. The top is unzipped to the point where her brand-new boobs strain against the zip. The audience are finishing their hot drinks. She is smiling, as well she might be. Her sheeny brown hair is tucked behind her ears.

She doesn't say a word about the Chinese gardenias. Taking my free hand, she pulls me through a set of double doors into near total dark. She leads me up some steps. I use the darkness to imagine Zoe as a gross pancake stack, worming up the stairs. She stops briefly on a landing. To my left, down a short corridor, a thin dash of light at floor level implies the shape of a door.

"That one goes backstage," she says, continuing up. At the top of the stairs, she opens a single door.

The control room is hardly lit, darker than romance. She clicks on a long-necked lamp; it gives off a blue light like the ones in the train station toilets that stop heroin users from seeing their own veins. It gives the room the feel of being deep underwater.

"Welcome to the boudoir. Make yourself at home." She rolls a leather-padded office chair toward me. I can see it has air suspension. "As guest of honor, you may also have a spinny seat."

I hold the flowers out. In the blue light, the white gardenias glow the color of X-rays.

She shakes her head.

"They're Chinese gardenias," I say.

I doubt anybody ever gave Pie a bouquet.

I'm still holding out the flowers.

"Give them to me at the end," she says.

The upper half of the far wall is taken up with plugs protruding from rubber-rimmed holes. It looks like an oversized version of the whack-a-rat game in the marina arcade. But with the plugs hanging limp and dead.

"That's called the patch bay," she says.

Beneath the plugs is a coral reef of yellow, green, and blue leads, bunching together, sticking out at all angles.

Zoe says, "Check out me cans."

She's wearing leather-trim headphones that have a microphone attached. The mic bobs in front of her lips like a mosquito.

"I said, *check out my cans*," she says.

I exaggeratedly perv on her tits.

"Thank you." She slips her headphones to her shoulders. "We call headphones *cans*."

"Great joke," I say.

I never thought I'd see the day when Zoe would deliberately draw attention to her own body.

"It's techie humor. We spend a lot of time in the dark."

Her sound desk sits in front of the window: there are rows of sliders, knobs, and a single golf-ball-shaped roller. A computer screen displays rectangles of block color: red, blue, green.

Through the window I can see into the audience; blue side lights run down the steps. The stage, brightly lit from above, is made from interlocking pine floorboards. Most of the audience are in their seats; one man is standing up, removing his jumper in silhouette.

Using both hands, she repositions four faders, steadily lowering the house and onstage lights; the man quickly sits down; the audience focus on the stage.

"It's terrible but I'm so fucking bored of this play now." She jabs a rubber button on the control desk and then slumps into her leather chair. I sit down as well. "I know I shouldn't get bored because it's the Holocaust yadda yadda but I can't help it."

She flips a switch on a squat black box that looks like what I imagine an old transistor radio would look like. A red light pings on. She lifts her headphones from her shoulders to her ears and says, "Aaron sugar?"

Onstage, the narrator is wearing a dressing gown, sitting in an old brown armchair. He is supposed to be missing a hand but I can tell it's a trick of the sleeve.

"Aah-ron?"

She gazes blankly down at the stage.

Her shoulder bag is under the table, unzipped and gaping.

"Just wanted to say hi," she burrs into the microphone.

I have a quick look for a purple diary but all I can see is a hairbrush, a fat black wallet, and a tube of E45.

"I've got a special friend with me tonight. Say hi, Oli."

She looks over at me. I stay perfectly still.

"He's waving," she says.

As she flicks the switch on the black box, the red light dies.

"I can talk to him but he can't talk to me because the audience would hear," she explains. "He's the stage manager."

"I thought he was an actor."

"Ooh, I'll tell him you said that. Aaron hates actors."

She leans over and presses a single button on the sound desk. The narrator's spotlight fades. Zoe waits for a few seconds before pressing the same button again. A yellow wash comes up over the stage.

"So, wow, sound and lighting director?" I say, doing my impressed face. It's important for Zoe that I appear to buy into her new life.

"Yeah, you can just call me Houdini." She waggles her fingers like an evil wizard. "Basically, I digitally preprogram all the lighting changes so that all I have to do is press the *Go* button on cue. Not so mysterious."

"Oh. Still, that's really cool."

"That's why I always get really bored up here. I end up just mucking around with Aaron."

Aaron must have been the one who taught her how to fit in.

During the first big musical number we wheel our chairs up close to the sound desk so that we can see all of the stage. This is the bit of the play where the Jewish theater company are practicing for their upcoming performance. Some of the Jews keep getting the song wrong and messing up the dance moves. But it's not particularly funny.

Zoe introduces me to the cast.

"Those girls singing are part-time lesbians. They had a threesome at the last cast party. Nathan, who plays Kruk, he's only fourteen, claims he's a pedophile stuck in the body of a boy. Owain, the short one on the left, is a sleaze. Arthur, who's playing the dummy, he's a slut but we love him. Jonny—the one talking now—is sweet and beautiful and in love with Arwen. Arwen's playing Hayyah—the one with the red hair—she is in love with herself mostly, and a little bit with Jonny. Aaron hates everyone and sleeps with everyone in equal proportion. Honestly, this lot are unbelievable. Our last cast party was basically an orgy."

"Yeah, wow. Because there's an orgy scene in the play."

"I know, you wouldn't believe the amount of sexual tension after a whole day rehearsing that scene."

"Ha ha."

She swivels her chair to face me.

"Or even worse: watching your friends rehearsing an orgy."

"Ha."

I turn mine to face her.

She makes a lot of eye contact. I think she has been watching too much theater; this whole thing feels stage-managed.

"So have you got a girlfriend?"

"No, we broke up but I think that was for the best, in the end," I say, since we're trading clichés.

"Oh shit, I'm sorry."

She skits her chair toward mine. Our knees dock.

"There's no point having a boyfriend or girlfriend at our age. Me and Aaron went out for a bit but it was just pointless—we both knew that we wanted to have other people. In Versive, everyone goes with everyone. We're all still friends."

She has certainly convinced herself. I bet he cheated on her.

"Yeah," I say, "like a commune."

She reaches past my arm and presses *Go*. A spotlight comes up on Hayyah, the beautiful redhead. She starts to sing.

I remember this bit of the play. The song's called "Swanee"—a jazz number by George Gershwin. Kittel, the SS officer, forces them to play the song even though jazz is banned by the ministry for culture.

"When did you break up with your girlfriend?" she asks, touching me on the knee.

"About six months ago," I say, still watching Hayyah as she twirls across the stage. She is substantially more beautiful than Zoe.

"Oh. What you need's a rebound."

She flicks the switch on the transistor box; the red light blips on. She holds the microphone to her lips.

"Aaron, you'd like to have sex up here, wouldn't you?"

She smiles at me.

"Don't you think this would be an amazing place to have sex?"

"Who are you speaking to?" I ask.

She pulls the headphones down to her shoulders.

"Who do you think?" she says.

I look at her. Her ears have turned a dark crimson. I can't help thinking of the times that me and Chips talked about what it would be like to have sex with Fat: Chips with his hands down his pants, making the farty, squelchy noise with his foreskin.

She leans toward me. "You can see them but they can't see you. You can hear them but they can't hear you."

This is the bit where the Jewish actors are choosing costumes for their play. Weiskopf, an entrepreneurial Jew, has recycled the clothes of people who died in the war. He says that all the blood's been washed off and the bullet holes have been darned. I liked the character of Weiskopf. He makes the best of a bad situation.

She drops the headphones into her lap and puts her hands on my knees.

"You're embarrassed," she says.

She moves her hands up to my thighs.

I am embarrassed; Sharon Stone as Catherine Tramell in *Basic Instinct* was more subtle than this.

"I'm not embarrassed," I say. "It would be an *amazing* place to have sex."

The more she comes on to me, the more I think of her in the dinner hall with a gob full of turkey burger, taking a sip of Orange Squash anyway.

"What are you thinking about?" she asks.

Her tongue sneaks out to wet her bottom lip.

This is also the bit of the play where Kittel announces that the Führer will accept no increase in the population of the Jewish race and, therefore, Jewish families are only allowed up to two children. The chief of the Jewish police is using a stick to count the number of each family's children. Father, mother, child, child. The third child gets sent away, offstage, which means that he is killed.

"Logistics," I say.

I have no condoms. I will have to use the rhythm technique.

"Logistics?" she says, leaning toward me. She takes a quick glance at the stage—the surviving family members have just finished a depressing song—before reaching past me to press the magic button. The stage darkens; a reading lamp picks out the narrator, who's asleep in his armchair. One person in the audience tries to start a round of applause but nobody else is up for it.

She pulls a lever to lower her chair; there is a shush of air escaping as she descends.

Onstage, they are clearing the set as the narrator snoozes. I watch two men heave off a suitcase.

She lifts the headphone mic close to her lips. Resting her forearms on my thighs, she leans into my crotch as she speaks: "This is your thirty-second booty call."

My chair rolls backward slightly. She yanks me back toward her by my belt loops. I don't own any belts.

Zoe holds one ear of the headphones against her skull and listens.

She raises an index finger. "When I say go, you press the Go button, okay?" she says.

"Yup," I say.

She can't even see the stage.

"Go," she says.

I poke the rubber lump with my forefinger.

A mellow light bathes three ghetto girls; they are hanging out by a pram.

"And again," she says.

I press again.

The narrator wakes up as a dusty brown light puddles around him.

"Now we've got three minutes till the next cue." She reaches under my chair and pulls a lever. The chair hisses down as my eye line sinks out of view of the stage. She's certainly planned this all meticulously.

"Mind these," she says, putting the headphones on my head.

She stands up, unzips her top, and lets it fall off her arms.

Through the cans, I can hear the dialogue onstage but I can't see who's saying it.

"I've got rather a headache."
"Take a sequence of head baths. You'll never suffer again."

Zoe's T-shirt says *Prozac* on it as if it were a washing powder logo.

"A sequence of head baths?"
"Yes! The sequence is: put your head in water three times, take it out twice."

As she yanks off her T-shirt, it gets caught on her large head. I take this moment to have a really good look at her belly. There's still a fair bit of give, her flesh tucks into her belt, but, yes, I'm willing to admit that she may be attractive.

She pops the T-shirt over her head and throws it on the floor as if nothing has gone wrong. Her boobs are big, they bulge from her bra. The blue light gives her skin a semifluorescent sheen.

Pulling the headphones off my head, she slots them back round her own neck. She adjusts the microphone so that it hovers near the side of her mouth like a thirsty fly.

She speaks very clearly, as though reading from an autocue: "You know you need a special theater license to show nudity."

It's a bit sad, but I do have an erection.

She smiles with her teeth slightly apart, her tongue mousing out, as though she is about to laugh. She straddles me tightly, pressing her legs round my belly. The chair absorbs the pressure with a *humph.*

"So you'd better not tell the authorities about this," she says, yanking at my T-shirt.

"Fuck the authorities," I say, getting into it.

"Now, I want you right up inside me," she says, arching her back. She's supple. I hold her at the waist. She moves my hands onto her tits.

"Uh!" she uhs.

She is very responsive.

Up close to her body, I examine the gentle curves at her sides and on her upper arms.

She is ruffling my hair frantically.

"God!" she says.

Me and Chips used to joke that it would be like having sex with a custard slice.

I do have an enormous hard-on.

She gyrates her hips; her bum and thighs rub my cock through my trousers.

"You're so fucking hard," she says.

She rolls her head around on her neck like a boxer warming up.

She whispers in my ear, "Tell me that you wan' fuck me hard, make me sweat."

In the excitement, she misses out a word.

"I want to fuck you so hard that your body drips with sweat," I say, grammatically.

We have not kissed yet. I lean forward and kiss the space in between her tits. She smells slightly musty. Like someone who has spent three weeks in the dark.

I put my hand on the crotch of her cords; it is difficult to define her clitoris—each thick rib could be the sweet spot. She doesn't seem concerned.

"Uuuh, yeah, fucking right," she says, leaning into my ear again. The microphone prangs against my neck. "Now say that you want to lick me, to eat me out."

I can't help thinking of the filling in a chicken and mushroom pie. Or a Calippo.

"I want to lick you out."

I kiss her tits through her bra. I can make out the shadows of her nipples.

"That's it—lick my tits!"

I tongue her scratchy, synthetic bra. The polyester makes me want to retch.

She smiles and writhes.

I feel quite close to coming so I think about all the skinny bodies looking through the barbed wire at Auschwitz.

"Tell me that your dick is hard. Tell me that you're hard for me."

I can do one better.

"My dick is stiff as a Nazi salute for you," I say.

"Hmm, mmm, ooooh," she groans.

Her thigh is squishing my erection.

She pushes off the floor with her legs and we roll and spin across the room, knocking against the desk.

Her belt is held with two complicated-looking clasps so I just keep rubbing the crotch of her trousers as if it were a magic lamp.

She groans, long and shuddery; her breathing cuts in and out.

I don't bother about undoing her belt, I just shove my hand down the top of her trousers and delve into her knickers. Because she is so close to me, I cannot turn my palm toward her and have to settle for using my knuckles as a makeshift sex tool.

She glances across at the red light, glowing like a clitoris, on the transmitter.

I move the top of my hand back and forth against the tacky, hairy space between her legs.

"Nh," she breathes.

I try and nestle my knuckles inside her.

"Okay!" she says, before stiffly pulling my hand out.

She leans over to the transmitter and flicks a switch; the red light fades.

She stands up, shakes her hair, plucks her bra.

My penis is chomping at my pants.

"Oh fuck, I've just realized. I haven't got any condoms."

The audience applaud. Some of them stand up, their heads appearing in silhouette.

"What do you mean?"

"I forgot them."

"Don't worry," I say. "I'll get one from the library toilets."

She picks up her Prozac T-shirt and slips it on.

"Shit, look, I'm really sorry. Don't forget your flowers, babe."

She turns to the desk and adjusts some of the switches.

I can feel a little bit of pre-cum, wet against my belly.

"Come on, Zoh. It's all right," I say, feeling suddenly helpless, desperate.

"It'll look pretty weird if we come out together. You go down to the foyer and wait for me," she says.

I watch her turn a couple of knobs. She told me that all you have to do is press the *Go* button.

Onstage, Hayyah is singing and dancing.

"Oliver. You should go. The show's almost finished anyway. This next bit takes my full concentration."

I walk down the stairs in the dark, repeating the words *full concentration*.

Mr. Linton, my history teacher, says we should be careful about using the phrase *concentration camp*.

I sit at a table in the foyer with my stolen flowers and my erection. My eyes sting from coming out into the daylight. It is still early afternoon.

I'm aware of having been part of something devious.

Buchenwald was known as a concentration camp, because it was a place where a high concentration of prisoners lived; they were used as slave labor to build weapons. The extermination camps—Auschwitz being the daddy—were designed purely for gassing and massacre.

I sniff the back of my hand. I nuzzle the flowers for contrast.

It would be easy to believe that Zoe and I are going to spend the rest of our lives together.

Mr. Linton said that one fifth of the prisoners in Buchenwald died or were killed; many were used for dangerous medical testing. So to call Buchenwald a concentration camp is almost to suggest that it was not also a place of extermination and death.

I smell my hand. I smell the flowers.

I look at the clock on the wall. The play's still got another ten minutes to go.

I think it's her relationship with Aaron that is the problem. I need to sort this out.

I stand up and hobble back through the doors toward the control booth. I stop at the landing, halfway up the stairs, and take a left through the heavy soundproof door. I close it delicately and walk along a gray corridor; there are doors on the left side only. I go to the end of the corridor and down a stairwell. At the bottom is a fire exit and a set of gray double doors.

I pull them apart and step into a large, high-ceilinged room. The wall on my left is made entirely of chipboard, supported by wooden struts. A slim door has been cut into the wood. On my right-hand side is a paint-flecked kitchen counter that runs along the wall, stopping at another fire exit.

I hear voices from the stage:

"A world ruled by God. Divine justice. Wishful thinking. Who is there to punish us, destroy us, scatter our people?"
"The civilized nations."

My stiffy starts deflating.

The dialogue seems to drift in and out, like listening to a radio play with bad reception.

The sound of the actors' voices is muffled—they could be talking about anything.

On the far wall, a large steel air-conditioning pipe climbs to a box-shaped vent, painted orange, fronted by a slatted grill. Bits of dead shows are piled in a corner: cardboard trees, bad charcoal portraits, Roman columns made from polystyrene. Grubby Nazi uniforms and a wooden rifle hang from a clothes rail that stands in the center of the room. Next to the rail is a kind of half ladder, half crane on wheels—a bit like the machines they use for taking pairs of trainers down from power lines.

Hayyah—the hot one—is singing a song. I recognize her voice.

We're dragged through the mud
And we're swimming in blood
Our bodies can't take any more.
So stand and unite—move into the light
You see how our people betray us.

All over the floor, yellow tape has been stuck down to make seemingly random shapes. A sheet of tarpaulin has also been fastened to the floor; it's splattered with brown, gold, and black paint.

The stage door handle turns silently. Aaron backs into the room, headphones on his head. He is carrying, not pushing, a pram. He keeps his back to me as he lifts the pram into a parking space of yellow tape on the floor. He is wearing baggy jeans and black Converse shoes. The back of his T-shirt has a list of tour dates on it. One of them says, *Swansea Patti Pavilion 5/6/97.*

I hold the flowers out and wait for him to turn around. I know what I'm going to say.

He is stifling laughter.

"I can't believe you," he says quietly.

He turns around and sees me. His eyes are blacked with mascara. The mascara has not run. His T-shirt asks, *Therapy?*

"I've come to explain—"

"Shhp." He puts his finger to his lips. He tiptoes toward me over the tarpaulin and whispers in my ear.

"Whatever you are going to say, you have to say it very, very quietly."

It must be getting near the end of the play. There's a brief drumroll, leading into a big sing-along:

Never say the final journey is at hand
Never say we will not reach the promised land

It's the rebellious Jews singing a rousing resistance song.

Aaron pulls his headphones off. He has small ears.

I whisper, "Zoe and I went to school together." I decide not to mention her nickname. "And I wanted to help her out with a pamphlet but she changed schools before I could give it to her. Then I came here because I was worried that she would never change and she seduced me, which was not difficult because I am still getting over my previous relationship."

He hushes me with his palms. I relower my voice.

"I've just realized that she did not want to have sex with me but, in fact, only wanted to make you jealous and angry because that is the sort of person she has become. And I'm sorry. I didn't know what she was doing. Have these flowers."

Our tomorrows will be bathed in golden light
And our enemies will vanish with the night.

He puts his hand on my shoulder.

"I'll just be one moment," he says.

He picks the rifle and the uniform off the rail and slips out the door.

On the counter are a number of empty wine bottles, bags of nuts and bolts and a book titled *The Story of the African Form.* On a piece of hardboard pinned above the sink the outlines of various tools have been painted in white: a paint roller, a wide brush, a hacksaw.

From the stage I hear Gens calling out, "Stop it! Stop playing!"

The music and singing stop.

Aaron comes back in, smiling lightly, one ear of his headphones on, one ear balanced on his temple.

He speaks very quietly, almost mouthing the words.

"Oliver, you don't need to be sorry. Zoe's a bitch. Aren't you, Zoe?" He raises his eyebrows, waits for a moment, and then nods. "Zoe says yes, she's a bitch. She was just fucking you around."

"I know she was; *I realized.*" I step toward him and put my hand on his shoulder. "She was using me to get at you. It was an elaborate trick."

"Look, Oliver, basically, the thing is, me and Zoe have way too much time on our hands. Everyone else gets to have this orgy scene and we're the lemons who get left out." He lowers his voice to a whisper: "She bet me that she could have sex during a show. We thought it'd be funny."

From the stage I hear: "And another, and another, yet another! You go to the opera, nothing but Jews."

I speak through my teeth. "But we didn't have sex."

"No shit—Zoe's no actress."

I can hear the tinny sound of her laughter coming through the cans. He puts his hand to his headphone again, listening to something, then he puts his lips very close to my ear:

"Look, I'm sorry, Oliver, no hard feelings. Why don't you keep those flowers?"

Two girls appear through the stage door, leaning on each other, trying to stifle laughter. They are dressed as prostitutes. They stop giggling when they see me.

One of the girls waves at me. The other one hisses, "Who's this?"

"Oliver from Derwen Fawr," Aaron whispers.

Their mouths turn into Os.

"God, Zoe is *awful,*" says the girl. Her dress has fallen off her right shoulder. I can see a couple of ribs and a collarbone.

They lean on each other.

From the stage, I make out some of the dialogue:

"Comrades, dear comrades. I proclaim the Kingdom of new freedom. We are free of this bloodsucker."

"Don't worry about it, love," says the other girl in a motherly way. "Zoe's a virgin, anyway."

They link arms as they start smiling. They watch me.

Aaron carefully leans on the bar across the fire doors; they swing open onto the car park behind the theater. It is bright outside.

"Oliver—why don't you go out the back way before everyone comes offstage?"

From the stage, I hear: "A brilliant effect. Magical! Bravo, gentlemen."

I console myself that I have been tricked by actors.

The two girls can't take their eyes off me.

"You could do better than her, anyway," says the one with the bones. They are both better-looking than Zoe.

We hear: "Load gun! Ready!" and the *ka-chuck* sound of a gun being cocked.

I want to behave like a child. I want to shout something about Nazis or Jews. Something like "Gas the fucking Jews" but I can't. I want to be juvenile. I want to do something for children.

I pick up an empty wine bottle and hold it above my head.

There is the sound of loud machine-gun fire from the stage. I wait for it to finish.

They are murdering them.

I don't lob the wine bottle at the ladder, where it would shatter and reverberate to the back rows. I don't smash the wine bottle against the sink and then dig the cut glass into my spare wrist.

Instead, I run out the fire door, and I follow the arrows for the car park's one-way system, and I keep running until I'm halfway across the car park before throwing the bottle—it is liebfraumilch, made in the city of Worms—dropping it, really, onto the damp tarmac.

indoctrination

On the way home through Singleton Park, I get involved in some crying.

I am still carrying the battered white flowers; the tips of the petals are ripped. I decide to walk along the path that me and Jordana used to walk with Fred, the martyred dog. But I walk the route in reverse—anti-clockwise—and as I pass each landmark I lay down one of the tatty white flowers. When I am very sad, I tend toward symbolism.

I imagine that she will be walking the same route—but clockwise—and also putting flowers down, and our hands will meet as we both go to weave a flower into the railings by the entrance to the botanical gardens.

It's bright and the park is busy: there are dog walkers, a hexagon of people playing Frisbee in direct sunlight, a youngster on a bike looking pleased with himself although his training wheels are doing the hard work.

I climb up into the rock garden and place a flower in the uncomfortable alcove where me and Jordana used to snog.

I lay a flower at the fork in the path where we once argued about which way was the more direct route. A golden retriever appears from around the bend and bumbles dumbly toward me. I wonder if the owner of the dog will be Jordana or, at the very least, a beautiful woman. I wait. Appearing from behind the wide, veined leaves of some tropical plant, I see that the owner is a man. He is about fifty, with no hair. I have never seen him before. I feel strange to be standing still at the fork of a path, holding a handful of flowers.

The dog jogs toward me, sniffs at my penis, then at the flowers.

"Tim, leave the gentleman be."

I stay still. I am a gentleman. The dog is called Tim.

The gates to the botanical gardens are locked. The old man has gone home for a snooze. I thread a flower through one of the links in the chain lock.

I put one flower on the doorstep of the Swiss cottage. It is a red wooden house with hanging baskets, two chimneys, and a white picket fence.

Another dog appears—a Scottie—sniffing along the fence, checking for piss scent. I think of how much easier it would be to accidentally-on-purpose bump into Jordana if, first, I could detect the smell of her piss and, second, she were prone to marking out territory. The Scottie's owner is a woman—short blond hair, a light suntan.

I reach the dense umbrella-shaped tree with the tiny white flowers that we used to agree would be the ideal place to take cyanide capsules. I lay a flower to rest against the trunk. There is a bench that is positioned under the tree's canopy. The plaque says:

Dedicated to the lifelong friendship of Arthur Morey and Mal Brace.

We used to sit on this bench and joke about Arthur and Mal being homosexuals. And then we'd touch each other.

There was one time when we were hiding in the rock garden, setting fire to things, and we watched two men go behind a bush. At first we thought it was cool because we were about to witness a real, live drug deal. But then they didn't come out for minutes and the sound they made was of men playing squash.

The only exit from our hiding place would have led us right past them so we stayed in total silence until they finished. It took four minutes and thirty seconds. The first man came out from the bush and he had his hands in his pockets. The second man waited for about twenty seconds then he walked out and he was grinning like it was the greatest day of his life.

There are some flies knocking around and the smell of leaves.

I sit on the bench and put my head in my hands. I think about what would be the most interesting way to commit suicide: a sky-dive onto a Kremlin steeple, hanging from the Hanging Gardens of Babylon, falling on my own sword at the annual Singleton Park medieval re-creation battle. I ruffle my hair and rub my eyes. I want to make it clear to passersby that I am unhappy.

I think that, now we're on revision break, the next time I'll see Jordana will be in the exam hall. And after that, who knows where she'll go. She was threatening to go to Swansea College and study sociology. She said she was interested in people. And I may not even stay in Derwen Fawr for sixth form. My parents suggested that I might like to go to Atlantic College to study the International Baccalaureate. I have noticed something totally pointless: both words are thirteen letters long.

I think that if Fred were still alive then at least I could have waited here for a couple of days and eventually, Jordana would have turned up. We could have had a chat on neutral ground.

I go inside my head and have a fantasy about someone—maybe a dog walker, maybe a woman, maybe a man—noticing that I am unhappy, sitting down next to me and telling me a story about their life. The story would be ridiculously traumatic. Maybe someone very close to them had died. Died in front of them. Maybe they watched their teenage son or daughter die. Or maybe they were driving the car and their only son was in the backseat, directly behind them, and he had not put his seat belt on and they had not checked whether he had put his seat belt on, which they normally would remember to do, but they were late for yoga—yoga, of all things—and they drove quite quickly and another car pulled out in front of them and although it wasn't exactly the parent's fault, they knew that it would probably not have happened if they had been driving more slowly, and it was quite a bad crash, but not so bad a collision that it made seat belts irrelevant, and their son wasn't wearing a seat belt and his face went into the plastic headrest—it was one of those old square Volvos with the hard plastic headrests—and it was enough to send his nose back into his brain and leave him dying and ugly on the backseat; meanwhile the driver of the other vehicle was already out of his car, rubbing his sore neck, stumbling onto the grass at the side of the road, and the narrator of this story, the parent, was still stuck, strapped into the front seat with a sore neck and a damp neck and a face full of airbag, and is asking the question: "Oliver?"—oh my God, their son has the same name as me— and they're saying, "Oliver, Oliver, are you okay?"

I stay with my head in my hands until the color of the sky catches up with my mood.

I concentrate on how hungry I am. I think about my stomach eating itself. I bite a chunk from the inside of my cheek. I will swallow anything.

I think about Zoe. About how much she has improved.

I hear some loud barking nearby. I lift my head up. A gray greyhound is glaring at me, straining at its leash, barking arrhythmically. I see the inside of its mouth, its tonsils.

It is being dragged away. The taut lead stretches out of sight behind a wide oak tree. The dog's toenails scuff through the grass as
it tries to get purchase.

I stand up and take a few steps so that I can peer around the
tree. I see a girl walking away across the lawn, one arm stretched out
behind her, gripping the leash. The dog is barking and leaping,
fighting the pull at its neck. The girl is in a tug-of-war with it, leaning forward just to keep her position.

It's getting dark but I can see that she has brown hair. I walk a
step closer. She has brown hair. She is using one of those retractable
leashes.

I start running toward her across the grass.

"Jordana!" I say. "Jordana!"

For this will be that bit where it is getting dark and I mistake a
girl for Jordana—a girl with brown hair and a retractable leash—
and when the girl turns around I will see that her face is nothing
like Jordana's and she will ask if she knows me and I will look traumatized and say, *No, I'm sorry, no, you don't know me, nobody knows me.*

The dog runs with me, yapping at my heels.

The girl doesn't turn around. Her arm is still out behind her
even though the leash is now slack. I notice dried blood and scratch
marks on her wrist. I stand back. The dog is panting, watching me.

She turns around.

I state the obvious.

"It is Jordana," I say.

She's wearing a black jumper with red stripes down each arm
and a pair of muddy tracksuit bottoms. In her spare hand she is
carrying a see-through plastic bag full of dog shit. Her hair is un-
washed.

My belly is cramping. It's making me wince. Jordana looks at
me with what I hope is sympathy.

I explain, "I've been thinking about telling people that I've been
thinking about killing myself."

She doesn't say anything. She presses a button on the leash that reels the slack in. The wire slithers back into the plastic casing like sucked-up spaghetti. Without taking her eyes off me, she takes a step toward the greyhound, bends her knees, and lets it off its leash. It bolts, sprinting off toward the pond. The sound of its paws thumping against the grass is reminiscent of my current heartbeat.

"Are you okay?" she asks.

"Yes."

"Okay," she says. "I saw you over there but I didn't think you would want to speak to me."

"I've just had my fingers inside a girl."

She doesn't say anything.

"It was a practical joke," I say.

Jordana's skin has got worse again. She wears a choker of in-flammation.

"When did your skin get worse?"

She rubs her wrist against her hip bone. She still has a bag of dog shit in one hand.

"Why have you got a dog?" I ask. I'm just talking. "I thought you're allergic to dogs."

"Oliver," she says.

"Where's your boyfriend?" I say.

She's blinking.

"Your skin's looking bad."

Her lips have disappeared into her mouth.

"Your skin's looking *bad*. It's probably the dog."

I take a small step toward her. She thinks about flinching.

"I don't care about my fucking skin," she says.

"It's okay," I say. "After we broke up, I realized that our relationship will not matter when I am forty."

Jordana makes a throaty noise.

"You're a fucking cunt, Oliver."

She throws the bag of dog shit at me. It is a girly throw but she still manages to hit me on the neck. I do not flinch. It makes soft contact, a moment of gut-fresh warmth against my collarbone.

It's amazing because, by all accounts, she was the one who cheated on me and yet, look how easy it is to make her rub her eyes with her free hand until her eyelids swell like overcooked conchiglie.

"You're a fucking cunt," she says.

She has irritated her eyes, as well. They look red and sore.

I could tell her: *You are rubbing your eyes with a hand that was carrying dog shit.*

She looks at me for a moment and I think that she is going to set me alight or beat me up but then she starts running away. She's not very fast because she has one hand held to her face, grinding her eye socket. I jog after her across the grass.

"Go away!" she yells.

I keep following her.

"Go away!"

She's actually screaming.

"Don't be mental!" I say.

She keeps running, following the path next to the tall stone walls that protect the botanical gardens.

I feel exhilarated. And I'm smiling because I lifted the scab off and it turns out that Jordana and I did have an emotional connection.

Her trousers are catching on the bottoms of her trainers, getting tugged down as she runs; I see the first suggestion of her arse. A short length of lead is dangling out behind her like a tail. She reaches the big, green bottle bank and disappears behind it.

I stop and listen. There is the faint sound of her lungs.

She is tightly curled up in the dark behind the bottle bank. Some of her hair has fallen across her mouth. The ground she is lying on is muddy and bare. The dog lead looks like it's coming out from her belly now, like an umbilical cord. There's a fug of vinegar and beer slops from inside the recycling bin.

I think about what I ought to say. I know I don't have to say I'm sorry because she was the one who cheated on me and she was the one who dumped me and she was the one who threw dog shit at my face.

"I'm sorry," I say.

And again: "I'm sorry."

It only makes her worse—she nuzzles the dirt.

I lie down next to her; I am the serving spoon, she is the tablespoon.

"Let me smell your fingers," she says wetly.

She grabs my forefinger and sniffs it.

"I can't smell anything," she says.

"Try my knuckles," I say.

She snuffles them, one by one.

"I'm happy for you," she says.

"What happened to your boyfriend?"

"Nothing."

"Oh."

"His name is Dafydd. You wouldn't like him."

"How long does he last?"

"That's not important."

He's a fucking marathon man.

"How long does he go for?"

"Oliver, I can't tell you that."

She even respects him. I feel my stomach twist.

She holds my hand to her mouth. Her teeth knock my knuckles.

"Who was the lucky girl?" she asks with a bitterness that makes me happy.

"Fat."

"Who's Fat?"

"You know Fat. Used to be in our school. Fat. Pie."

"You mean Zoe?"

"Yes."

"Urgh, she's fat," Jordana says, suddenly snort-laughing through the wetness. It is a sound I have not heard in months.

"She's not that fat anymore," I say.

"Yehright."

"It's true."

"Why did she leave anyway?" she says.

"She's not fat anymore."

"Parents didn't think Derwen Fawr was good enough?"

"It was because we pushed her in the pond."

"She fell in the pond," she says.

"On about? We pushed her."

"I didn't push her," she says.

"Oh."

"Have you got a hard-on?"

I am a serving spoon. I am a ladle.

"Yes."

"Okay."

I try to recognize a new smell that is coming from the recycling skip.

It's blood.

I take another, longer sniff and think back to my mother taking the hat off her middle finger with a handheld blender. The smell of the bloody kitchen tissue.

"Ah fuck. Frieda!" Jordana yelps, jumping to her feet and backing away.

The greyhound is at my feet, panting. It has a small duck in its jaw. The duck's limp neck lolls around like a semi-on.

"Oli, get up!"

They called their new dog Frieda.

Frieda pads toward my face and drops the bird in front of me as I lie still on the ground. The bird's feathers are slick: spiky with blood and saliva. There's a strong smell of drying pond water. The feathers around its shoulders are fluffy and newborn-looking, like cotton wool, while those on its wings are more battered. Its amber beak is slack and open.

"You called her Frieda."

"In memory of Fred," she says. "Stand up, Oliver, oh God!"

"You're allergic to dogs," I say.

"I know!"

"Why have you got a dog then?"

"Get up!"

"Is it a replacement for your mother?"

"My mother is not dead!"

"Why have you got a dog then?"

Frieda nudges the bird toward my face as if to say: *Here, this is for you.* I am touched. Frieda's torso expands and contracts, the skin pulling tight around her rib cage.

"Why have you got a dog then?" I say.

I am hungry.

Frieda's tongue flops over the edges of her mouth, like sandwich ham that is too big for the bread.

"Because I like dogs," she says finally.

"Wow," I say. I hadn't expected that. I remember why I fell in love with Jordana.

It is past the watershed by the time I get home. My parents are watching TV.

I go straight to the larder, open the door, and, taking the key out of the lock, I step into the darkness. I lock myself in.

I take a deep breath. The smell is an emulsion: fruity pots of shoeshine, musty stiff brushes, a sweet, moist waft from the gasoline-style tankard of Grade A Vermont Pure Maple Syrup, and an acid tang from jars of homemade Seville Orange Marmalade.

My parents' lifetime collection of plastic bags looks like a large white cabbage, hanging from the back of the door. Each bag contains another bag which contains another bag—starting at Habitat, down through John Lewis, Debenhams, Sainsbury's, Tesco, Sketty Butchers, WHSmith's, Uplands newsagent, Boots, and so on into infinity or close enough. I realize that if you really wanted to kill yourself, you wouldn't bother with megaton pyrotechnics or hiring the Red Devils to write a suicide note in the sky. You'd just do it. With a Tesco bag tied around your neck, in a poorly stocked larder.

But I don't want to kill myself. I'm just very hungry.

I pull down a packet of Bourbon Creams and sit on the tiles with my knees up to my chest. These packets are notoriously difficult to open. I scrabble at the seal, flicking at the plastic. I have no thumbnails. I get nowhere. I start to feel overwhelmingly sad.

I give up on the Bourbons and grab a small microwave chocolate pudding. I rip off the cardboard outer packaging and peel back the thin plastic tab. I shove two fingers in—it's the consistency of foam. I eat the sponge off my fingers, going quickly, knowing that at the bottom of the cup is the chocolate sauce.

My gullet spasms. It is remembering how to digest.

I lick the goo from my fingertips. I think of Zoe in the old days.

The edge of my unhappiness softens. There is a gristly but manageable lump somewhere in my torso.

I try to focus on something positive. My experience with Zoe has made me sharper. Every year, I will track her down using the Internet and telescopes. It will be a healthy competitiveness.

My GCSEs are more important than my first relationship. My first relationship, which will not matter when I'm forty-three. Jordana would just have distracted me from my revision. My GCSEs will decide how the rest of my life pans out. In job interviews, they will not ask me whether I am still on good terms with my ex-girlfriend.

Jordana told me that her mother's fine. She also said that she didn't think it would be a good idea for us to meet up again. She said that if I really needed to speak to her I could send her an e-mail. I told her that it would probably be easier for me just to wait around in the park until she turns up.

She walked away and told me not to follow her. She said she was going to bury the duck. This is the sort of person she has become.

I did not offer to help dig. I was far too hungry for that.

port talbot

My parents are not pressuring me to revise for my GCSEs, which I think is highly irresponsible.

One of my main problems is that mathematics is not nearly as interesting as Port Talbot Steelworks, which I can see from my bedroom window, just beyond the docks.

I look at it and think of Mrs. Arlington constructing the world's ugliest simultaneous equation on the blackboard—all numbers, dashes, scraping, and chalk dust.

Port Talbot by night is GCSE maths as it ought to be taught—an equation with glitz: pipes run through the air unsupported, kinked at wacky angles just for the fun of it; rows of giant, bracketed smokestacks, wrapped in ladders, scaffold, long division; there are billowing yellow flames, dense blue flames, and sometimes, on a good day, a flame of toxic green. X equals one of the thousands of orange carbon lights that cling to every structure: the points of a line graph awaiting connection. There are tall, thin towers, dirty at the top like chewed-on pencils.

They should have a picture of it on the front of our textbook. They should include it in school trips. They should encourage us to go there for work experience: a fortnight in overalls.

And once I have stared at Port Talbot for long enough then I type the number 07734, which spells the word *hELLO* when you turn the calculator upside down. 7734 spells *hELL*. And 77345 spells *ShELL*. Which is the name of a garage that my parents boycott.

My parents like to blame Port Talbot for a number of local problems: leukemia, lymphoma, asthma, eczema, brain tumors, and the lack of investment in Swansea city center. There is a stretch of houses between the motorway and the steelworks that Dad calls Melanoma Way.

I used to say, *I do not believe in scenery.* This is still true but I would send postcards home of Port Talbot by Night.

rhossili

I am eating a plum on a gun installation. My father sips from a thermos. My mother nibbles a Rocky Robin.

We are at the top of Rhossili downs, with our legs hanging over the edge of a pocked concrete platform, looking out to sea. My dad told me that during the Second World War, these platforms were built into the side of the hill to be used as early warning lookout points and ground-to-air gun placements.

It is windy but very clear: the sky is full-on blue. Three paragliders are floating just above the horizon and, behind them, a thin dishcloth of cloud.

We are not going on a proper holiday this year until after my exams. Mum said that she "didn't want to interrupt my flow."

So in lieu of somewhere foreign, my parents and I have been going for walks on the weekends and I am doing my best to remain calm. I say things like, "Oh yes, I'd like to go for a walk," and "Cool, Mum! A walk!"

We have exhausted most of the other Gower walks—Mewslade

to Fall Bay, Whitford Sands, Caswell to Langland—and so, today, we are doing Rhossili. It is very brave of us, as a family, because at one end of the down is Llangennith, home to Graham and Mum, the surfing lessons and the wee-woo. It is also the place where Jordana had a serious conversation with an older boy called Lewis, who seemed nice, which was the middle of the end for us. To the south is Worm's Head. And beyond that, a few miles around the coast, Port Eynon and Graham's house and the broken porthole window. So this is the Tate family showing that we are strong like oxen.

We parked up next to the village church and walked down the steps onto the beach. We didn't talk much as we walked along. Mum did well not to mention surfing or whether the waves were good or bad.

We passed a group of learner surfers in a circle around their instructor. You can tell the beginners because they use enormous blue polystyrene boards. They were practicing their stance, pretending to catch waves on dry land.

We walked on the hard, damp sand. There were hundreds and thousands of those tiny, translucent sand shrimp. They usually only appear when you start digging a hole but today they were everywhere, just lying out on the surface, catching rays. With each step that we took, the shrimplets would jump. They were not jumping in terror or respect or anger because primordial creatures don't make such judgments. They felt the vibration of a foot landing on sand and they made a simple choice.

Sometimes they would jump into my shoe.

Then we turned up to walk through the dunes and climb Rhossili downs, which is a hill—steep enough for a neck sweat—that rises up behind the beach. This is where we stopped for our picnic, at the gun installation.

"Who would want to attack Swansea?" I ask.

"Swansea was a very important port," Dad says.

He finishes off the cashews, tipping the corner of the packet into his mouth: salt dust and nut crumbs tumble in. I watch him chew.

"It was the fifth city on Hitler's hit list," Mum says. She is not a historian.

"Wow," I say.

The wind is making Mum's weak tear ducts produce. She wipes the tears away with her sleeve.

"The guns were never used, though," Dad says.

Mum starts packing our rubbish into a Sainsbury's bag: scrunched-up foil, an empty bag of McCoy's Salt and Malt Vinegar, three banana skins, and the wrappers from four Rocky Robins. She stuffs the plastic bag into the green rucksack and hands it to Dad for carrying. He dons the rucksack without fuss.

My parents are a well-oiled machine.

We stand up and start back toward Rhossili village.

"Look," Mum says, laughing, "a political statement." She is pointing at one of the walls of the crumbling bunker. Some graffiti-artist-slash-poet has sprayed three words in red paint: I EAT MEAT. My dad laughs as well. They are sharing a moment.

I feel sorry for my parents, in a way.

We step off the concrete and back onto the uneven grass. I stomp on a molehill that gets in my way.

Dad walks faster than both of us. He tends to go on ahead and then every ten minutes or so, he'll let us catch up. He starts to accelerate away.

"Have you heard from Jordana recently?" Mum asks.

It is fine, I am enjoying this walk. I am calm.

"Yes, I bumped into her in the park the other day."

The wind makes our voices sound ethereal.

"Oh right. Is she okay?"

"She seems okay," I tell her. "Things are still pretty raw between us."

Mum nods. We lean into the wind as we walk.

"Her skin seemed worse," I say.

"Maybe it's exam stress."

"Or maybe it's the dog. She's got a new dog."

"What breed?"

"Greyhound," I say.

"Lovely dogs," she says.

"It's not a replacement for her mother, though," I say. "Her mother's still alive."

I feel grown-up. Like I could talk about anything. I could ask anything.

"Right. I've got a question," I say.

"Okay."

"Me and Dad are in a house fire."

"Yes."

"Now, given the hypothetical situation that we are both equally saveable, then who would you go for first?"

"I'd go for you," she says.

"Cool."

"But I'd feel bad for your father."

"Yeah."

We go single file—me first—as the path cuts through a patch of purple gorse. We see Dad in the distance, starting to make his way down to Rhossili village.

I proffer some more information: "She's still with her new boyfriend, Dafydd."

"I'm sorry," Mum says, and she rubs my back as we walk along.

"I hate him even though I haven't met him," I say, over my shoulder.

"That's understandable," she says.

As the path opens out again, we see a group of people watching the paragliders. A bit further downhill, two men are tending to a purple parachute laid out on the grass—it billows like a jellyfish; its tentacles are attached to a man wearing a jumpsuit and a helmet.

I expect Mum to remind me that these relationships mean nothing when you are forty-three. Or to at least wheel out a cliché:

There are plenty more fish in the sea. There are fish but also whales and crustaceans and shipwrecks and a dozen or so submersible military vehicles.

"I did like Jordana," she says.

Dad is waiting for us in front of the Worm's Head Hotel.

"Shall we have a little explore toward the worm?" he says.

"Worm me up," I say.

He starts off along the cliff path.

I wait for Mum while she puts on her terrible purple fleece.

The wind drones. I play at being italicized: opening my zip-up top into wings, leaning forward, propped up on a gust.

Mum is now wearing the world's worst piece of clothing. She puts her arm through mine, as if we are man and wife. I try not to feel ashamed.

We walk on the gravel path. Sheep chew grass on the cliff tops. They cannot suffer from vertigo because their brains are not sufficiently developed. A sheep cannot imagine a sudden slip of the hoof, the whoosh of adrenaline, seeing its own life in flick-book montage with barely enough time to be very disappointed.

We walk past a family in matching lemon yellow sailor's anoraks. They are of Asian origin. The children pose for a photo next to a ram.

Mum gets up on tiptoes to speak into my ear. I have just recently grown taller than her and she likes to make a point of it.

"Every year, at least three people die along these cliffs. Blown clean off," she says.

"I'll be very careful," I say.

"I was just telling you the statistics," she says.

I look at her face. The short, curly hair at her temples is being blown into Medusa snakes.

"Don't lie to me. You'd hate it if I fell off here. You'd be gutted."

"I'd get over it," she says, grinning.

This is amazing.

The path spreads into a plain as we walk past the National Trust information lodge. Dad has already gained some distance on us. He reaches a ridge and is a clear silhouette, severed at the knee by the horizon, his corduroy trousers flapping. He disappears over the other side. From here, it looks as though he could be stepping out into nothingness, ending it all.

The sky has turned a cooler, lighter blue. The single strip of cloud has grown from dish cloth to duvet. The sun is dropping faster now. I pretend that time is speeding up.

We step up onto the ridge, experiencing the wind's full potential. I would compare the feeling to being in a fight, but that comparison is beyond my experience.

Beneath us, there are shallow steps to the left that lead toward Worm's Head. The Worm can only be reached during low tide. The tide is high. To the right, Dad's following a steeper path cut into the rock; it zigzags down to the disused lifeboat hut, clinging to the cliff.

"They say that this shack is haunted," Mum says.

"Who says?"

"They say."

We follow Dad round to the right. As we dip below the ridge the wind suddenly cuts out.

"Do you have any primary evidence?" I ask.

Mum's hair settles back against her skull. We adjust our balance in the lack of bluster. It's like stepping off a boat onto dry land. My mum still has me by the arm.

"They say that the old lifeboat man wanted his son to become a lifeboat man too." Her voice is clear. "And one day they were out on the boat. The father was teaching the son how to be a lifeboat man."

"You should practice this story in your head before you tell it."

We take the steps together, careful to stay synchronized.

"All of a sudden, a storm came rolling in from Ireland," she says.

"Storms don't come from Ireland. This is going to be like one of your jokes. You're going to mess up the punch line."

"The father wanted to get the boat back to land immediately but the boy said that, if he was going to learn to be a proper lifeboat man, he would need to learn how to handle difficult conditions."

"Valid," I say.

"But the father was not convinced—he said that they needed to go back to the hut straight away. The son pleaded with him." She puts on her whiny teenager voice: " 'Dad, I'm ready, I swear to you. I'm ready.' But he was not convinced."

"This is basically the plot of *Karate Kid*."

"The father said, 'You're not ready yet. Sorry, son, we're taking her back in.' "

"That's good, Mum, because boats are female."

"But the boy was really stubborn. He's your age, fifteen, sixteen, and he thinks he can do anything."

"Are you trying to make me relate?"

This is the sort of thing Mrs. Riley does in religious education. *When Jesus was your age . . .*

"And the boy won't help his father take the boat back in. He's stormed off below deck."

"Stormed off. Nice."

"And so the father sets about steering the boat back to the lifeboat hut. But the storm's become more powerful than he first anticipated and he's having trouble hooking the boat in, on his own."

"Why wouldn't they just take the boat back to the beach, rather than trying to moor it to a precarious shack against a cliff? That's just dumb."

"So the father runs below deck and pleads with his son to help. He says, 'Son! She's closing in!' "

"Storms are female as well."

" 'We're gonna have to park her up on the beach!' he says."

"They're having a domestic in the middle of this storm. You're just making this up as you go along." I cup my hands around my mouth and yell to Dad in my Hollywood voice, "*Pop! Help! She's closing in!*"

Dad is peering in through the windows of the shack. He doesn't look up.

"Cheesy," I say. "This ghost story is chee-zee."

We reach the bottom of the steps and approach the hut. It's still just about white but the paint is flaking off. I look in through a small, smashed window. The shack looks charmingly spooky from far away but when you get up close you realize that it's just an old shed: it smells of piss and there are broken Heineken bottles on the floor.

"So the son comes back up on deck. But by this time, the storm has really taken hold. The waves are towering, pushing them toward the cliffs. And in the battle to save the ship, the boy is thrown overboard."

"He's wearing a life jacket, of course," I say.

"Yes, he is. But they are too close to the cliffs. And before the father can pull his son out, the boy gets tossed against the rocks. He gets flung against the cliffs and his father can't do anything but watch."

"That's just not convincing. You should have at least let the tension build a little," I say.

Dad's standing next to the mechanism that they used to tow the boat in: a hook hanging from a kind of crane that sticks out over the water.

"And the boy's dead, or soon to be dead, still floating in his life jacket, with his desperate father screaming at him to pick up the life rope."

"Why didn't the father dive in?" I ask.

"Because then they would surely have both died."

"It would have been a nice gesture."

It's too sunny and clear to be scared of anything. I could watch *Hellraiser* in this light, no problem. This is Ouija weather.

I can see why someone wrote a ghost story about this spot. In fact, it would probably be in my top-three best hypothetical spots to commit suicide. And on a day like this, you couldn't do much better. I imagine the coast guard's helicopter spotting the body, waves crashing into the cliffs below, seagulls at my eyeballs already, a pod of seals mourning from the water. And the coast guard has a high-quality video camera and they sweep past and the shot goes out on local news at first but then it gets picked up by the international news corporations and photos of my corpse are being constantly downloaded from the net and soon it's back on the *News at Ten* and CNN under the pretense of a story about how messed up the Internet is—and how upsetting for the family—but actually, it's such a beautiful helicopter shot that they'll find any excuse to show it.

"And so his son died," I say. "And the old man survived the storm then hung himself from this beam?"

"Correct," she says.

"Yawn," I say. "I'm not frightened."

Dad is standing on the edge of the concrete foundations. He is peering down, watching an ongoing grudge match: the Waves versus the Rocks.

"It's hanged, not hung. He *hanged* himself," Dad says. He steps back, turns around. "Who are we talking about?"

"The creepy old lifeboat man," I say.

"Oh yeah, that's true," Dad says.

"Shut up it's true," I say.

Dad looks at me blankly. There is the sound of the waves slapping and butting.

"He had spent years of his life saving people on the Gower coast and then his son drowned while under his supervision. He hanged himself," he says.

"And now he haunts these shores," I say, wiggling my fingers in the air and making a horror face.

"Oliver," he says disapprovingly.

The sunlight is coming side-on: making half his face bright, half of it dark.

"My fault," Mum butts in. "I thought it was a ghost story."

Dad looks at her. "Jill, that's terrible."

She bares her teeth.

"It's true. It happened," Dad says. "In the eighties."

"That is awful," she says. "Why did I think it was a ghost story?"

I put my head on her shoulder.

"Because the thought of losing your beloved son—i.e., me—is *so* terrible that even when you hear about it happening to other people you have to convince yourself it's not real."

I notice that the sun is setting. I do not believe in scenery but still, there it is.

"It's an absolutely stunning day," Dad says.

The sun dissolving against the horizon like aspirin. A bright, white path of light on the surface of the water.

Mum leans into my arm.

"You might be right, Oli," she says.

I feel a little bit ill at the vastness of the ocean. There are dark patches and lighter patches on the water. The dark patches are shaped like continents.

"Why are there bits of water darker than other bits?"

"Maybe something to do with the currents," Dad says.

"Imagine all the mental things that live down there," I say.

Particularly those at the deepest parts. Voluminous jelly creatures that could squeeze through a keyhole but have mouths so wide they could swallow a whale. Pressure makes no bones. I consider telling my parents that I want to become a marine biologist; it's already one of the most commonly proposed career paths among my schoolmates.

The sun is setting. The light is yolky and warm.

"You know they used ultrasound during World War Two to detect submerged objects," I say.

I am standing in between them, shoulder to shoulder.

"I didn't know that," Dad says. He is a Welsh historian.

The sun is setting. All the colors are there.

"How deep is the ocean?" Mum asks. Her real surname is Hunter. Jill Hunter. The sun is setting.

"Not sure," Dad says.

I like it when my parents do not know things.

Goldfish grow to fit the size of their bowls.

"The ocean is six miles deep," I tell them.

The sun is setting.

And it's gone.

acknowledgments

I wrote the majority of this book while studying creative writing at
the University of East Anglia. I am very grateful to all the tutors
and students there for their help and encouragement. In particular,
I'm thankful for the expertise of John Boyne, Megan Bradbury, Andrew Cowan, Doug Cowie, Sian Dafydd, Patricia Duncker, Seth
Fishman, Paulo Mellett, Michèle Roberts, Clive Sinclair, Joel Stick-
ley, and Luke Wright. Particular thanks to Tim Clare whose pa-
tience, enthusiasm, and friendship have been invaluable. Also, I
would not have been able to write this book without the Curtis
Brown Prize and the assistance of the AHRC.

For energy, support, and attention to detail, I would especially
like to thank my agent, Georgia Garrett. Hefty thanks are also due
to Simon Prosser, my editor. I'd also like to thank Francesca Main,
Emma Horton, and everyone at Penguin; Philippa Donovan, Rob
Kraitt, Naomi Leon, and everyone at AP Watt; Bruce Tracy, Dan
Menaker, Ryan Doherty, and everyone at Random House; and
Claire Paterson. I posted the first chapter of this book—when it

was just a short story—on ABCtales.com; the response it received had a large part in my decision to write *Submarine*. I'd also like to thank Lara Frankena; in the chapter "Apostasy," the twigs that spell the word "help" are taken from her poem "Vipassana Meditation Retreat, Ten Days' Silence."

For their support and for living with this book, thank you: Fran Alberry, David Rhys Birks, Ben Keeps Brockett, Simon Brooke, Toby Gasston, Ally Gipps, Alison Hukins, Matt Lloyd-Cape, Gregg Morgan, Alastair O'Shea, Dylan O'Shea, Emily Parr, Ian Rendell, Laura Stobbart, Maya Thirkell, Hannah Walker, and Mial Watkins.

To my family, for their encouragement and love: Mum, Dad, and my sisters, Anna and Leah.

about the author

Joe Dunthorne was born in 1982, and
was brought up in Swansea, Wales. He now
lives in London. He is the author of the
novels *Submarine* and *Wild Abandon* as well as
the poetry collection *Faber New Poets 5*.